FROM A

DISTANT

PLACE

A NOVEL

Don Carpenter

NORTH POINT PRESS
San Francisco 1988

North Point Press
850 Talbot Avenue
Berkeley, California
94706

This book is dedicated to
Klyde Young

FROM A

DISTANT

PLACE

LIFE

Jackie Jeminovski lived in a fine home, in an old development north of Manzanita Canyon, just a few blocks from downtown Lincoln's Grove, in Marin County. The development was all three- and four-bedroom houses, built quickly after World War I I for the families of returning veterans. Now, forty years later, these houses were worth a fortune. Jackie's street was typical, with its artificially curved roadway, no sidewalk, mailboxes on posts out at the curb, lush greenery almost hiding the houses from view. All the streets in the subdivision had names from the war. Jackie lived on the corner of Halsey and Funafuti, her front garden as lush and beautiful as anybody's, with its outstanding feature a fan trellis of bright red bougainvillea hiding the front porch. There were beds of calla lilies next to the house, and a big lawn sloping down to the roadway. A good-sized backyard was hidden by the double garage, with more flower beds and a small vegetable garden. It was a nice one-story house of white stucco, with green false shutters and a natural shingle roof turned dark with age. Steven Jeminovski bought it for his bride and the family to come, in the middle 1960s. He paid $30,000 for the house, which at the time seemed like a lot of money.

By now everybody figured Jackie's home must be worth at least

$200,000. And Steven Jeminovski must have been generous in child support and alimony, although of course that must have come to an end. Steven was a lawyer specializing in personal injury cases. He lived in Venice, in Southern California. Everybody thought Jackie owned the house, that she was a great success story, an independent woman who had spent twenty years keeping house and raising children, and was now free to live out her life as she pleased.

Jackie knew the story. People told her all the time that she had beaten the system. What they didn't know was that she had sold the house to Steven years ago, the payments equalling the rent, and the lump sum, her capital, going for her little green Jaguar sedan and her living expenses. She was doing the one thing her father had told her not to do—she was living on capital. And the capital was about gone. She was living in a big empty house with nothing to do all day but drink. It was really time for a change, she kept telling herself.

Jackie was crazy to go on living in that big house. Four bedrooms and nobody came home anymore. She had thought about renting out a couple of the rooms, but her pride got in the way. She was really a small-town girl, and her idea of respectability did not include renting out rooms to strangers. And there was something else. She would have to clear up some personal habits a little before any strangers started running around in her private home. And she had heard enough about roommates to know that men would always end up sitting on the edge of your bed at three in the morning telling you they loved you, and women would take your boyfriends and eat your food out of the refrigerator. Young ones were too wild. Old ones were too set in their ways.

I am just too screwed up for roommates, she thought. But the fact was that she liked to start out her day with a bottle of Green Death, Rainier Ale, which was practically harmless. But she knew it gave her bad breath and people thought less of you. When men stayed over she either skipped her ale or for some reason they would both have something to drink. Men liked to take women, especially good-looking women, out to breakfast after a night together, show 'em off to the boys lined up at the bar nursing their hangovers. She liked to go to Perry's down in Mill Valley and start the day off right with Eggs Benedict and a Ramos fizz. But that was only on weekends, and it had been a while since anybody stayed over anyway.

She could get a job; in fact, she wanted a job. But she could no longer work in her profession as a stewardess because it had been too long. Steven hadn't made her quit. She had been delighted. Just thinking about it made her remember with sad amusement how she and her two sisters had planned to get out of Kansas. She remembered them, on the third floor of the old Salina house where they were raised, all in their white nightgowns, the endless prairie twilights after bedtime, sitting on Jackie's bed next to the window. They would become stewardesses, working their way up to the international runs, where they would meet and marry rich men. Out of the sky and into the money. It was all going to be wonderful.

The funny part was that all three had done it. Well, not exactly, but close enough. Jackie had become a stewardess, Jill had begun as a waitress in San Francisco after Jackie sent for her, and was now a real estate woman in Arlington, Texas, which her husband owned, or nearly owned. Jackie could always go live with her sister. Sure. And the baby, Joey, who hadn't been quite as cute and pretty as her sisters, came to California and after only two weeks found a husband. She was now working on her third husband, or was it her fourth? Joey was living in Hong Kong, where she had a part interest in a human hair business. Life was certainly strange. Joey still wasn't that good-looking, and she had a sharp tongue, and was tighter than J. P. Morgan. Some baby sister.

Well, Jackie had raised a family. Why didn't her children take care of her? Why didn't she want her children to take care of her? Why would she rather jump off the Golden Gate Bridge than let her children give her one dime? Easy. Because her children didn't like her. She had not done her best, and it had not been good enough. She tried to be the Great American Mom, at the center of a big happy nuclear family, and it had not worked. What a relief.

Her last major attempt to be Mom had been on Thanksgiving, when she really pulled a stupid move by inviting her entire family to assemble at her house for the traditional turkey feast. How this idea had gotten into her head she did not understand. Just one day she started thinking about having the children come, if they would, and then Steven, and then the others, a half-drunk daydream about the whole family in a warm fugue of togetherness. She could just see it, even smell it, the air crisp outside, persimmons turning orange on leafless trees . . .

She was sitting on her favorite barstool, next to the picture window in the front of the Happy Hour. She liked to watch the passing parade. Although today the parade was running by, in a heavy gusty rainstorm. She was sitting next to her friend and sometime lover Al Burke, a big blond happy man of fifty, who taught English to foreign students at San Francisco State.

"What are you doing Thanksgiving?" she asked Al.

He grinned at her, his handsomeness undimmed by age. "Turkey day? Why, are you offering me a free meal?"

"Sure," she said. "You know what would be great? Instead of a turkey, let's get some of those exotic game birds. There's a place up in Sonoma that specializes in pheasant, grouse, or we could get a goose and roast it. Roast goose, Al!"

"Sounds great to me," Al said.

Oh, they were going to get a goose and roast it, they were going to buy dried cornstalks and ears of dried maize, dried gourds, and make a real Thanksgiving centerpiece, but as the big day grew closer and closer and nothing done, she panicked and ordered two big turkeys from the Grove Market. It had been a terrible mistake for her to rashly invite all those people. She was not a Thanksgiving or Christmas kind of person. When she had been working for American she had spent most of her holidays at ski resorts, partying. When she had been a housewife she had made all the usual holiday dinners for her family, and they often had guests from inside or outside the family, but never a big party, just enough to crowd the dining room, with cardtables set up for the children. But after a while, they all stopped pretending that the holidays meant anything more to them than time off work or school, and so the dinners stopped, just pooped out after a while, with this one or that one not home or not interested.

Why did she feel guilty every single time she thought about her children? Did everybody feel like that? Probably.

It turned into quite a long day. She had not meant to invite so many people. Anyway, the idea had been not so much having the big Thanksgiving dinner for the family, but letting the family know she was still alive and kicking, still ready to throw open the front door and holler, "Come and get it!" That's what her poor dead mother back in Kansas might have said. "Come and get it, before the hogs come in through the windows!" Good old Mom, practically the only member of the family who didn't show up. Jackie assumed, in her near hysterical state, that Mom didn't come only because she was buried too deep.

One problem was that as Thanksgiving approached, Jackie kept telling people she was having a big dinner, and they would look away or mutter something, and Jackie would have to invite them, too. "Oh, come on by!" she said to she didn't know how many people, and you can guess what happened. Maybe the spirit of the season got to her. It had been fun talking to her sisters on the telephone, drinking Green Death, curled up on her big long couch in front of the fireplace, smoking a little marijuana somebody had given her, listening to her sisters' voices over the long-distance crackling that seemed just as bad from Texas as it was from Hong Kong, hearing their excuses and just for the hell of it rising to every challenge:

"No, bring the kids. I have plenty of room!"

Or, "Think of it as a vacation! Oh, come on, I haven't seen you for so long . . . I *miss* you!"

Derek and Diedre, her own children, had been harder to get in touch with. Diedre lived in Oakland with her husband, and Derek lived in the city, on the edge of Chinatown. Nobody ever seemed to be home when she called Diedre. With Derek, she had to just send a postcard and hope he got it. Diedre and her husband both worked for the telephone company. Any time Jackie spent with them was an ordeal for all three. They would just sit there and not say anything. There was not much to say. Diedre had been a sweet child, but she had grown up into Jackie did not know what. Diedre was aggressively ordinary, and so was her husband, who had stolen her right out of high school. They both planned to stay with the telephone company all the way to retirement.

Jackie had no proof of it, but she suspected that Diedre was mad at her for frittering away all the money. There hadn't been that much money, but Diedre seemed to think her father was a wonderful generous man, and that somehow Jackie had screwed things up. Derek was different. He seemed to dislike both his parents. Derek had never been a sweet child. He had been a strange, silent baby, and if he was no longer silent, he was strange enough to make up for it. Derek was small and uncoordinated, and cut high school so much he finally quit during one of his many suspensions. He moved to the city, where he worked at one terrible job after another. His face was unformed, almost blank, his eyes small and brown behind dark glasses. Jackie loved him, but she didn't like him much. Her sorrow as a parent was that she did not seem to like her own children. She tried not to let them know this. Part of the idea of the Thanksgiving dinner was to show them that she loved them and that they belonged to a family.

People started showing up Tuesday night. The first surprise was her father, seventy-one years old, coming in from Salina. He telephoned from the airport but refused to sit around and wait for Jackie to come and pick him up. Instead he took a $35 cab ride and showed up at her door with an armload of Christmas presents and an old battered suitcase. "Hello, Daddy," Jackie said.

"Let me in and give me a drink," said her father.

Both her sisters arrived the next day. Jill brought her family, hus-

band Tom and two teenage daughters, Dorothy and Eileen. Sister Joey came in from Hong Kong alone, her face guarded behind thick glasses. Joey was heading for divorce.

"I hope you aren't planning to marry a Chinaman," their father joked. The squinch-eyed look Joey gave him was, to Jackie, a dead giveaway. "I hope he's rich," she said later, and got the same look from Joey.

Wednesday night was quiet. Jackie assigned bedrooms, and they all went out to dinner together, to the Hick'ry Pit, and by midnight only the three sisters were left, drinking beer and talking. Joey finally relaxed and told them about her life in Hong Kong. All three sisters had been little golddiggers, but Joey had really gotten into money.

"Are you rich yet?" Jackie asked her.

"I've been a millionaire for a couple of years," Joey said. "Hong Kong millionaire, that is."

"Will you come home when you're an American millionaire?" Jill asked. Jill was plump now. She had always had the best figure, and somehow she still did, although Jackie's was the one everybody commented on. Jackie was proud of her figure. She weighed the same at forty-five as she had at twenty.

Joey said, very businesslike, "There's no hair business here. I know how to buy and sell hair." Actually, Joey could be fascinating on the subject of hair. "The best most expensive human-hair wig in the world is eventually going to turn red," she said. "All human hair is basically red."

"My God, you don't say!" Jill exclaimed, but Joey didn't get it.

Jackie could hear the two teenage girls talking to each other as she passed their bedroom door. She smiled to herself.

The next morning bright and early Al jogged over as he had promised, to help with the turkeys. But he wasn't needed. Instead, he down with the family to breakfast, and then offered to take Jill's band Tom Phillips and the old man for a drive around Marin Cou It was a clear day, although hazy at sea level, and they drove up top of Mount Tamalpais for the view, using Tom's rented Pon

"Pig heaven" was the old man's comment, as they gazed out over the homes of four million people. Al kind of liked Jackie's dad. Spent his whole life working for the railroad, and now, just in time for retirement, there was no more railroad.

Al liked Tom Phillips, too, his favorite kind of Texan, soft-voiced, humorous, hard to fool. And rich. Jackie's sisters had done real well for themselves, as far as Al was concerned. It was nice to know that whatever other problems Jackie might have, there would always be money. If it came to that, her sisters would surely take care of her.

When they got back, the middle of a fine Thanksgiving morning, three more guests had arrived, Derek, Diedre, and her husband, Jerry Ledbetter. Al knew Derek, and here he was, offering a damp hand and peering up at Al from behind dark glasses. Jerry Ledbetter was big, bigger than Al, with a big dumb face and big hard hands. "What smells so good?" Jerry asked, and that broke the ice. Everybody started babbling, and Al wandered into the kitchen. Jackie had two regular ovens, an electronic oven and a toaster oven, and they were all in use. The big table in the middle of the kitchen had been used for chopping fruits and vegetables, and was now covered with salad in bowls and beer bottles. The night before they had picked up several pies from the Hick'ry Pit, which was famous all over Marin County for its great pies, especially peanut butter pie and pecan pie. Jackie bought three big pecan pies and three Dutch apple pies, instead of the usual pumpkin and mince pies, which she hated anyway.

By two in the afternoon, when they were supposed to sit down, the house was packed and people still coming in the door. Not only had all her relatives come, so had everybody else—local people, denizens of the various bars from San Rafael to Sausalito, but thank God most of these people brought something with them, a bottle of wine, a casserole, anything to keep from being empty-handed. In the kitchen the sound level escalated upward and there was no place to put anything. Between the double garage and the kitchen there was a laundry room, and this became an improvised pantry. It was three days before Jackie found a Pyrex casserole dish full of macaroni and

cheese sitting in her dryer. The sideboard in the dining room became
a buffet, with stuffed eggs, celery stuffed with pimento cheese,
cheese puffs, stuffed green olives and pitted black olives, cut-glass
dishes of hard candy and peanut brittle (somebody brought five
pounds of peanut brittle), sweet pickles, Italian antipasto, brie, Til-
lamook cheddar, Monterey Jack, and even some feta cheese. In the
living room, Jackie's father had set up a little bar of two cardtables,
covered with bottles of liquor, long tubes of plastic glasses, and underneath, a galvanized tub full of ice. Beer kept coming in by the
case, but it never lasted very long, and the plastic-lined garbage cans
out back were full long before people started to eat.

The last person to arrive, not counting the people who were just
wandering in and out, was Steven Jeminovski, always good at making entrances. When he pulled up out front, there happened to be a
vacant parking place in the driveway, which was just his luck. His car
was a brand-new silver Mercedes sedan. Jackie felt a thrill when she
saw him getting out of his car. He was an exciting man, even now,
with his dark hair streaked with silver, his dark eyes covered by sunglasses. He grinned at Jackie through the window. Of course he was
here to see his children. Just as they were here to see him.

Derek certainly was. He didn't care about Thanksgiving, except
for the food, of course. He intended to eat himself sick, and then take
home as much food as he could stuff into his pockets. But the important thing was to see his father and get some money out of him. Derek
loved his father, of course, but he also knew his father was a danger-
ously charming person. The trick would be to get the money out of
him before the old man charmed Derek into not wanting the money.
But he did want the money. He lived in a hole in the wall on Jackson
Street, a real fucking hole in the wall, with the smell of Chinese cooking everywhere, a sour cabbage smell he hated with all his heart, and
it was time to move. But he was temporarily out of work. His last job
had been driving bagels around to restaurants, a job that not only
started far too early in the morning but lasted all day, and at three-
fifty an hour, you actually lost ground. At least Derek couldn't keep

up. He always had trouble with money. He hated money, but he knew he had to have it. Not only was he going to hit on his father, he was going to case the possibility of going through the women's purses. The women would put their things on his mother's kingsize bed, and if he could find the right moment, he would lock himself in the bedroom and frisk the purses. He had never done this before, but a friend of his had told him about ripping off purses at his mother's dinner parties. It sounded to Derek like a good way to get money, and the trick would be to not take too much from any one purse. Thus he could remain undetected.

Derek went out the front door to shake hands with his father, but his dad got him in a big bearhug, right in front of the picture window where everybody could see them.

"Hi, Dad," he managed to say. Steven had him off the ground, and he struggled to get free.

"Help me with the packages," his father said. He opened the trunk of his car and started handing wrapped Christmas presents to Derek. "Yours is the little red one," his dad said. Derek swallowed his sarcastic remark. He could get together with his dad later on, maybe out in the backyard or something, and he didn't want to ruin the mood by being his usual nasty self.

"What about the suitcases, Dad?"

"I'll stay at the Tamview," his father said.

More people were coming out now, so Derek went inside and got rid of the Christmas presents by putting them in the top of the hall closet with some old hats. Then he wandered down the hall to the last bedroom, where the girls were. His cousins, Dorothy and Eileen Phillips, from Arlington, Texas. They were in their teens and both so beautiful Derek could not get them out of his mind. The door to the bedroom was closed. He stood close to the door, hesitating. Derek imagined he could smell the girls through the door, making him almost sick with desire. Finally, he knocked.

"It's Cousin Derek," he said. Did you fuck your cousins? Only if you got the chance. They would go back to Texas full of stories about the great little guy they met in San Francisco (or near San Francisco) who taught them so much about the world, and who was such a great lover they couldn't resist him, and both of them slept with him as many times as they could . . .

"It's me," he said to the door, and when it opened he put on his coolest grin and said, "How about letting me in?"

Eileen, the youngest one, peeked out at him through the crack in the door. "We're still dressing," she said.

"All the better," he said, but she shut the door.

At first Jackie was upset that so many people were coming by. She hadn't meant her invitations so literally, but maybe it was just the law of averages, and after a while she relaxed. Some of the people coming by brought not just a covered dish or a bowl of salad, but their own turkeys, already roasted, in big roasting pans, which were all over the kitchen. The table in the dining room was completely taken up with food, so that the lack of chairs went unnoticed, and people got their plates full and just stood around eating. Jackie had a vision in her mind of turkey and people flowing into the house, and turkey bones and carcasses flying out the windows until the whole yard was piled high with bones.

Jackie tried to be a good hostess and tried to see that everyone was comfortable and fed, but there were just too many people, and so about three in the afternoon she just gave up, got herself a plate of stuffing covered with gravy, and found a place to sit down. People kept coming up to her and telling her she was throwing the best party in years, and this pleased her.

It did not seem to matter that the party was out of control. No one cared. Football played on the television, and somebody thought it would be a good idea to have a poker game, so they cleared the wreckage off the dining room table, took out a couple of the extra leaves, and somebody found Steven's old army blanket that they used to take to the beach. Cards appeared, and the game began. Derek was hot to play, seeing all that real money coming out, but he didn't have enough money himself. It would have been very uncool to try stealing from the purses in the bedroom, because there were always people coming and going. Besides, he hadn't seen any unguarded purses. And he hadn't yet been able to get his father alone. Now his father had taken off his jacket and was sitting there in a white shirt playing poker. Derek was sure, after watching the game a while, that he could win a fortune here. Derek had been playing poker all his life.

Also in the game was Jackie's baby sister Joey, with a pile of bills held down by stacks of quarters, dimes and nickels. They were playing table stakes, pot limit, and there was a lot of goddamned money on the table, they didn't know, didn't realize, how much money. Derek's Uncle Tom from Texas, also in his white shirt, with his string tie, must have had a couple of hundred dollars in front of him, sitting there blinking fatly at his cards, he probably didn't even know how to play real poker. Derek imagined everybody in Texas played that jive-ass game with four cards in the middle of the table and three in your hand, or wild card games. Derek had been trained by his father in the precise odds of regular stud and draw poker. This game should be easy pickings, if he could only get in.

Local people kept sitting in, losing all their money, and getting out, so that after a while there was a hard core of winners, all playing on other people's money. This made the game pretty wild, and Derek was going crazy with the desire to play. All the more when his mother sat down in a chair vacated by some poor sucker and says, "I want to play, somebody give me some money," and all the other players threw money at her, except for her sister Joey, whose pile of bills now looked an inch thick. Derek stood behind his mother, sipping from her bottle of ale, and watching the game. After a while he tried his mother's trick, saying in a joking tone, "Hey, how about somebody staking *me*?" But nobody did.

Then one of his cousins, was it Dorothy or Eileen? touched him on the elbow and beckoned to him with her finger. He followed her down the hall to the girlsmelling bedroom, his heart unable to believe his possible good luck, but there in the bedroom was the other cousin, and the two girls sat him down on the bed and said to him, "We decided you could tell us who everybody is." They had such lovely little accents.

"Just a bunch of assholes," he said, and saw the girls look at each other. Maybe he ought to cut down on the swearing.

"We know the handsome man in the dark blue suit is your daddy," one of them said.

"Yeah," Derek said. "But I don't know anybody else. Local people. I'm from San Francisco myself."

"What kind of a car do you have?" the other one asked him. They were beautiful but hard, Derek decided.

"I don't have a car," he said. "You don't need one in the city. It's a burden, actually."

"You don't have a car?" There was a chill in the soft little Texas voice. "All the boys we know have cars."

"I guess so," Derek said miserably.

The poker game was down to six players, and there must have been a thousand dollars on the table. Al Burke didn't consider himself much of a poker player, but he had come into this game with a little over forty dollars, and immediately started winning. In the early stages of the game, when people were getting in, losing, and getting out, Al played cautiously, expecting to be wiped out at any moment. You couldn't bluff, because somebody was bound to call, so Al sat tight and waited until he had cards, and then *Wham! Bam! Thank you, Ma'm!* By the time those of faint heart or thin wallet were out of the game, Al had over three hundred dollars in front of him, money enough to make the game actually thrilling.

The other hard-core finalists were the three sisters, Jackie, Jill, and Joey, Jackie's ex-husband Steven, and Jill's husband Tom, a plump goodnatured man who probably had more money than everybody else put together, and who was really worth going after. Jackie had told Al about her rich brother-in-law, who was supposed to have won his fortune playing dice in the hold of a troopship coming back from Korea, but who had actually made it in the Tokyo black market, selling PX golf clubs, steam irons, and whiskey to the Japanese. He was going to be a hard man to beat.

Jackie for one needed the cash. They had given her about fifteen dollars to start, and she had been lucky as well as careful. Now she had nearly a hundred and fifty dollars. She wanted to quit. She wanted some of the champagne that was being passed around, but didn't ask for any because champagne gave her such a nasty headache. Wine always made her feel bad the next day, where she could drink ale or vodka all day and all night without much trouble. But she wanted no problems tomorrow, because she was the one who was going to have to get up bright and early and fix breakfast for everybody. Right now all she had to do was play poker, protect her winnings, and have a good time.

She and her sisters had played poker all their lives. Jackie played like a man, her father told her without further explanation, and now he stood watching his daughters, refusing all invitations to play. "Muh butt hurts," he said, walking around the table with his hands clasped behind his back. Jill played like an amateur, smiling, acting as if she didn't know what was going on, asking, "What's the bet?" or "Is it my turn? I'm sorry!" and other irritating things, including her most irritating remark, "Oh, did I win?"

And the baby, Joey, the Hong Kong millionaire, played as if she were starving. Joey talked very little, just sat blinking behind her glasses that were so thick she couldn't wear contacts, throwing money out and pulling pots in with the same jerky silent moves, her slender fingers constantly working, either playing with her money or tapping the blanket.

Probably the best player, though, was Steven Jeminovski, and if his luck had been a little better, he might have walked off with all the money. As it was, he left the game a couple of times, which might have broken his luck.

The first time Steven left the game, it was to drive down to the Tamview Motel and get a room for the night.

"The Tamview?" Tom asked. "Where's that?"

"Right down the road," Steven said as he counted his money and put it away.

"Maybe we should have a room, too," Tom said to his wife.

"You have a bed here," Jackie said.

"That's fine for the girls," Tom said.

"You don't have to come along," Steven said. "I'll get you a room." He drove down to the motel some time after dark. The bar was crowded, and he could hear music and dice cups as he crossed the thickly-carpeted lobby. He had to wait at the desk for the deskman to come in from the bar, looking frazzled.

"I'd like a couple of rooms," Steven said briskly. "One for me and my wife, one for Mr. Tom Phillips and his wife. I'll register for both."

"We have no rooms available," the man said without looking Steven in the eye. He was a thin, sallow-faced man, about thirty-five, getting a little bald. Not worth a hundred. Steven brought out his sheaf of bills, and, carefully passing up the hundreds, selected a fifty and passed it over to the clerk.

"For you," he said. "Happy Thanksgiving."

The clerk slipped the fifty into his pocket and then pulled his nose. Without looking up he said, "I still don't have any rooms."

"Yes, you do," Steven said.

After a moment, the clerk said, "Yes, sir," and Steven signed for the rooms. He walked into the bar. The holiday merrymakers were well into Thanksgiving, and the waitresses in their red satin hotpants were being kept on the go. Steven stood next to the waitress station at the bar.

"I'll have a gin and tonic," he told the bartender. One of the two girls working the bar was tall and very pretty. Steven began a conversation with her by saying, "Do you know a really good steak place that stays open late?"

"There's Denny's," she said, looking at him to see how he reacted. Steven grinned and shook his head. "Anything a little less well-lit?"

"You'd have to go to the city," she said, which of course he already knew. The next time she came back to order drinks, she gave him a smile. "On business?"

"No," he said. After he finished his drink, he waited for her to come back. "What time do you get off?" he asked.

"Two o'clock," she said, and smiled, waiting.

"Could I buy you a steak after work?"

"Uh, okay, sure. My name's Karen."

"I'm Steven," he said. He grinned warmly at her, mock-saluted, and went back to the party.

The second time Steven left the game, it was to talk to his son. Steven imagined Derek wanted to borrow money. He always did. Steven didn't usually cave in to his son's requests, but this time he decided to lend him fifty dollars, if he should ask for that much. Maybe he would even win something.

"I need some money, Dad," Derek said. They were standing in the backyard. It was dark and cold, and Steven in shirtsleeves was almost ready to shiver.

"Somehow, that doesn't surprise me," Steven said. His son was a terrible negotiator, damn it.

"I'm sick of my life!" Derek suddenly blurted. He was surprised at himself, but there was something in his father's tone that pissed him off. "I thought I could make it in the city, but I can't. You were right, Dad. The lack of an education is really hurting me. I know, the way I talked before. I was stupid."

"It's nice to hear you admit it," Steven said. "Maybe that's the start of something." He was definitely cold now, and was ready to give Derek his fifty dollars and go in the house. But Derek kept talking. He really sounded agitated.

"I have to get out of where I'm living," Derek said. He was cold, too, and wondered why he was blabbering away at his dad. Something inside him had snapped. Maybe being back home with the suburbanites is what did it. He did not know, he only knew he didn't want to go back to his tiny dirty smelly apartment. "I have it all worked out," he improvised. "I have to get a better job, I have to get a better place to live, I have to get into college, because, Dad, I know now that I'm not getting anywhere without my education. I know I can't get into a good school because I screwed up too much, but I think maybe that was a good thing for me, because it taught me the real value of education. I know I'm smart enough to pass, it's only a question of getting in there with purpose and getting everything done right. To do that I need to take a whole new look at myself. I'm behind, Dad. I just need to get some money to get on my feet, get a firm base, work days and go to school nights until I can get into college, and then really settle in to getting my education. I don't know if I can make it to law school, but . . ."

Steven was a little confused, and his feet were really getting cold. "What are you talking about?" he asked, a little sharply. "Going to law school? I thought you hated lawyers."

"No, not me. Not lawyers. I guess I was talking about the kind of lawyers everybody hates, you know, the kind that gets in there and screws everything up. But not the *other* kind of lawyer, the kind that works to make things *better*, to *improve* society . . ."

"I thought you hated society," Steven said humorously.

"I *do*, but I only hate it because it's so *bad*. We *need* good people going into the law, to turn things around, you know? I'm not saying I'm right for law school, but right now I'm *determined* to make something of myself, to get back on the right track again. I'm sorry, Dad. I guess this comes as kind of a surprise. But please. I really need your help."

They stood in the backyard watching their breath for a while. Derek was amazed at himself. Where had he gotten the nerve to speak? Was this true desperation?

"How much are we talking about?" his father asked.

What the fuck. "Ten thousand dollars," Derek said.

More silence. Then his father said, "Ten thousand dollars?"

"For everything. And I'll never come back on you again, I swear. Figure a new apartment, first and last month's rent, cleaning deposit, moving costs, but that won't be much, I'll do most of it myself, and I need new clothes for getting a new job, and I really can't get around looking for jobs unless I have a *car*, but it doesn't have to be much of a car, just a little car, a few bucks for that, mostly just the new apartment and some stuff to go in it. And a car. And some clothes. Is all. And college."

After some time, Steven chuckled and said, "I thought you wanted some cash to get into the poker game."

"I *do*," Derek said. "I mean, I *did*. But then I got to thinking this might be my last chance to see you face-to-face for a while, so I thought I better bring up the important stuff that's been on my mind, you know, kind of put it out there on the table. What I really need," he said lamely into the silence. His father chuckled again, mist coming out of his nose. Did he think this was funny?

"I really mean it!" Derek said, as he felt his last chance fading away.

"I know . . . I know . . ." his father said. "Here's fifty dollars." The hand came out of the pocket with a single bill in it. "Maybe you can win the ten thousand playing poker."

Derek felt the money in his hand, and something cold, colder than the night air, moved into him. "Thanks, Dad," he said. It had been a hustle, a shuck, but he really meant it. At least while he was babbling he had meant it. Now his father was gone and he was alone in the backyard. It was foggy and it felt like snow, although it never snowed around there.

When Steven got back in the game, he found a new player, another lawyer, named Richard Kreach. Kreach was dealing five-card stud. He was a thickset man, muscular rather than fat, with a lot of dirty-white hair, a ruddy complexion and a grizzled Mexican-style mustache. Kreach was wearing an old army field jacket over a black sweater. Steven was glad to meet him.

"You're in music, right?" he asked.

"I'm in deep shit right now," Kreach said, indicating his face-up card, a nine.

"Deal me in!" came the clear young voice of Derek.

By one-thirty the game had seven players, and everybody else had gone home or gone to bed. Eileen and Dorothy had stopped watching the game and gone to bed. Joey had quit winners and gone to bed. Steven looked at his watch and said, "I have to quit now." He smiled flatly at his son, and his son smiled flatly back. Derek had no time for his father. He was three hundred dollars ahead and in the middle of the best poker game of his life. The beauty of it was that he knew now he was outclassed on all sides, but being outclassed seemed to be bringing out the best in him, so instead of playing his usual game of conservatism alternating with wild, almost insane betting, he played the colder yet more exciting game of paying attention to every card, every bet. This game was shark-eat-shark, and he loved it.

Steven got up from the table, having lost eighty-one dollars, and Tom Phillips said to him, "I'm not ready to quit yet, but my wife is tired." Tom smiled over at Jill, who folded her hand and started counting her money. "I wonder," Tom said to Steven, "if you would be so kind as to drive Jill down to the motel?" So Steven found himself in his car with his exwife's sister, the voluptuous Jill Phillips. He had made a couple of passes at Jill over the years, mostly a long time ago, nothing he couldn't pretend hadn't happened, and she hadn't responded with anything but harmless flirting. He wondered what would happen if he took her to the door of her motel room and gave her a little kiss goodnight. Would she respond? If she did, he could ask her over to his room for a nightcap. He had a bottle of Martel's in the car somewhere. Brandy, my dear?

Then he chuckled to himself. He had a late date with Karen the waitress, which is why he quit the game losers. Karen. Maybe if he worded it right, he could get both Karen and Jill into bed with him. Wouldn't that be entertaining? Let's see, he could take Jill to her room, leave her, go pick up Karen, no . . . the logistics were too complex. And besides, he didn't know when Tom would be quitting the game. He didn't know how things were between Tom and Jill, maybe he was being set up. Anyway, he had Karen waiting. Or actually, just getting off work. He wasn't more than a few minutes late. He could take her to Denny's for a steak. She might complain, but once they were in the Denny's parking lot and the gastric juices were flowing, what was she going to do? Anyway, she'd feel great after eating. Then back to the motel for a glass of brandy.

Steven turned and looked at Jill's lovely profile, with its little dewlap chin and the voluptuous promise below. "Tired?" he asked.

"I'm so tired I could sleep in a phone booth," she said. Try as he would, Steven could not find anything sexy in her remark. In fact, she did look tired. He decided not to proposition her. Steven hated being rebuffed, although it did not happen that often. He remembered the first time he had made love to Jackie. She wanted to rebuff him. But she didn't. Across the street from the No Name bar in Sausalito, in the Bank of America parking lot, in the front seat of his car. He had been driving a little MGB then. He smiled to himself. It must have been difficult, but where there is a will, there is a way. Jackie had been so innocent, for a stewardess. He was just coming down off a big victory in court, a kid on a skateboard running into a negligence owned by the City of San Mateo. Really good money, and he must have been radiating something, because all the women in the No Name were after him. But Jackie had been on his mind since the first time he had seen her. Still beautiful, but untouchable now. Steven felt a twinge of regret. Well, no use dreaming . . .

The bar was still open when he got into the lobby, but when he went looking for Karen the barman said, "Sorry, we're just closed." There were a couple of drunks in the corner, and a waitress was talking to them. Not Karen.

"I was supposed to meet Karen," he said.

"She left," the barman said.

Sitting alone in his room with his bottle of Martel's, he wondered if he might just give Jill a ring. But no. He sipped the brandy. Bad stuff. But it would help him get to sleep. He thought about going back to Jackie's and the game. No, fuck it. He went to bed and was asleep in minutes.

By this time of the morning, his son Derek was doing very well. Steven would have been proud of him. He had run the fifty dollars up to five hundred, and now he was holding his own against some very tough, very educational players. He had been sandbagged once by Richard Kreach, who had checked what looked like a pair of nines, and then when Derek had bet twenty dollars on his aces, Kreach raised him sixty dollars and really pissed him off, because even though he knew he had been had, he couldn't do anything about it. He had to call. And so he went ahead and called, and of course Kreach had the third nine. But that had been quite a while ago, and Derek was back up to strength now, waiting for the right hand to make a killing. Looking down at the thick pile of bills covered with stacked coins gave him a real sense of power. With this kind of money he could do some things.

Then came one of those coincidences that happen every so often in poker games. As Richard Kreach put it, "I think everybody's got the winning hand. Isn't this wonderful?"

But that was later, after the draw. Al Burke was dealing his usual round of California poker, no openers, check and check out, which meant you had to bet before the draw, or fold. Al dealt himself three little threes, an ace and a queen. The ante had been a dollar (they had long since quit fucking around with quarter antes) and Jackie to Al's left bet a dollar, which everybody called, no raises, it seemed to be a routine hand to Al, who bumped ten dollars, the size of the pot. Three threes seemed to be a very good hand in this game. Big pots had been taken down with less, far less. Al bet the pot not only to clear out the inside straights and small pairs, but to set the hook into anybody who still wanted to play. To Al's surprise, everybody wanted to play, and the pot went to sixty dollars before the draw.

With that kind of response, Al wanted to throw in his ace-queen and hope for the fourth three. But he knew he would have a better chance of catching another ace than the final three, so he threw away only his queen.

"Cards?" he asked the table. This was going to be fun!

Jackie took one card, so she was dangerous. Jackie wouldn't be holding junk, she was too good a player. Her son Derek, in his dark glasses, also drew one card. Al didn't know what to think about that; he would have to wait and see how Derek acted after the draw. Tom the Texan drew three cards, so he had a high pair, probably aces. Poor Tom had been second-best all evening, and a large amount of the floating wealth around the table had come from Tom. Then Richard Kreach stood pat, and Al's heart sank, figuring the rock lawyer for a straight or flush, but more likely a straight, because Kreach had proved over the last couple of hours to be a pretty conservative player, in spite of his bullying ways, and he hadn't raised Al's raise.

"One card for the dealer," Al said quietly. When he had been a kid playing poker, this had been the best time to cheat. All the other kids would be looking at their new cards, and you could take whatever you wanted off the bottom of the deck and no one the wiser. He smiled in remembrance of those wild kid games, and happened to look up to see Kreach watching him.

"Off the top, pardner," Kreach said without smiling, and Al felt a powerful twist of guilt. He took himself one card, ostentatiously off the top, and shuffled his hand together to mix up the cards, but the first card he peeked at was the newcomer—the three of clubs. Hmm. He looked around at the others examining their new cards. The game had grown awfully quiet. Al shuffled his cards loosely, and then fanned them. Four threes and an ace. Hmm, again.

"Check to the raiser," Jackie said, and everyone agreed, checking around to Al, who bet sixty dollars, the size of the pot, the maximum bet. Al was not certain of winning except in his heart. In his heart he knew he would win. In his mind he knew he had a very good chance of winning, with all the factors carefully and scientifically weighed. But his soul gave the orders, and his soul told him to bet and keep betting until hell froze over. If you play straight poker, and you don't play that often, you aren't going to see that many fours of a kind in your lifetime. And so you are going to bet them all the way, or why the hell are you playing?

"I'll raise a hundred dollars," Jackie said quietly. Jackie threw in the one hundred and sixty dollars, leaving her with only a few bills and some quarters. She had drawn one, and must have hit. No one but a blockhead would try to bluff now.

Derek closed his cards in his hand and then fanned them open again, as if checking the spots. Then he did it again, and started counting his money.

"Shit or get off the pot," Kreach said. "A fucking kid like you shouldn't even be in this game; come on, bet your fucking bet or fold the fucking cards."

"Make it two hundred," Derek said, raising forty dollars. If Derek was betting two hundred dollars. . . . Al felt even more excited. What if they both had four of a kind? It was mathematically remote, but far from impossible, especially with this many players, and nearly every card in the deck in play.

Texas Tom, who must have sweated off forty pounds since dinner, put his two hundred dollars into the pot quickly and with no fuss. "Call" was all he had to say. Then Kreach, who had taken no cards, but who hadn't raised, either. Now he looked around the table at the other players and said, "I hate to do this." He put four one-hundred-dollar bills into the pot. He looked at Al. "Three-forty to you."

Al counted his money. He had just over two hundred dollars in front of him. He was glad. If he had had more money, he would have had to put it in. As it was, he pushed the two hundred into the pot. "I'm all in," he said.

That was when Kreach made his remark about everybody having the winning hand. The betting and raising went on until everybody was shypot except Kreach and Tom. Tom's white shirt was stuck to him, his face pale, but still kindly. He could get well on this hand. As for Kreach, he seemed to have an endless supply of one-hundred-dollar bills, and had been continuously winning since entering the game. Al had seen him that afternoon eating from a heaped-up plate and loudly cheering the football game, and then later after the poker game started, Kreach had been sacked out in one of the bedrooms, snoring away. Now here he was, the last player willing and able to raise.

"Is that it?" Kreach demanded. "Is everybody in?"

Al had gone shypot first, so he turned up his cards first. He didn't really think he had a chance. "Four little threes," he said quietly.

It was too important a hand, and obviously the last hand, so instead of just throwing in her cards, Jackie spread them, a heart flush, leading with the ace-king.

"I had you beat, Mom," Derek said tiredly. He turned over a full house, three nines and two jacks.

"Well, I ain't dead yet," Tom said, and turned over four tens and a six.

"You bastard," Al said, not unkindly.

"I'm the bastard," Kreach said, and fanned out a small straight flush, dealt to him pat, the four, five, six, seven and eight of clubs.

Everyone was quiet as Kreach pulled in all the money.

"I guess that's the game," Jackie said into the silence. "I'm just as glad. It's been a long day."

"You look tired," Al said to her.

"God damn fuck shit," said Derek, looking down at the few dollars in front of him. "I had over six hundred dollars."

"That's really too bad," Kreach said, as he continued to sort his money and the others continued to watch.

"How much did you win?" Derek asked.

"None of your business," Kreach said. He rapidly counted out some bills and passed them over to Jackie. "For the house," he said.

Jackie picked up the bills. "What's this?"

"Just some money," Kreach said. "Thanks for having us all over. Even though you didn't invite me personally, the word was out. Usually I hate Thanksgiving."

"It's daylight," Derek said.

"Does anybody want a turkey sandwich?" Jackie asked.

Nobody did.

Jackie was alone now. The weekend was over, everybody had gone home, and Jackie was alone in her bed at three o'clock on Monday morning. She had gone to bed too early, but there had been nothing else to do. The house was clean. She had spent all day Sunday cleaning house and drinking ale, playing records at top volume. Now the only signs that there had been a big party were the six bulky green plastic bags out by the mailbox, waiting to be picked up, and the assortment of dishes and pans Jackie had scraped and cleaned and which now waited to be picked up by their owners. Al had called and volunteered to come over and help, but she lied and said she didn't need any. In fact, she was both tired of people and terribly lonely, all at the same time, and Al's cheerful grin would have driven her crazy.

Insomnia was an old companion. Jackie counted the hours until she could get up and begin her day. Three to four. Four to five. Five to six. Six to seven. Four hours. Jackie wasn't good at things like time and dates. She had been once, but not anymore. She was slowly losing her mind, but nothing dramatic. Just duller and duller, until she has to count on her fingers. If she got up and had a bottle of Green Death, would it help her to sleep? Jackie thought about going ahead and getting drunk again, maybe a couple of shots of vodka and a couple of bottles of ale, and then crash. She would probably wake up around ten in the morning, muzzy and hung over. She didn't feel particularly hung over right now. A distant headache, feelings of guilt, worthlessness and fear. In other words, she felt normal. There was no reason for her to lay off the booze. She didn't have to get up at seven. She could stay in bed if she wanted. But there was something terribly wrong about that. If she stayed in bed, she would just die there. Not sudden death. Rot. She would shrivel up and die.

But if she got up and went to the refrigerator and opened the door and took out a bottle of ale and popped the cap and put the bottle to her lips and tilted it back, ah, she would already be dead and rotten. Just not ready to lie down. But she *was* ready to lie down. She was already lying down. There was no reason to get up. One more bottle wouldn't make that much difference, she couldn't get away from her own mind, so why bother? ESCAPE TO FREEDOM, HAVE A BEER. Would it work?

Like all of Jackie's problems, which she didn't even want to give names to, problems so overwhelming that they couldn't bear looking at unless Jackie was a little drunk, and of course when she was a little drunk, her problems didn't look like problems anymore, and she could forget about them and go on pretending she was still nineteen and had the world by the tail. Well, she was not nineteen, she was forty-five. When she had been a child, working out her life in advance, she had seen the career, she had seen the meeting of the right man, the marriage, the house in the suburbs, the children, all that she had seen very clearly. What she had not seen was this. She had run out of plans and she was only forty-five, with about forty years to go and nothing to do.

Except drink. All her life Jackie had been a sexual woman, but she had expected that she would gradually grow less and less attractive to men, and that as her attraction dimmed, so would her desires. But that had not happened. Nothing happened the way she planned it. Jackie was still getting hit on regularly, but she was losing interest fast. Unless she was drunk. Then she could get pretty wild. But people didn't do that stuff anymore. It was too dangerous. Jackie had managed to get this far in life without sexual disease. She would like to make it all the way.

She was worried about her daughter Diedre. Diedre acted so strangely. Was it fear? She seemed to crave security so badly. Now she was chained to a machine forever. Not a drill press, a computer, but Jackie could not see the difference. When Jackie had been Diedre's age, she had been free.

She had been flying all over the world, running around with girls just as goodlooking as herself, and men with futures, big goodlooking men who skied and surfed and flew choppers and drove fast cars . . . Looking back, had it really been like that? She had always been so proud of her stewardess years; it had seemed like such a clean thing. But not anymore. You didn't have to be hot to be a stew any-more. They were nothing but flying waitresses now. Back when Jackie had been flying, stews had cachet. Poor Diedre wasn't that goodlooking, of course. In Jackie's time, Diedre could never have gotten a job with American. Even then she would have had to go to work for the telephone company, or something like the telephone company. She and her telephone company husband would have had chil-dren, and Jackie would become a grandmother. She had been wait-ing to be a grandmother. That was the next step in her life. What she hadn't known about was the big empty space between Housewife and Grandmother, and she guessed that she would learn that being Grandma wasn't all that hot, either. She didn't mind being a grand-mother. She liked little kids. She liked them a lot more than she liked big kids.

Derek. If she was going to think about Derek, she would certainly have to get up and get an ale. She looked at the clock beside her bed, just as the number silently clicked over to 3:06. She threw off her coverlet. She was wearing panties and an old tee shirt. The air felt good against the skin of her legs; gently she waved one leg in the air, as if getting ready to get up. Derek had been so unhappy after the poker game. Derek broke her heart.

Why couldn't she be nicer to him? He had enough trouble in the world without Jackie getting on his case, too. But maybe if she had gotten on his case a little more in the earlier years, he might not have turned out so strangely. Not badly. She refused the notion that De-rek was a bad kid. He just hadn't found himself. He was such a bril-liant kid sometimes. And so stupid. Or maybe none of it was his fault. He had played wonderful poker, Jackie had been so proud of him, and then he lost it all. But she did not blame him. After the game he could not keep from begging money from Jackie, and with all the money Richard Kreach had given her she hadn't been able to refuse, and had given him too much, a hundred dollars. Kreach had given her three hundred dollars. She wondered what he expected for it, and then took the thought back. Maybe Richard Kreach had given her the money for the reason he said. "For the house." It didn't matter, Jackie was still in the hole from the party, and thank God the house was finally clean. She should get out of this big house. It had been far too big when they moved in, and now it was far too big again. But Jackie hated to move. Not moving was part of her dream of life. You found your place and you stayed there. Like her father in Salina. Jackie owed Steven two months' rent. He had been very sweet about it. She wished Steven and Derek got along better. It had been worse, though. Maybe everything was getting better.

The bedside radio played faint rock music. Jackie wondered if she should get up for a bottle of Green Death. She wondered if the way to do it was to get married again, only this time for different reasons, this time for companionship as well as money, or call it security, never call it money. She still had the classy body, the breasts that were just a little larger than they were supposed to be, the eyebrow-lifters that had gotten her preferred treatment all her life. She put her leg down without getting out of bed. Maybe that's a sign of will power. Or laziness. She could marry Al, not that he had asked her. But as much as she liked Al, maybe even loved him a little, she did not want to live with him. Be frank, honey. It's early in the morning. You don't want to marry Al because Al is a poor man. Yes, but. There was more. Sweet sunny Al was also sort of strange, to be perfectly honest. There were sides to Al she didn't understand. Maybe it was because he was so ambitionless. He seemed content to teach a few classes and spend the rest of his time fucking off, fishing, reading, daydreaming, hanging out in bars playing chess. Al was strange. No, Al was a good guy, she really loved him, but he would be her friend rather than her husband, in that wonderful future that is about to start as soon as the sun comes up. Oh wonderful day to come.

There was another choice, she thought without emotion. She could always kill herself. She remembered the suicide of the actor George Sanders. "I've had enough," he said in his note. What a fine thing to say. Don't worry about me; I've had enough. There were knives in the kitchen. Jackie shivered and pulled the covers back over herself. No knives, please. Did she have any pills? Two or three #4 codeines, left over from her last trip to the dentist's. No death lurking there. No guns in the house. Women seldom shoot themselves anyway. Poison or jump off something. That was how women did it. Maybe she should commit a man's suicide. "Jackie did it like a man. She blew her fuckin' head off."

Jackie ran her thumb along the edge of her front teeth, feeling the chipped place where the lesbian had popped her in the mouth that time in Denver, and then followed her around all the rest of the night apologizing and calling her a saint. Jackie hated dentists but was too polite to let it show when she went in for her checkups. Dentists were strange. Either they were trim little sadists wearing aftershave, humming away, enjoying themselves, singing out for the nurse, always telling Jackie what fine teeth she had, except for that one chip, of course; or they were sad-eyed men who seemed trapped into the act of dentistry as much as she was. Her current dentist was this last kind, and he agreed with her that the chip gave her face character. The dentist before this one had killed himself, she remembered. Speaking of suicide. Tim, his name had been, Tim Kaiser or something. Doctor Kaiser. It had been years. Back in the old hippie days, with the dentist in tie-dyes and sandals. The Jefferson Airplane booming over the sound system, ferns hanging where you could see them as you lay there being worked on. Tim had those sad eyes, too, but doped-up sad eyes. He had fallen in love with his own medications. Apparently he had been filling up on percodan every morning, before looking down into all those frightened eyes, all those open mouths, and would keep popping Percs all day long, two and three at a time, and then in the evening to calm himself down, to remove the taste from his own mouth, he would sit in his dentist's chair, let it all the way back to the most relaxing position, and turn on the laughing gas. The moment must have come when he grew tired of the routine. They found him in the morning, in his chair, the gas still on, but the tank empty. They knew it wasn't an accident, because he hadn't turned on the oxygen, just the nitrous oxide. He had gone out on a blast of pure happy gas.

Maybe that would be a way of doing things. She could turn on the gas. Make sure all the pilot lights were out, then leave the oven door open. She didn't want to stand there bent forward with her head in the oven. Her ovens were up high, and if she did that she would probably fall back as soon as she was unconscious, and lay there on the floor, maybe even waking up before she died. But she could seal off the house, turn on all the gas outlets, take all her pills, have a drink and go back to bed. After a while, the gas would fill the house. The gas was heavier than air, so it would silently pour out of the ovens and off the stovetop down onto the floor, where it would gather in pools and streams, slowly moving from the kitchen to the dining room, to the hallway, to the bedroom . . . and she gets a little drunk and a little high from the pills and forgets about the gas and lights a joint, BLAM!!!

Nothing left at the corner of Halsey and Funafuti but a couple of rose bushes. Chunks of Mrs. Jeminovski seen flying over the Redwood Highway . . .

As a matter of fact, gas was too dangerous. She might want to blow herself up, but not the neighbors. Suicide was out of the question anyway. She had not had enough, she decided once more. She looked at the clock. 3:16. It really was time to get up and get that bottle of ale and stop fighting the whole universe. She had to get up anyway, to pee. She visualized the inside of the refrigerator. Was there a bottle of ale in there? The trouble was, there was so much stuff left over from Thanksgiving. She could see the tops of milk cartons, but she also saw the tops of two bottles of ale, green bottles with green and gold foil on top. But did she actually see them, or did she dream them up? She would have to go look to find out. She could feel her chest go cold with panic. What if there wasn't any? What if she had gone to bed without making sure there was ale in the house? Her fucking memory!

She would have to get dressed and go down to the Seven-Eleven. Sure. Nearly four A.M., walks into the store. Nobody there but a couple of black kids or something. The clerk. She buys, what? Toothpaste, quart of milk, sixpack of ale . . . They would all know. "Drunk old bitch!" the kids in her mind yelled at the woman in her mind. No Seven-Eleven. Al? She could go down to Al's and knock on his door. He must know. Everybody must know. No. She could not see herself showing up at anybody's door. She was a beautiful woman. Beautiful women do not show up at people's doors. They make calls, and people show up at *their* doors. Who could she call? Who would be so glad to hear from her that he would gladly get up out of a warm bed to bring her a sixpack? Wait. There was the vodka. She relaxed. The vodka in the freezer. Even if there was no ale, she could have her vodka. But isn't that horrible, having vodka at four in the morning? Just to get to sleep? Why had God forsaken her?

What was that? *My God, why hast thou forsaken me?*

That was what Jesus said on the cross. With the nails in his hands and feet, things didn't look so good, did they? Poor Jesus. She didn't much believe in God anymore, but she could never give up her Jesus. She knew him too well. When she had been little. You never get over it. Jesus up there sweating, his eyes wild with disbelief and pain. "My God! Why hast thou forsaken me?" Hey, the joke's over. It was just a ritual. We don't have to go through with it. Hey, let me down. Hello? *Hello?*

Jackie smiled and threw back the covers. She sat up, actually sat up. Apparently she was going to the bathroom, and then to the kitchen for a little something to drink. She felt a ripple of guilt, as if somebody were watching her. The baby Jesus, of course. Watching to make sure she didn't get away with anything. But the truth was, nobody was watching her. Nobody minded if she got up and had a bottle of ale. There were no children asleep in the bedrooms of her house. There was no job waiting, no husband to send off to work, nothing but emptiness, self-pity, and the little baby Jesus.

"Okay, Jesus," she said aloud. "Let's have a drink."

YOUNG PEOPLE

The first time Derek Jeminovski saw him, Burns was being hauled out of the Gayety Theater on Turk Street by two policemen. The cops were typical San Francisco cops, big and beefy, with red angry faces. Burns was a tall thin kid about Derek's age, with a shock of peroxide hair. The cops banged out the double doors of the porno theater and slammed Burns against a parked car. Burns had a silly loose grin on his face until one of the cops snapped the cuffs on him tightly, and then Burns let out a scream, his mouth wide, showing a lot of jagged teeth. He looked right into Derek's eyes and winked just before one of the cops turned him around and took him by the front of his dirty white tee shirt and double-slapped his face.

"Don't scream," the cop said. They led Burns off down the street, the kid skinny between the two big cops. Derek felt a blossoming of rage and fear at the sight. He had been on his way to this room in the Greenleaf Hotel just up Turk. But now he didn't want to be alone, so he ducked into Doakie's Cafe on the corner and sat at the counter.

Doakie's was a hole in the wall with six stools and two narrow little booths. This time of the afternoon there were a couple of Iranians or something in one of the booths, an old guy drunk at the end of the counter, leaning against the wall and grinning at nobody, and the old

Vietnamese woman behind the counter cooking her own lunch on the grill in the front where people could see the food cooking through the window. Doakie's was a hangout of Derek's since he moved from Jackson Street to the Tenderloin. He asked for a cup of coffee, and the old woman drew it for him and put it in front of him without ever looking him in the eye, and went back to her eggs and sprouts, or what the hell. Derek tried to calm down. He was very much afraid of the police these days. He wondered what the tall guy with the wide mouth had done in the porno theater. Maybe he hadn't done anything. Maybe they were just picking him up there on a tip. The kid didn't much look like a criminal, but Derek was getting smarter every day, and you couldn't tell what anybody was from the way they looked.

Another of Derek's hangouts was the Tivoli Billiards, across Market Street, practically the only place where anybody would talk to him. A lot of the people who hung out at the Tivoli were criminals, or so they told it, and Derek could believe them. One of them even tried to sell him a hotel key, promising that the girl in the room only wanted a guy to bring her a little weed or some coke or even a pint of whiskey, but Derek declined to buy, grinning with embarrassment at the thought that he was so obviously a pigeon.

Derek did not think he was a pigeon. He was just new around the Tenderloin. When people got to know him better, they would realize that he, too, was a criminal. But Derek was not the kind of criminal who boasts about it at the local poolhall. Derek's crimes were a little too petty to brag about. Derek these days made his living walking all over the city busting into newspaper machines. He had run from a police car once, and been chased by a meter maid once. You had to hit the changebox a sharp blow with the screwdriver to bust it loose, get a crack open, and then you had to shake the goddamn box for the money to drop out. At the end of a good day Derek would have a pocketful of quarters, dimes and nickels, mostly quarters. On a really good day he could make twenty or thirty dollars, which was terrible money.

He kept remembering the six hundred dollars he had lost playing poker at his mother's house. What a humiliation. And he kept remembering that his father was rich, and would not give him any money. He would get the money later, when his father died, but that made no difference to his father. Derek was supposed to find his own way in life. Then, when he inherited his father's money, he would be ready for it. Well, Derek was ready for it now. He wondered what his father would think if he got arrested for busting coinboxes. His father was a lawyer, but not the kind that would do Derek any good. His father specialized in pleasure-related accidents.

Derek took a sip of his coffee, to make more room in the cup. Then he filled the cup again with cream and sugar, the poor man's milkshake. He still had to go stealing today. He had about three bucks on him, and two twenties stashed in his dinky hotel room. He hated his hotel room. The Greenleaf was a Patel hotel, run by the endless Patel family from India. The room was a slot, with a broken bed and dirty sheets and blanket. The sink in the corner smelled of a thousand years of indiscriminate pissing, and the dirty walls smelled of death. Derek paid seventy-five dollars a week to stay there. The only time the place was anything like quiet was in the daytime. At night there were funny noises and frightening noises, people drifting around the corridors, murders happening, screams in the night, strangers scratching at your door. Derek did most of his sleeping between 4:00 A.M. and noon.

Seeing the blond kid dragged off by the cops made Derek think about his own criminal career. Now that he had learned how to break open the paper boxes, he knew it was only a matter of time before he was caught, arrested, and sent to jail. He dreaded the thought of county jail. Derek knew perfectly well that as a slender kid of twenty he would be Raw Meat in jail. There was no privacy in San Francisco county jail, too crowded with every kind of bad criminal type. Derek knew he would be raped, fucked in the ass, given AIDS, and killed. He would be so much better off in a straight job. But every day his clothes got shabbier and his ability to put on a straight hype grew less and less, and he would sleep till noon, eat a stupid breakfast of Hostess cupcakes or some such shit, and go hunting for harmless newspaper machines to kill.

The next time Derek saw Burns was at the Tivoli Billiards. It had been a bad night for Derek. His various criminal activities had failed him all day, and the three-fifty he spent on a bad-tasting hamburger at Doakie's left him with eighteen cents. He had his bed in the hotel room, but that was all, and on Saturday if he didn't come up with the weekly rent, he would be out on his ass. Naturally, the cheap hamburger did nothing to cut his hunger. It was funny. He had noticed it before. That last meal before you go broke always leaves you hungry as hell, like, you'll never eat again. "The condemned man ate a hearty meal." I'll bet he ate a hearty meal. Scoff scoff scoff, got anymore of that lemon pie? I'm still HUNGRY!!!

So death and hunger were on his mind as he aimlessly walked around the Tenderloin. Tonight he was dressed in jeans, black Reeboks, and an old tweed jacket that somebody had given his mother and his mother had given him. His mother might be a source of money, if Saturday came and he still hadn't managed to get any money. He was not really worried about hunger, an old Marin County boy like Derek. In Marin County you learned a lot of oddball facts about life, such as the fact that people don't starve if they don't eat right away. When Derek had been a kid all kinds of Marin County people were fasting all over the place, and they would go twenty or thirty days without solid food. Of course they drank orange juice and such shit, but some of them went on water fasts and could last amazing lengths of time without eating. The secret was to drink plenty of water and not move around too much. But maybe his mother would loan him some money, if he told her how desperate he was. But she was broke, too, he knew. Not real broke like he was, she could always tap Dad, or something. He really wondered how his mother made it, sometimes. The big house, the big car. The money must come from his dad, he decided once again, and so there was nothing wrong with Derek hitting her up for some of it. All she had to do was hit the old man up again. Derek sure wasn't going to call his dad. He had done it before, always the collect call, the joke about maybe not accepting the call, then the jokes about never calling except when he needed money, and then the jokes about everything else, but never the money.

The Tenderloin was noisy that early in the evening. The sidewalks had plenty of traffic, hookers and cops, bums, muggers, pimps, old people, Vietnamese kids running around screaming and laughing, johns in their john clothes looking for hookers, and cars full of johns cruising the district, pulling up at the corners to talk to the hookers and open the car doors for them, money changing hands, the johns driving the hookers up a couple of blocks to a dark street where they would lean over and give blowjobs for twenty, thirty bucks, four-minute sex, and half the time the poor fucking john did not know whether the hooker who blew him was a woman or a queen, half the so-called female hookers down here were guys in drag, and the other half were mostly these black chicks who would stick you as quick as blow you, yet Derek had this fantasy he couldn't shake, about the young white hooker he meets casually on the street, and they end up loving each other.

Because Derek was starved for love. The truth was, he had only been laid a few times in his young life, and only once by a civilian, which had been back up in distant Marin County when he had been eighteen, when he had worked for a short time as a kitchen helper in a dirty little hippie hangout in Larkspur called Eggmont's, and one of the older women who worked the counter had hauled him home with her one night to this tiny place underneath somebody's house, a little mother-in-law, she called it, and fucked him on her thick white rug. She must have been at least thirty, and knew all about sex, but when Derek came around after he had been fired and tried to get her to fuck him again she just laughed and said, "That was just for fun," and wouldn't take him seriously. Bitch whore, he thought, not really meaning it. Actually, he had liked her a lot. I learned about love from an older woman.

Now as he wandered around the Tenderloin he occupied himself by staying alert and making sure he didn't give off any victim vibrations, you could get scragged around here for eighteen cents, and keeping an eye out for the girl of his dreams. There were plenty of hookers out. Young ones, too, but always something missing from their faces, he did not know what to call it. His legs ached from a fruitless day of hunting, and this drove him to the Tivoli Billiards. It was better than going home, even if he didn't have enough money to buy a cup of coffee.

They wouldn't let bums into the Tivoli anymore, and Derek only got past the barrier because he was an old regular, at least old enough a regular to know the creep at the gate.

"Buzz me, Louie." *Bzzzzt*, and he was in.

The giant room full of pool, snooker and billiard tables was pretty empty. There was a game going at the open snooker table in the front of the place, four guys playing for two dollars a corner; a couple of old guys playing billiards down at the end of the room, and three or four guys at the counter. The game machines were unattended except for this tall kid in a black leather jacket, black jeans and a shock of peroxide hair. Derek didn't recognize him when he first came in, but after taking a piss and sitting watching the open game for a while, Derek got up and wandered over to the machines to watch, and saw that it was the same guy he had seen getting rousted out of the Gayety.

Burns was playing one of the pinballs, bumping and cursing. He had a bottle of beer on the glass, and some quarters, and a pack of cigarettes. Derek stood with his hands in his hip pockets, watching quietly. After a while Burns would look over at Derek when a shot went well or badly, grin, say, "Ain't that a bitch?" or something. Finally the quarters were gone. Burns slapped the machine hard enough to tilt it.

"So much for that shit," he said, and wandered over to the counter with his beer. He left the cigarette pack behind, and after a moment, Derek picked it up. He wanted the cigarettes; he hadn't actually quit so much as gone on an economy drive. But the idea of stealing a half a pack of butts did not appeal to him. He walked over to the counter, where Burns was ordering coffee. Derek waited until the old China-man went to get the coffee.

"You left these on the machine," Derek said.

Burns looked up and grinned widely. "Thanks!" He had an inter-esting face, not handsome or anything, but very expressive, and his eyes were big and blue and intelligent. Burns grinned at Derek and shook the cigarette package until a couple of cigarettes and a rolled joint fell out.

"I guess you deserve a reward," Burns said grinning. "Wait till I blow down this coffee. You want a cup of coffee?"

Derek hesitated, and Burns said, "I'll buy."

Derek sat down next to the tall thin boy, and Burns yelled at the counterman, "One more coffee, Charlie!"

"I seen you the other day," Derek said.

"Oh, yeah? Where at?"

"The Gayety." Derek grinned. "You were coming out."

Burns frowned in remembrance, then brightened. "Oh, yeah. I remember you. I winked at you."

"Yeah."

"Just to show I wasn't scared, you know?" Burns laughed. "I wasn't scared, either. I was so full of smack. I guess the girl behind the counter called the cops. I was just sitting in there watching the porn, eating popcorn, having a good time. Then here come these cops. It was very funny."

"Smack, huh?" said Derek, who couldn't think of anything else to say.

"My first time. Smoked it, brown stuff, not really smack. Mor-phine. But much better than real smack, they tell me. Okay, we'll fin-ish our coffee here and then go outside and find a nice quiet spot to split our joint here. This joint I got from a lady, and my guess would be that it's good shit, maybe the best. It's not smack, but it's something."

Derek smiled.

"They call me Burns," the tall boy said. "I don't know why."

"Is that your name?" Derek said stupidly, and regretted it immediately, but the other boy just grinned. "Burns is my name, and *burns* is my game . . . "

"I'm Derek Jeminovski."

"Jesus Christ, who laid that on you?"

"The Derek or the Jeminovski? My mother called me Derek. My old man's the Jeminovski."

"It's a great name, Derek," Burns said. "Here, have a cigarette. I have a first name, too, but nobody uses it. James. Jim. Jimmy fucking Burns. But call me Burns."

"Okay, Burns," Derek said. He put one of Burns' Pall Malls between his lips and Burns lit a match for him.

"Sorry, my Dunhill lighter's been pledged as a security," Burns said.

"That's all right," Derek said. "I don't mind."

"That's good," Burns said. "You come to this dumb fucking poolhall much? I've never seen you before." He grinned again. "Except that one time at the movies."

Derek laughed. "What'd the cops do with you?"

"Well, they asked me what all the trouble was back in the movie house. They had me in their car. They weren't such bad guys. I told 'em candy really got me off and maybe I must have gone crazy from too much candy. They let me go."

"Where you from?" Derek asked.

"Me? I come from Stockton. Have you ever been to Stockton?"

"Not me," Derek admitted. "I'm from up north."

"North where? Oregon?"

"No, Marin. Lincoln's Grove."

"Oh, a Grover, huh? I've heard about Grovers. Grover cowboys. Cowboy drag, BMWs, joggers."

"Yeah, real assholes. I couldn't wait to get out."

"You should try Stockton. Everybody who isn't a fucking Mexican says, 'Shoot,' and spits on the ground. Plenty of work, though, if a man wants a job, plenty to do in the Valley. Beets to hoe, plenty of sugar beets. You ever been to L.A.?"

"No," said Derek. "My dad lives down there, but I never went down there. When he moved I was too little."

"I've been there a couple times. Hollywood, that's the town, man, you think Market Street's fucked up, you should see Hollywood Boulevard. You think Castro's gay? You should see Santa Monica Boulevard. Fifteen miles of fags. On a warm night you can smell poppers a mile out to sea. And you better not mess with those fags down there, either. They are tough. But L.A.'s great."

"I heard," Derek said.

"That's a lot of cream and sugar, Man," Burns said with a sly grin. "Little coffee milkshake, huh?"

Derek blushed, and with a pang of fear he remembered he only had eighteen cents.

"It's okay," Burns said. "Let's go out and smoke our doobie."

They walked down the long, wide staircase to Market Street, passing a slumped-over drunk sitting on the steps. When they got to the street Burns looked back up at the drunk. "I'd roll his ass, except that he's a cop."

Market Street was pretty crowded. People were coming out of movie theaters, and others, mostly foreign-looking to Derek, just swarmed up and down the big, wide sidewalks aimlessly, looking into the litup windows of the stores, coming and going from the bars and restaurants, always a lot of action downtown, which was one of the reasons Derek loved San Francisco and hated Marin, especially Lincoln's Grove. Boring. Nobody out without business. Nobody like Derek to be found. As he walked down the street with his new-found friend, Derek thought for a moment about the friends he had left behind, his fellow Grovers, mostly in college or working. Some dead. He remembered his friend Willie from high school, Willie the Rock they called him, big muscles, big grin, didn't give a fuck for anything or anybody, died when his VW bug flipped over on the

Rosemont curve in Mill Valley. Nobody hurt, but the Rock was dead, his big head smashed to a pulp. Other friends? No, not many, and no deep friendships. Dates? Girls he had loved and left? None, except in his dreams. The Grover girls looked for a little more than Derek could offer, it seemed. Grover girls want a man with prospects.

As he was thinking these thoughts he was surprised to see Burns put the joint in his mouth and stop briefly to light it, his hands cupped around the paper match. He took a deep drag and handed the joint to Derek. As they walked along through the late evening crowds they passed the joint back and forth. Instead of pinching the joint between his thumb and forefinger, the way everybody else did with marijuana, Burns held it to his mouth between his first two fingers, as if it was a regular cigarette. Derek did it the old-fashioned way, and Burns laughed at him.

"You look furtive, Man," he said. "Act like you're smoking a regular cigarette, and people will think that's what you're doing."

"I get you," Derek said. The marijuana was starting to work. "That's enough for me," he said.

"Okay, I'll eat the roach," Burns said. "Let's stretch our legs here on Market Street for a while, really walk along, okay? And then we'll get something to eat. How about that big German place on Turk? They have a turkey dinner, how about it? Oh, money, right? Sorry about that. I have a few pesos, but not enough for the two of us."

They walked fast down Market, although because of the dope Derek felt as if he was walking into a stiff wind, or in slow motion. It was all he could do to keep up with his new friend with the long legs.

"Wait," Burns said. "I have enough money to buy us a couple of beers, and we can talk about what to do. Do you have any ID? You're not twenty-one, are you?"

"Not quite," Derek said. "I had some ID but I ran it through the washing machine and turned it into pulp."

Burns laughed. "Nice dope, huh? I can see you handing a wad of pulp to some cop. Anyway, I know a place."

They turned south off Market and went a block or two, turned up

an alley where there was a bar called the G&G. It was full of dark
wood and old men in suits banging dice cups, a couple of women but
all old. Burns led Derek to a table in a dark corner of the bar. When
the old waitress came over Burns said, "Two beers, please." She
didn't even look at them, just mumbled, "Yessir," and went for the
beers. Derek told himself to remember this place.

"Ha, it's nice to be seated in here out of the cold," Burns said, although it wasn't particularly cold out.

"Yeah," said Derek. "That's smooth dope. Still comin' on," he
said, hoping to flatter Burns.

"This girl gave it to me. I'm amazed. People don't give good dope
away. It costs too much. You're from Marin, huh? They grow a lot of
dope over there."

"Yeah," Derek said. "Up on the mountain. Pot patches."

"Make a goddamn fortune," Burns said. "Four or five ounces of
good smokable weed for every plant, maybe a hundred plants in a little patch, call it four hundred ounces just to be on the safe side, and
what do you have? What's the shit going for now? Sixty a quarter,
that's two-forty an ounce, we're talking a hundred thousand bucks
here, for hauling a little water, picking a few leaves."

"It's not that easy," Derek said defensively, although he did not
know what he was defending. Marin County maybe.

"I don't give a fuck how easy it is," Burns said coldly. He stubbed
out his cigarette almost angrily, his mouth tight. "The trick is to rip
the fuckers off."

"Huh?" said Derek.

Now Burns grinned at him, and it was not a nice grin. "You know
where any of these pot patches are?"

"Sure," Derek said. "Up on the mountain. But you can't rip these
guys off. Not anymore."

"Why not?"

"Because they got guns, pitchforks, booby traps, all kinds of shit.
Some kids ripped off some Stinson Beach farmers a few years ago,
remember that?"

"No," said Burns.

"Well, they did, kids from South San Francisco or Daly City, came up at night in black vans, caught the growers by surprise, held 'em down with guns to their heads, right after the poor guys picked their crop. Nobody got hurt. Nobody got caught. The cops didn't find out about it till everything was all over."

Burns seemed fascinated, and Derek was pleased at being able to entertain his host. The marijuana made him talkative, and he told himself to shut up. But he was still pleased with his story.

"That's great," Burns said after a long sip of beer. "Some fucking greaseball from down there figured how to burn the bastards. How much do you think they got away with?"

"At least a million dollars' worth," Derek said.

"It takes planning," Burns said. "A handful of guys. Guns. Trucks. Find somebody to deal the shit off to, but that wouldn't be hard. You could be our inside man. You know these bastards. You could kind of hang out, find out where the plants are, who's guarding, all that shit, and then right after the harvest, bing-bong, here we come, Halloween masks, we could all wear the same mask, Freddie from Elm Street, or no, Miss Piggie, how would you like to see five or six guys with guns wearing Miss Piggie masks coming at you?"

Derek could not stop laughing.

"Well?" Burns said seriously. "Are you up for it? We could make a fucking fortune. Your end would be at least, what? Two hundred thousand? How would you feel about two hundred thousand, huh?"

Now Burns was laughing, his wide mouth even wider, his eyes big.

"Gee, great," Derek said. "But harvest time is about six months from now. You think we got enough time to plan this thing out right? I mean, these things take time, don't they?"

"Six months?" The light went from Burns' eyes. "I can't wait that long to get rich. Six fucking months." He began tapping his long fingers on the black Formica tabletop.

This is a moody guy, Derek thought. They sat quietly for a while,

Derek looking around the little bar. Even though the waitress hadn't asked for ID, Derek decided he wouldn't want to hang around here anyway. Everybody was too old. No girls. No hip-looking guys. Except of course at their table.

"Wait a minute," Burns said, almost coldly. "What do you *do*?"

"What do I do?" Derek asked. "For a living?" He thought about the screwdriver in his left hip pocket, and thought for an instant of telling Burns about going around knocking off newspaper racks. But it was so cheap, so small-time . . .

Derek grinned in what he hoped was a sophisticated way and said, "Oh, you know. This and that."

"You mean you're a thief?" Burns asked. "It's okay. I do a little stealing myself, from time to time. Everybody's got a little larceny in their heart, including, amazingly enough, myself. What kind of thief? Are you *packing*?"

"Packing a gun? No," Derek said, being casual, as if he normally did pack a gun, but just didn't happen to have one on him at the time. "How about you?"

Burns grinned. "What would I need with a gun? I have my looks, my personality, my brains. I don't need a gun. I've had a few guns in my time. The best gun I ever had was an old British Webley thirty-eight. That little fucker fit into my hand perfectly."

"Ever shoot anybody?" Derek asked, and immediately regretted it. Burns looked pissed off at the question and shut up, staring down at the table. Their beers were finished, and Derek thought about saying thanks and goodnight, but didn't. He didn't want to go back to his room, not just yet.

Finally Burns answered. "No," he said quietly. "I never shot anybody." More quiet, and then, "Maybe a few dogs and cats." He giggled, and Derek giggled, too.

"Let's get the fuck out of here," Burns said.

They walked up Market Street side by side, not speaking. It was about ten o'clock, not late, but there were very few people on the street. At the corner of Market and Third, Burns stopped, his hands jammed into his jacket pockets. It was a little chilly now.

"Thanks for the beer and the smoke," Derek said. He wanted to shake hands, but didn't know how Burns would take the gesture.

"You need money, don't you?" Burns asked.

"I sure as hell do," Derek said.

"You want to rob a store?"

"Huh?"

"You want to rob a store? That's where I'm headed. Two guys are better than one."

"Uh, not tonight," Derek said. His feet were getting cold, and as much as he did not want to end this unexpected evening, he was scared by what Burns asked. Burns just stood there. Black leather jacket, black jeans, he looked like somebody who would rob a store. "I just can't," Derek said lamely.

Burns' face softened, and he put a hand lightly on Derek's shoulder. "I understand," he said. "Catch you later on, Dude." He turned and began walking up Market. After a few minutes, Derek followed, not to catch up, but because that was the direction of his hotel.

Derek crossed Market at Fifth and started up Turk Street, past the hofbrau Burns had talked about, the one with the big turkey dinner. Derek passed the place all the time. There were always big hunks meat, beef or turkey or ham, slowly roasting in the window, turning on a rotary spit. The window was dark now, but Derek averted his eyes anyway. A beer and half a joint had made him hungry as a child. The eighteen cents in his pocket was worse than having no money at all. What could you do with eighteen cents?

Turk Street was busy at this time of night, compared to Market. Johns and hookers made up a lot of the traffic, but there were always plenty of bad people out, looking for action. Derek's game was to keep his eyes to himself, not make eye contact with anybody who might react, yet at the same time to keep looking for the girl of his dreams, the young pretty white hooker who would become his love. The trouble with looking for love among the hookers was that if they caught him looking they might think he was a john, so they would smile and step into his way, and he would have to mumble something like "No, thanks," or, "Sorry," or some other lame excuse for not going with the girl. And they got pissed off. Some of them would threaten you. One black hooker had really scared Derek one night just by saying to his back, "*Cut* you." Derek wasn't even sure she was talking to him. He had looked at her one second too long because she was so outrageously beautiful, in a white satin blouse tied up so he could see her bellybutton, and old cutoff jeans that bulged tightly at the crotch, long sleek legs . . . "*Cut* you."

Derek desperately did not want to go into the Greenleaf Hotel, up two flights of stairs to his little slot of a room. The hotel was still a block away. Why was he walking so fast, if he didn't want to go home? There was an old guy down on the sidewalk, Derek had to walk around him. The guy must have been about fifty, white whiskers showing, old dark blue suit coat, checked shirt, brown pants, one arm outstretched, as if the guy was reaching for something. Derek thought about cartoons of guys out in the desert reaching like that for a mirage. Derek thought about giving the guy a quick frisk, to see if he had any money, but of course just stepped around him and kept on walking, thinking, he's probably a cop anyway, and there's too many people around anyway, and I don't have the guts anyway, and this last thought made his face redden as he remembered Burns' casual offer, "Want to rob a store?"

"Sure, let's go." Why hadn't Derek said that? He would be with Burns now, and they would be walking into some little store with some Middle Eastern greaseball behind the counter. In his mind Derek saw Burns pull out a gun and hold it on the guy behind the counter, and then the daydream fizzled. He was at the hotel, its front darkened to discourage loiterers, but still there was a male hooker leaning against the doorway. "Hi," the hooker said.

"Hi," Derek said, and started up the stairs, filling with dread at the thought of the long night to come, a night of hunger and self-hatred. Why was he such a coward?

Walking down the long dingy corridor with its naked 15-watt bulbs, he could hear television and radio music, not entirely unpleasant sounds. There was nobody in the corridor. Derek was more afraid of this corridor than he was of Turk Street, sometimes. At last he came to his own door, and opened it with his key. He flipped on the light, another 15-watt bulb, high up on the flaking ceiling, too high to reach. Derek had thought about buying a better bulb and putting it in himself, but he never did. The thought of going down and talking to The Patel behind the desk, getting the stepladder and all that, depressed him, and so he did nothing. His room under the dim light looked terrible to him. The sink in the corner. The cardboard closet, with his few clothes on rusty hangers. His cardboard box of stuff next to the closet. The unmade bed with its grey blanket and yellowish sheets. The chair.

Derek undressed down to his Jockey shorts and was pissing in the sink when the noises from the next room started, noises of lovemaking. Derek could hear almost everything. The man was grunting and the woman wheezing, and as they rolled around they bumped into the common wall. Derek sat on his bed, trying not to listen. It didn't turn him on, it made him sad. Desperate old people, fucking away in this cheap hotel. God damn. How awful. What would happen to Derek when he was old? Would he be rich enough to avoid this terrible fate?

Derek quietly, so as not to disturb his neighbors, crawled in between the clammy sheets. He put his hands behind his head, quietly thinking, when suddenly from the next room, "You goddamn bitch!" and a really loud thump against the common wall. The woman cried out, not loudly, and Derek heard what must have been slaps. The guy was slapping her, and she was whimpering. Derek started breathing hard; this was more than he could stand. He could see the guy, big and fat and hairy, and the woman, small and thin, both of them old, at least forty. Derek wanted to beat on the wall and yell out for the guy to stop or Derek would come over there and beat the shit out of him. But Derek kept quiet. Why? Because he was a coward.

After a while, the noises from the next room stopped, but Derek did not stop thinking he was a coward. He had liked Burns. A nice friendly guy, funny with those long arms and legs and his big wide grin and his funny way of talking. Derek wondered if he was really an armed robber. Sure he was. Where do you think he got his money, working in a bank? He had been so friendly, too. And Derek needed friends. Derek wanted to see Burns again, see if he was still friendly. It would be good to have a friend. But Derek didn't want to show up at the Tivoli looking for Burns without any money in his pocket. That would be a repeat, and Burns would think of him as a bum. No, the thing to do was to get some money, enough money to be able to go in there, find Burns, and offer to treat him, buy him a beer or something, turkey dinner even. Something. But not broke. There would have to be some way to make money. He had to get a racket of his own, not this shit of busting paper racks, he was going to get nailed doing that one of these days, and for what? A handful of quarters? Fuck it. A racket. A racket. There must be something he could do. Something.

Well, start at the beginning. Where was all the money? The money was in the banks, or in the cash registers of businesses. These places were guarded, but people still ripped them off. Derek saw himself walking into a bank armed with nothing but a note. "Give me all the money, or . . . " Or what? ". . . Or I'll run out of here like a rat!" Somebody in the next room was snoring. The guy on the other side of Derek was a Vietnamese man who never made a fucking sound. Ha, joke. Never made any kind of a sound, just came and went, with a slight bow if you ran into him in the corridor, the Corridor of Sudden Death. Oh, shit, this was not getting any banks robbed. How does one man, and a little one at that, rob a bank all by himself? Easy, he walks in with a piece of paper, not a dumb fucking note, but a check. The check looks good, the guy has identification, everything goes smoothly. But where would Derek get a blank check, where would he get fake ID, where would he get the nerve to walk into the bank? Hmm. He could find a blank check somewhere, but not fake ID. You had to buy that. His own fake ID which had been washed into pulp had been an army reserve card, which wasn't much good anyway, since he didn't have a driver's license to back it up. His own driver's license showed him as twenty, and had expired anyway. His mother wouldn't let him drive the Jag after the second time he drove it and put a scratch on the left side pulling into the Seven-Eleven in front of the guys.

Sleep would not come, in spite of the marijuana and beer. He wasn't even hungry anymore. He just lay there on his back. Sounds came from the Corridor of Sudden Outrageous Death, but he hardly listened.

After a while he heard a scraping noise at his door, and then a voice: "Bobby?"

Derek did not answer, and for no reason at all he felt cold fear. People had scratched at his door before, sometimes asking for Bobby, whoever that was, or just scratching. He wondered again who Bobby was. He wondered why the people scratched instead of knocking. Then after a while a drunk woman came down the corridor, bumping against the walls and cursing. It flashed into Derek's mind to open the door, grab the woman, pull her into his room and fuck her. Rip her clothes off, she was so drunk she wouldn't be able to stop him, and Derek could fuck her and throw her back out of the room and in the morning she wouldn't even remember who did it to her. Or that anybody did anything to her. He laughed quietly to himself. Let the bastard in the next room listen to Derek for a while, see how he liked it.

This left Derek nothing to do but jack off. His hand was on his cock and balls anyway. Almost always when he was laying there trying to get to sleep, he would grab hold of his cock and balls, for security maybe, he did not know. He squeezed his dick to see if it would react by swelling. It didn't. He dreamed up the drunken woman as a beautiful although old black woman, maybe forty, in his room now, and he was not ripping her clothes off, they were undressing each other and kissing, Derek kissing her neck, but no. It wasn't working. What would work? Derek ran through his regular fantasies, girls he had known, girls he had seen, girls he made up, but nothing seemed to work. Derek sighed. Too fucked up to jack off. Well, that was all right. He was against it on principle anyway. He only did it to keep his dick from rotting off, anyway. What he really needed was a woman, a love, somebody to put him on the track and keep him there, somebody like his mother, oh, shit, there it was again. One of the reasons Derek had trouble jacking off was he kept thinking of his mother. Without wanting to, of course. But his mother had a really beautiful body, and when Derek got to thinking about women's bodies he had to fight to keep from thinking about his mother's. He could remember times seeing her half-dressed and wishing he hadn't because of the inflamed emotions he would have to put up with for a while, bad emotions, of course, the dirtiest word everybody knew was motherfucker, wasn't it, and Derek sometimes could not help his mind starting in on some vicious rotten fantasy about being naked with his mother. It never got further than that, thank God, but that was far enough. And his sister Diedre, who he not only fantasized fucking but peeked in her window trying to see her naked ever since she started to blossom. She was two years younger than Derek and already married and working over in Oakland. Derek had never seen her place. He did not like the goof she married, Jerry Ledbetter. Big guy, but with undefined muscle, just a big white blob of flesh. Cowlick and his mouth always open. Telephone company lineman. Maybe he could get Derek a job. But no. Derek had had job interviews before. "Sorry." He always gave himself away. Said something, did something. He was not cut out for corporate employment. Those fucking computers scared the shit out of him. He couldn't do math, so there was no place for him in modern society. Except as an artist or a criminal. The arts bored him. He liked to read and go to the movies, but he knew he had no special talent, not even a talent for acting. Acting would be the easiest of the arts to get into, but he knew he couldn't act. He had tried it in high school, just to meet girls, but he got scared just going out on stage, even when he didn't have any lines, and he didn't get anywhere with the drama girls, so fuck it, fuck the arts, and welcome to a life of crime. Only there, too, was stagefright, and Derek was a middle-class boy and hated the petty shit he did for money, and finally drifted off to sleep.

He was sitting at the counter at Doakie's drinking his first cup of coffee at around eleven the next morning when he remembered he only had eighteen cents in his pocket. The coffee he was drinking cost forty cents, and the refill he always had cost another twenty cents, and he could feel his face reddening. No money! Would they make him do dishes? By standing up and craning his neck just a little he could see the old Vietnamese in the kitchen scraping off the dishes, sticking them into a machine, no, they would call the cops, this was the Tenderloin, twobit scams like not paying for your breakfast were not tolerated down here. Derek looked down into his half-full cup, feeling about as depressed as he had ever felt in his life. His whole life had been like this. Would it always be like this?

There were people sitting on both sides of him. Eating their goddamn breakfasts. He knew the woman behind the counter, and she knew him. They nodded to each other when he came in. But she was Vietnamese. Derek drank off the last of his coffee. He would walk to the front, to the cash register, and try to explain as quietly as possible. But when he stood up the old woman smiled at him and said, "No refill today?"

"Ah, no," Derek said. He walked to the cash register and everybody in the place looked at him. The woman behind the counter wiped her hands and smiled at him, waiting for his forty cents.

"I don't have the money," he said.

The woman smiled, showing two gold teeth. "You forget money? No matter, come back later!"

The air outside was delicious. It made him feel cocky. Maybe it was the coffee. Maybe it was the sunshine, it was a beautiful day, and the Tenderloin this time of day was like any neighborhood, the people on the street were familiar, the traffic light, look, there was a striped cat running across Jones Street and under a parked car. Derek filled his lungs with precious air and started walking up Jones. He would make money today. He would make money if he had to knock somebody down and take it.

As he walked uphill the muscles in his legs felt good from the work. He walked a lot, and it was giving him good legs. He was pumping right along, and had just crossed Sutter Street when he happened to look into a parked car and see a bunch of camera equipment in the backseat. He saw in the same glance the back door lock was up. Without thinking or even looking around, Derek opened the car's back door as if he owned the car. He picked up a camera with a bright neck strap and an aluminum case like a suitcase. There was some other stuff but he left it alone, closing the car door, slipping the camera strap around his neck, turning around, and walking down Jones back into the Tenderloin. Those first few steps, before he crossed Sutter, were extremely exciting. He did not feel fear, only excitement, and if anybody had yelled at him he would have burst into laughter and started running, he was sure of it. But nobody yelled, and he was away.

Derek went back to his room and sat on his bed to look at the loot. *Loot!* Derek had stolen a few things in his time, but nothing this expensive-looking. The camera was a Hasselblad, which meant nothing to Derek, except that it looked so good, so rich, that he knew he could get at least fifty bucks for it. The metal case was lined with foam rubber cut to hold lenses. There was a big one, a couple of little ones, some stuff he didn't recognize, and a space for the camera. Derek put the camera into the case, closed the case, hefted it, and wondered where in hell he could get money for it. A pawn shop, sure, but better money could come from a camera shop. Derek tried to remember where there were any camera shops around there. Then he decided to get out of the Tenderloin to get rid of the stuff. He was still pretty excited. He told himself he would have to calm down, make himself look casual, like a photographer selling off one of his cameras. The trouble was, he didn't know how much to ask. He didn't know anything about cameras. But he knew he was having a run of blind dumb luck, and he knew in his heart that everything was going to be all right after all. And just think, an hour ago he had been so depressed he wanted to commit suicide.

The first pawnshop Derek walked into was south of Market, on Sixth Street. Its windows were full of watches, rings, and cameras. Inside, half the store was taken up with rifle racks and glass counters full of pistols. It was still early in the day, and Derek was the only customer. The man behind the gun counter was big and soft-looking, with receding black hair, grey skin, and a white shirt. The man rested his hands on the countertop as he seemed not to watch Derek, who knew he should have gone right up to the man, put the aluminum case on the counter and started to bargain, but instead lost his nerve and walked slowly around the pawnshop looking at junk, racks of guitars, leather suitcases, brass musical instruments, a big set of shiny blue drums, all kinds of crap, before he finally approached the man, Derek's head down, looking at the pistols in the counter.

"Can I help you?" the man asked.

Derek swallowed and put the aluminum case on the counter, fumbling with the catch. Finally the case came open, and Derek turned it so that the pawnbroker could look. The man's eyes widened for a second and then closed down. He picked up the camera and looked it over carefully. "Nice," he said. He put the camera back and picked up the big lens, looking through it out toward the street. Derek's crotch was hot and his feet cold. He wanted very much just to run out of the place, but he stood his ground, hoping his hands and legs would not start to shake.

"Hasselblad, huh?" the guy said. "Just a minute, okay?" He put the lens carefully into the case and went to the back of the store, through a curtain. Without thinking, Derek closed the case and hauled ass. This guy was calling the cops, Derek was certain. He

walked up Sixth to Market, the back of his neck hot enough to fry
eggs. The guy had taken one look at Derek and one look at the camera, and decided to call the cops. Maybe find out if the camera was
stolen by the serial numbers or some such bullshit. Or maybe the
camera was already reported as stolen. The jerk who left it in his car
and the car unlocked must have thought his stuff was safe, he was
only going to be a couple of seconds, and he gets back to his car,
ripped off in two seconds! The guy calls the cops, and every pawnbroker in the city is waiting for Derek to come in. What about a camera store? He remembered there was this huge camera store on
Kearny, where people came and went buying and selling cameras
and camera equipment, there was so goddamn much camera stuff
they couldn't possibly keep track . . .

Derek stood on the corner of Market and Third, wondering what
to do. This was where he had said goodbye to Burns the night before.
Was it only the night before? Yes. He could run up to the Tivoli and
look for Burns. Lay the problem on Burns, for half the money. But
no. Derek didn't want to, not because of the money, but because he
wanted to show up with a wad of money, not a big problem.

Fifteen minutes later he was in front of Brooks Cameras on
Kearny. The place was just as he had remembered it, packed with
customers and employees and cameras. Derek suddenly realized
that he was probably standing in the worst place in San Francisco for
a camera thief. He began walking rapidly up Kearny Street toward
Chinatown. His stomach was empty and growling at him. He felt as
if he was in some terrible nightmare, trudging through San Francisco with this heavy camera case full of expensive equipment he
could not get rid of without getting caught, sent to jail, raped,
AIDS, killed, etc.

Here was a crummy little pawnshop with a crowded dusty window
and an old Filipino standing in the doorway. Derek smiled at the
man, and the man went into the shop. Derek followed.

Instead of a glass counter the man went behind a chainmesh
screen with an opening you could pass things through. Derek put the

case up and slid it through to the little man, who opened it, and very slowly examined everything in the case. He and Derek had not yet spoken a word to each other. Faint music came through the curtains behind the man, and Derek thought he could smell orange marmalade. His stomach growled. If the little Filipino went behind the curtain or reached for a telephone, Derek was prepared to grab the case and run, he did not know where. He was starting to feel pretty jacked up.

"You want to pawn these things, or sell them?" the little man asked finally, shutting the case and looking into Derek's eyes.

"Uh, sell, I guess," Derek said lamely. God damn it! I should have been more definite! Shit!

But the guy said, "Five hundred, okay?"

Derek was stunned. "Okay," he said after a long moment. The man was counting out bills, three hundreds, two fifties, five twenties, and handed them to Derek. Numbly, Derek counted the money.

"You want a receipt?" the pawnbroker asked. There was a slight smile on his wrinkled brown face.

"No, thanks, uh, oh, yeah," Derek said, cool as a fucking cucumber.

"Cash deal, no receipt," the man said. "Everything okay."

Derek left the pawnshop dizzy with accomplishment. He had a great deal of money in his pocket. Damn near as much as he had won at his mother's house playing poker. Somehow, as he walked down Kearny toward Market, the money in his pocket became his, because he had lost all that money at his mother's. This was that same money, gotten back to him somehow by the workings of fate. It was his karma to have this money.

He took the steps up to the Tivoli Billiards two at a time. "Hello, asshole," he said to the geek on the gate, who buzzed him in without comment. Suddenly the smell of frying hamburgers hit Derek's nose, and his mouth filled with saliva. He sat on the first stool and yelled, "Fry me a burger!" to the frycook down the way. "Yo, burger," the cook yelled back, and Derek swiveled around to see who was in the poolroom. There were a lot of people, it was lunchtime, and the place was noisy and full of smoke, the high fluorescent lights making everything look weird, in a nice way. Derek did not see Burns, which was a little disappointing. But with money in his pocket, Derek could stand a little disappointment.

His hamburger came, smelling wonderful. "Strawberry milk-shake," he said to the counterman.

"You must have hit it big," Burns said, sitting down next to him just as he was finishing his burger.

"Hey, Burns, man," Derek said. "Wanna burger? Shake? Anything at all?"

Burns looked at him with that heavy-lidded look. "Sure, Derek. I'd like a beer. Coors."

"Bring a Coors for my friend," Derek said to the counterman.

"Well well," said Burns. "Last night you were broke, now you're buying the beers. What happened, or am I being crude?"

Derek laughed. He knew it would be fun to find Burns. And this day was going entirely his way no matter what happened. He could feel it, the luck, running all through his body. He laughed at Burns' curiosity. "Cashed in some securities," he said, and giggled. He took a big gulp of his strawberry milkshake. Jesus Christ! Did anything ever taste better? "Ahh!" he exclaimed, and grinned at Burns.

"I know that feeling," Burns said. "I know just how you feel."

"What do you mean?" Derek asked. "How do I feel?"

"Your eyes are lit up, you're grinning like a fucking ape, I'd say you pulled off some kind of hairy caper, pulled a gun on somebody and took all his money. Am I right?"

Derek laughed easily. "How'd you do last night? Did you stick up a store?"

Burns pulled a long face. "Naw, I just went home," he said.

"Well, that's okay," Derek heard himself saying. "I did pretty well." Making it as funny as he could, he told Burns all about his morning.

But Burns was strangely quiet while Derek told his tale. He sipped at his beer, and when Derek, to cap his story, took the folded bills from the pocket and peeled off the outside twenty to pay the check, Burns' eyebrows lifted only slightly.

"So it's real," he said finally. "I thought you were telling me a story."

"Why would I do that?" Derek said, grinning.

"But you shouldn't flash that roll," Burns said. "You never know who's in this dump."

"Yeah," Derek said. "I guess you're right." He cursed himself silently for being such a fool. He would not do that again.

"I can show you how to hide that money," Burns said. "They could search you for half an hour and never find it."

"Yeah?" said Derek.

"Yeah, come on down to the can." Burns got up and crooked his finger at Derek. Derek scooped up his change, leaving a dollar tip for the counterman, and followed Burns down to the men's toilet near the back of the poolroom. The place reeked of piss and disinfectant. There was an old man standing at the urinal, and Burns stood next to him. Derek washed his hands and combed his hair. He looked pretty good. There was something tough in his eyes that he hadn't seen before, or maybe it hadn't been there before. Maybe he was getting there.

The old man left the toilet. Derek turned around to see Burns grinning at him strangely. "Shake hands," Burns said. Not understanding, Derek automatically held out his hand. Instead of taking the hand, Burns grabbed Derek's thumb and bent it back sharply, driving Derek to his knees on the tile floor.

"Ouch, Jesus!" Derek yelled.

"Shut up!" Burns said, pressing the thumb painfully. Burns was very close to Derek and grinned down at him, his eyes wide and glinting with excitement. Derek's mind almost froze as he saw the knife in Burns' other hand coming toward his face, his right eye. Burns let go of his thumb, and Derek without thinking rubbed his hands together. "Give me the fucking money," Burns said. "All of it." Derek stared at him in disbelief. Burns grabbed him by the hair and the knifeblade was right there, threatening his eye. Derek could see the blade was sharpened on both sides and dirty, stained like a fishknife or something, and then Derek realized that the knifeblade had dried blood on it.

"The fucking money, punk!" Burns said coldly. Numbly, Derek got the money out and passed it up to Burns, who tucked the bills away, still holding his knife in front of Derek's face, the blade weaving back and forth like the head of a cobra. Derek's knees hurt and his thumb really hurt, it had almost snapped, he thought, and he was frightened. But not so much as he was disappointed.

Burns backed away toward the door, with that cruel glint in his eye. He's enjoying this, Derek thought, he's really getting off on it. Burns stood at the door, looking down at Derek.

"Get off your knees, man," Burns said.

Derek stood up, embarrassed, frightened, dusting off his pants stupidly, avoiding Burns' eyes, wondering why the fuck he didn't just leave, so that Derek could break down and cry. But no, Burns was grinning at him, and the sadistic look was gone.

"My turn to buy," Burns said.

"Huh?"

"Come on," Burns said. He held open the door. Derek passed him out into the poolroom, wondering what the fuck was going on.

"Let's get out of this dump, too many weird people around," Burns said to Derek's back.

They walked down the double staircase side by side. Derek was frightened and confused, but mostly he was depressed. No matter what he did, he lost.

About halfway down the steps Burns put his hand on Derek's shoulder and said, "You have a lot to learn, my boy."

"Are you gonna give me back my money?" Derek heard himself saying. Suddenly he felt Burns' big hand on his throat, and he was pushed back against the wall. There was that look again.

"Listen, there's something you got to get straight," Burns said tightly. "You may be a thief, but I'm a *robber*, get it? Your kind doesn't fuck with my kind. Not ever." He let go of Derek's throat. "Come on," he said.

Derek didn't know what else to do, so he followed Burns down the stairs to Market Street. They stood squinting in the sunlight for a moment, then both put on dark glasses.

"I better keep your money for a while," Burns said in his old lazy friendly voice. "You'd lose it in a minute. I'll be your banker, okay?"

They walked down Market among the midday crowds. Derek was beyond confusion and into a kind of surrealistic calm. "I'd rather be my own banker," he said.

"I don't know," Burns said in a teasing tone. "You made so many mistakes today, it's a good thing you're young and lucky, huh? Or you'd be in jail, or laying dead someplace. Do you have any idea how lucky you are?"

"Yeah," Derek said. "What mistakes?"

"I don't know," Burns said. "Maybe you didn't make any mistakes. But the Filipino pawnbroker, he's gonna want to see you again. I bet that camera stuff was worth a hell of a lot of money. He'll probably just deal the stuff off to the insurance company, make a quick grand or so for himself, buddy up to the authorities, all in all, a great deal for him and a good deal for you. Now he's got you out stealing for him, no?"

"I guess so," Derek said. He had not even thought about it, but now he had his own fence, a really important connection if he was going to be a thief. With a prickle of excitement, Derek realized that he was entering a life of crime. Oddly, he liked the feeling. At least it was something to do.

"Hey, come on, man, give me my money," he said to Burns. "God damn it, a joke's a joke."

"Money's no joke," Burns said.

"I stole it, it's mine," Derek said, and giggled.

"Well, that's true, of course," Burns said. "But then, *I* robbed *you*.

That doesn't mean I won't be generous. What kind of a guy do you think I am?"

Derek did not have an answer for that one. He almost had to run to keep up with Burns' long legs. "Where we goin'?" he asked.

"Down the street," Burns said. "Let's find a phone booth. I know a guy with a car. Now that we have a little money to play with, we should go out and play, don't you think?"

Derek did not know what to think. For some reason he was feeling pretty good, even though he had not figured a way to get his money back from Burns. He was not sure Burns was going to keep the money. After all, he could have just ripped him off and then left. He didn't. He seemed to be friendly. Maybe he was just teaching Derek a lesson.

"We could go to Reno," Burns said. "This isn't much money for Reno, but we could probably run it up into some real money, don't you think? You like to gamble? You ever play any roulette? It's a fantastic game, Derek. Totally calculated against the player, for the house. The only way to beat the game is to put all your money on one bet, and if you win, walk out. Toughest way to gamble in the world. Make one bet, the whole five hundred, or four hundred by then, we got to eat, buy gas, shit like that, but put the whole four hundred on one third of the board, down at the end. Win that bet, walk away with twelve hundred dollars, and fuck'em."

"What's the odds?"

"Let me call this guy," Burns said, as they came to an outdoor telephone. Derek stood waiting. They were almost to the Embarcadero. The idea of heading up to Reno was a little scary, with Burns holding the money, but what could he do?

"Let's go," Burns said after he hung up the telephone. "Should we take a bus? Fuck no, high class criminals take taxis." They had to cross Market to find a cab.

This was a part of San Francisco Derek had never seen, Bernal Heights it was called, down in the Mission somewhere, a district of sharp hills and twisting streets, old Victorians and Frisco-looking pastel apartment buildings. The cab let them off in front of an old garage cut into the hillside below a big old yellow Victorian that looked like a boarding house. The wooden garage doors were open, and Derek could see the back of a 1967 Chevrolet, painted yellow and black, with shiny chrome, a real cherry it looked like from the back.

"Come on," Burns said. He grinned at Derek and patted him on the shoulder. "This guy's a real nerd, sort of, so just be cool, okay?"

Derek followed Burns into the dark garage, sidling past the car. The hood was up, there was a worklight hanging down over the engine, and a young guy in a really dirty white tee shirt. The guy turned and blinked at them through rimless glasses, and Derek saw smudged grease on the lenses.

"Hi, fellas," the guy said. Pimples, not a lot, but enough. Light brown hair cut pretty short, biceps.

"Derek, this is my pal Kenny. Kenny, Derek."

"I'm Kenny Scheib, don't try to shake hands, I'm greasy as hell."

"Okay," Derek said. Immediately he did not like Kenny Scheib. They were about the same age, but Scheib looked really dumb, or innocent, or something. There was something about him that Derek just did not like.

"Kenny is my main man," Burns said, and that sealed it. Derek did not like this guy. Burns grinned at Derek wickedly. "Derek here is a sneak thief," he said. "We picked up a little stake, not much, but enough to have some fun. You up for a trip to Reno? You got anything planned?"

"Not much," Kenny said. "I have to ask my mom. How long we gonna go for?"

"Just long enough to make a shitload of money," Burns said.

"What if we lose?" Kenny asked.

"You fucking downer, we won't lose. And if we do, we'll rob somebody, kill their asses and throw the bodies in the weeds alongside the road. Okay?"

"Let me ask my mom," Kenny said. He was still wiping his hands on a red rag when he left the garage and went up the old broken cement steps to the house. Burns and Derek stayed down on the street.

"He's an asshole," Burns said. "But he has this car. He's kind of nuts, too, but I can handle him. I'm nuts, too."

"I guess," Derek joked. He did not like this with the new guy. Some greaseball with a car, that was all Derek could see. Big arms. Pimpleface. "He has to ask his mother?" Derek asked.

Burns grinned. "Maybe she'll pack us a lunch," he said.

"When will we be back?" Derek asked. He was thinking about his stuff in the hotel. He only had two more days on the room, and then his stuff would be put in storage, or stolen. His stuff, his cheap shit. He didn't really want to go back to that little smelly room, and now that he had money, he could . . . but he didn't have money. Burns had the money. Derek felt frustrated by this, but could not think of what else to do but go along, ride along, wait and watch. He didn't want to get away from Burns, he liked Burns, but this guy Scheib was something else. Boring. Dull. Stupid.

Burns pulled out his pack of Pall Malls, and shook one out for himself, then offered the pack to Derek. Derek took a cigarette and let Burns light it.

"You don't smoke much, do you?" Burns asked.

"Not much," Derek said.

"I don't see how you can do it. I smoke forty of these fuckers a day."

"I used to smoke a lot," Derek said.

Burns grinned. "Then you ran out of money."

"Naw," Derek said with a smile.

"I wish I had a joint. Maybe we could get some weed before we leave town. I don't have any connections in Reno. Or we could go to Tahoe, what's the weather like up there now?"

"Snow," Derek said.

"Fuck snow, we'll go to the biggest little city in the world, where they got heated rooms, heated pussies, hey, we could get laid in style if we won enough money, how would that be?" Burns laughed openly at the look on Derek's face. "Haven't been laid in a while, huh?"

"You know how it is," Derek said.

"Yeah, I know how it is."

After a while Kenny Scheib came down the steps wearing clean jeans, a tan leather jacket cut like a sports jacket, and a black tee shirt. He was carrying a paper bag.

"Your mom fix us a lunch?" Burns asked.

Kenny smiled, showing bad teeth, and said, "I just grabbed some fruit."

"You got any money?" Burns asked.

"Thirty bucks," said Kenny.

"Then let's roll," Burns said. "Derek, you get in back." Derek did not like sitting in the back, and he was really not happy about this trip, yet he felt good, excited. It was completely confusing. He and Burns waited while Kenny put down the hood, started the car, and backed out. The car sounded good, a deep rumbling.

"Isn't this the worst getaway car you ever saw?" Burns said. He held the seat forward for Derek. "You're the big guy. We're just your driver and bodyguard, get it?"

And off they went.

They were driving up the freeway toward the Bay Bridge. San Francisco glittered under the sun. Derek felt better than he had felt in a long time. He had not realized how lonely he had been. For some reason he trusted Burns. Burns might fuck him over, but he wouldn't really fuck him over. Derek had a lot to learn, that was all. And he had to stop being such a terrible coward and get rolling into life. He remembered the awful moments in the Tivoli Billiards men's toilet, on his knees staring at the blade of Burns' knife, dirty with blood.

"Hey, Burns," he yelled. "How come you never clean that knife of yours?"

Burns turned in his seat and grinned back at Derek. "Scared the shit out of you, didn't it?"

"You fuckin' ay," Derek said.

"Take the Fell Street offramp," Burns said to Kenny Scheib.

"What for?"

"I want to pick up a sixpack before we get caught up in traffic. You want anything from the store?"

"Beer is all," Kenny said. He laughed, for some reason.

They got off the freeway and went up Fell Street, through a black neighborhood Derek was not familiar with. Kenny kept saying, "There's one," but Burns kept saying, "No, keep going, out the Panhandle."

More twists and turns, Derek didn't pay much attention, thinking about his own problems, when Burns said, "Here, this one," and then, "Park around the corner."

They parked alongside a small corner store on a flat treelined street. Derek did not know where they were, just in San Francisco somewhere. "Come on, Derek," Burns said, and pulled the seat forward so that Derek could get out.

"Keep the motor running," Burns said to Kenny. When he straightened up he grinned at Derek. "You starting to catch on?"

"What's going on?" Derek asked. His heart was tight in his chest, and his feet starting to freeze.

"Come on," Burns said.

"What are we doing?" Derek said. His throat was tightening, but underneath all the symptoms of fear, he could feel a tiny red light inside him somewhere beginning to glow.

"We're gonna buy a sixpack, asshole," Burns said, but Derek could tell he was excited, even though his eyes were more heavy-lidded than ever. Derek followed, his whole body cold, into the little corner store.

All the details were unusually bright. It was a store with tall shelves making two narrow aisles. The produce was all in the front window, and the cold storage lockers were in the back, next to a curtained doorway. The liquor was all back of the counter, along with a small thickset Middle Eastern guy, probably a Palestinian, with a newspaper on the counter he was reading with the help of a magnifying glass. As they walked back toward the beer, Burns said in a normal tone, "Look around, see if there's anything you want for the trip." Derek looked around, but he was too intense to notice anything except that the produce in the front window all seemed wilted, and the tomatoes were bad-looking, with black spots and soft spots. It was like the produce in the Tenderloin stores, he thought idiotically.

"You want any cigarettes?" Burns asked in a normal voice as they both approached the counter. The man behind the counter kept reading his newspaper until Burns set down the sixpack of Coors.

"Is that all?" he asked.

Burns moved around the side of the counter, toward the shelves of liquor and cartons of cigarettes.

"I might want a carton of Pall Malls," he said, moving all the way back of the counter. The Palestinian frowned and said, "Don't come back of the counter," but by this time Burns had pulled his knife and quickly put one hand behind the man's head and had the tip of the knife pointed at the man's eye, just as he had done with Derek.

"We want all the money."

"I don't have any money," the man said.

Burns pushed the man away from the counter toward the front window, which was blocked with signs and goods. Without looking at Derek, Burns said tightly, "Tap the register, man."

On frozen feet Derek came around the counter. Burns was blocking the man, who was saying something with a thick accent. Derek did not know how to get a cash register open. His hands were shaking so much he didn't think he could do it anyway. "Hit the No Sale button!" Burns said, and Derek hit the button and the register opened.

A woman came through the curtain at the back of the store, small, shapeless print dress, black hair, wide eyes. She screamed something in a foreign language, and Burns said, "Tell her not to fuck up, or I'll slice you," and the man yelled something. Derek took all the bills out of the machine, there didn't seem to be that much, a few tens and twenties, a couple of fives, some ones. Derek stuffed the money into his jacket pockets, hearing the woman jabbering hysterically and Burns saying, "You better stand still, bastard," and the man: "God damn you kids!"

There was a wide drawer under the counter, and on impulse, Derek opened it. In among the papers he saw a revolver. Numbly he took the gun in his hand. It felt cold and heavy. He turned toward the jabbering woman, and when she saw the gun pointed at her, she screamed.

"Shut up!" the man yelled at her. Burns had been going through his pants pockets, and had money and a set of keys in his other hand. He still held the knife right in the man's face, and the man seemed hypnotized by it, as Derek had himself a hundred years ago.

"Don't come outside, don't call the cops, or I swear to God I'll find you and cut your guts open," Burns said as viciously as he could, and the two of them left the place, walking rapidly around the corner, just as a small man on a bicycle pulled up to the store, dismounted and entered.

"Let's get the fuck out of here," Burns said.

Derek's mouth was too dry to speak. He got into the back of the car, Burns got in, slammed the door, and the car took off smoothly, without a squeal of rubber.

Derek sat in the middle of the back seat, stunned. He had the gun and the money in his pockets. After a while, Burns turned to him, grinning sickly. "That's how it goes," he said.

"No shit," Derek managed to say, in spite of his cotton mouth.

"How do you feel?"

"Huh?"

"How do you feel, Man?"

Derek did not know how to explain it, even to himself. He felt wildly excited, more excited than he had ever felt. He was terrified, but the little red light was really glowing now. He grinned at Burns, his face stiff. They were a few blocks from the store.

Burns let out a long chuckling laugh. "Whoo," he said. "I always get a thrill." He turned back toward Derek again. "Okay, gimme the money and the gun, we'll count it and see how we did. I think I got at least three hundred out of the guy's pants."

Derek reached into his pockets. He could feel the bills and the cool pistol. "No," he said suddenly. "I copped this gun, I'm gonna keep it."

"Come on," Burns said, "I just want to look at it. What is it, one of those Saturday night specials?"

Derek took it out, holding it properly. It was an interesting moment. They were driving down this street of two-story apartment buildings. Derek held the gun, Burns looked back at him, his eyes glittering. Derek knew Burns wanted to grab the gun away from him, but there is something about holding a loaded gun . . . Derek looked to see if it was loaded. Yes, he could see the rounded tips of the bullets in their chambers, deadly-looking and somehow reassuring.

"It's a Smith and Wesson," he said. "Thirty-eight. Full of bullets."

"How much money did you get from the register?" Burns asked. Derek tucked the gun down into his pants. Was there a look of disappointment in Burns' eyes? Derek got out the money and started to count it. "A hundred and eight dollars," he said.

Burns had turned back and was counting. "I got three-fifty," he said.

"Money money money," Kenny said. Derek couldn't see his expression. Kenny must have known about the stickup, they were a pair, they did this all the time.

"Damn it," Burns said. "Only four-fifty-eight."

"What's the matter with that?" Derek asked. He didn't know what to expect. He had always heard or read in the papers that you only got a few bucks robbing these stores.

"You didn't lift up the drawer and look under, did you?" Burns asked, turning toward Derek. "There would have been big bills down there, asshole. We could have got a lot more."

"I didn't know what to do," Derek said. "I didn't even know about the holdup until it was half over." Derek laughed, almost cackled.

"It's not funny," Burns said. "That's where those fuckers keep their big bills. Any asshole knows that."

"I knew it," Derek said. "I just didn't think of it."

"You thought of the gun," Burns said.

Derek started to say that he hadn't planned to find the gun, but shut up.

"Go out Nineteenth," Burns told Kenny. At the next corner, Kenny turned right. Derek didn't know where they were, but he knew they were miles from the Bay Bridge, which was the way to Reno. Maybe they weren't going to Reno. He didn't care. He had money in his pocket, which he decided he would not give to Burns, and he had that gun tucked down under his pants. Pointing right at his dick. He wondered if the safety was on, or if the gun had a safety. He took it out. Yes, there was a safety, no, it was not on. Derek clicked the safety on and felt better. He had handled a few guns. His father had some guns, two shotguns, an octagonal-barreled .22, a Ruger .22 target pistol, and a couple of deer rifles. Derek had been too young when his father left home to have spent much time handling the guns. Now he put his .38 in his right jacket pocket. No use tempting fate.

"You know what?" he said to the others. "We left that sixpack behind." His throat was really dry. "Let's stop for something."

But Burns was silent, looking straight ahead and paying no attention to Derek. They were going south out 19th Avenue. At one stop a police car pulled up next to them, and while both cars stood waiting for the light to change, the three boys all looked straight ahead stiffly. When the light changed, Burns said in a low voice, "Roost!" and Kenny laughed, pulling out slowly enough to let the police car get ahead of them.

"Roost, huh?" Kenny said, and chuckled. "Burn rubber!"

"Yeah," said Burns. "Show those fucking cops."

"You know I never burn rubber," Kenny said.

"My throat's dry," Derek said. "Can't we stop for something? A Coke?"

Burns turned to him, his face serious. "We'll stop for something to eat," he said. "But I want you to know I'm really pissed off about that cash register drawer."

"You should have told me," Derek said flatly. He was scared of Burns, but he had to keep Burns from running all over him.

They turned off 19th at Irving and stopped at the Kentucky Fried

Chicken. While they were standing in line, Burns said to Kenny, "We could rob this place easily, don't you think?"

The girl behind the counter looked up at him and smiled. Burns grinned at her and said, "We won't, though. We just want chicken."

Derek got a big container of Coke and drank off half of it gratefully. It was delicious. When they got back in the car and on 19th again, he sat in the back and ate four pieces of chicken, wolfing them down as if he hadn't eaten in days. He used several paper napkins but still his mouth and fingers felt greasy. He hated that feeling, and hoped they would need gas soon, so he could wash his hands and face.

"Uh, where we headed?" he asked the front seat. Nobody answered. Derek sighed and sat back, watching the houses roll by. Pretty soon they passed San Francisco State, with a few students milling around out in front at the trolley stop. Derek thought of his mother's friend Al Burke, who taught here. And then of his mother, and wondered what she would think of him now. She would not be real happy, he decided. He could hardly keep his eyes open. There was a need to wash his hands and mouth, a need to take a piss, but he felt so sleepy from the greasy chicken that he closed his eyes. They had the car radio on, and he could hear the faint rock'n'roll over the traffic sounds. Burns and Kenny murmured to each other from time to time, and Derek fell asleep.

The run lasted three days before everything came apart. They never went to Reno. They never returned to downtown San Francisco. Instead, they drove south on 101 and eventually ended up in Los Angeles, but not before they had done some sightseeing and committed a few crimes. Derek began the run an almost innocent kid, who didn't know who or what he really was, and ended his three days with Burns and Scheib if possible even more immature and confused than before. But at least he knew one thing by now, he could take his cowardice in his hands sometimes and control it, get past it, and find himself in a world where nothing mattered but what he wanted. It was so exciting to be free of fear that Derek was really surprised he didn't kill anybody. The urge was there, he could feel it underneath everything, but for some reason, probably blind luck, Derek didn't kill anybody. And nobody killed him, either.

The gun had been a big problem. When Derek woke up to find himself in back of the car alone, parked in front of an International House of Pancakes in King City, he was really surprised to find the gun still in his jacket pocket. Why hadn't Burns taken it? Burns could have taken the gun and the money and thrown Derek out on the road, but he hadn't. Derek sat in the car in the darkness for a few minutes thinking about things, and when he did go into the IHOP it was to find his comrades.

The next robbery they tried was at a 7-Eleven in a little dusty half-Mexican town at the southern end of the Salinas Valley. Derek never caught the name of the town. It was late at night and the air was cold and crisp, the stars brilliant, far more brilliant than they ever were in the city. This was not a stickup for money, Derek finally understood, but for Burns' macho. Burns had been pissed off that Derek had stolen more than Burns had robbed. So, even though they had almost a thousand dollars between them, Burns wanted more. He wanted to commit an armed robbery, with the gun, and he didn't care if anybody got hurt or not.

This time the robbery was a little more clever, and not so off-the-wall. They plastered the car with mud, so it wouldn't look so cherry, and put mud over the license plate. Still they parked around the corner under a huge dark tree, hoping the car would never be seen at all. Kenny had wanted to steal another car for the robbery, but Burns laughed at him. "First you have to steal a pair of gloves," he said, "so you won't get fingerprints on the car you steal." They compromised on the mud.

"In a life of crime," Burns said, "you have to take a few risks." It seemed to Derek that the risk part was what interested Burns the most, even more than the money. And Derek could see why. Robbing stores was outrageously exciting.

They were jacked up anyway, even if they pretended to be cool. They jacked each other up. Burns seemed to be playing Derek against Kenny sometimes, just to piss them off. Burns was alternately very respectful of Kenny and then very insulting, calling him a nerd or a creep or a wirehead, whatever that was. Kenny would grin goodnaturedly, but never seemed to make eye-contact with Derek. Derek wondered how two such completely different guys could be friends, but all Burns would tell him was that they had "gone to school together." Kenny laughed at this, but didn't add anything. Derek finally figured out that they had been in reform school together, up in Ione, at Preston School for Boys.

"Think of Preston as a big cage, crammed with the worst kids in California," Burns said over breakfast the morning after the 7-Eleven. That robbery had not gone like the one in San Francisco. They had been lucky to get away with their lives, much less their freedom.

Burns had been tough with Derek. They were parked under the tree, getting themselves ready to go in. Derek did not know how to prepare himself, and he now partly understood why Burns had walked him into the other robbery without telling him anything. It was entirely different to know you were going into an unknown place to commit a robbery, and this time to be carrying a gun, pointing it at people, and maybe even having to fire it.

"You're a thief," Burns said. "You stole that gun, so it's yours, but you're just a thief all the same. Can you point that gun at somebody and use it if you have to? I don't know. Do you know?"

Kenny said, "I can use the gun. I'll go in with you."

Burns grinned in the dark. "You have to drive, unless you want Derek here to drive."

"No," Kenny said. "We can all go in, leave the car running, can't we?"

"No," Burns said. "You're not a fucking robber, you're a driver. I'm the robber in the bunch, don't you get it?"

Derek handed over the gun. After all, Burns hadn't taken it when he could have. Instantly, Derek was glad. Not only did he not have to carry the gun, he felt a thrill of comradeship at the smile Burns gave him.

"That's my man," Burns said. He hefted the gun. "Nice," he said. "Let's just hope we don't have to fire the fucker. We only got six bullets."

Kenny laughed easily, as if he had no nerves. Burns was acting like he had no nerves, and so Derek could not be the only one to ask fool-

ish questions or act stupid. "What about your knife?" Derek asked.
"I could carry that."

"My shiv is personal," Burns said. "I made it myself. Your job is to
get the money, when I push the guy out of his spot and give him the
oke-doke. And don't forget to look under the fucking drawer."

Derek promised he would not, but his heart was frozen in fear. He
only hoped he would act okay, not be a coward. Nothing else mattered now.

"Let's do it," Burns said.

A couple of minutes after Burns and Derek came into the 7-Eleven
another carful of guys showed up, young guys, all Mexican. Three
of them came into the store, laughing and talking. The young guy
behind the counter knew them, and a lot of kidding went on, in
Spanish and English. Derek and Burns looked over the brightly-lit
shelves. Burns got a couple of sixpacks, and so Derek picked up a big
bag of potato chips. He knew now they were not going to rob the
place. They couldn't. But Derek's mouth was terribly dry anyway,
and he went up to the counter and started making himself a big Coca-
Cola. The three Mexicans left with their stuff, and Derek heard the
sound of their car rapping, and then a spin of gravel as they did a
rooster. And were gone.

Derek turned to see Burns smiling charmingly at the young guy
behind the counter, a slim kid in a Hawaiian shirt, yellow and green
flowers. Burns pulled the gun and pointed it two-handed, his arms
straight out, at the kid.

"Get the money, pal," he said to Derek.

The next thing that happened was that Derek saw a thickset man
coming out of the back with a shotgun. Derek wanted to yell, but his
throat was too dry, but Burns swung quickly and started firing at the
guy, the shots like loud snaps in Derek's ear. Goods were flying off
shelves when the shotgun went off with a blam and wiped out half the
soft-drink setup, a piece of something hitting Derek on the forehead. The next shotgun blast hit the big glass door, blowing it to bits,
but Derek and Burns were already outside, heading for the big tree.

From behind them Derek could hear the man shouting in Spanish. Kenny had opened the passenger door, and they piled into the front seat. "Let's go!" Burns said in a tight voice. The Chevy slid a little in the gravel and then took off onto the dark road.

Burns was in the middle, holding the gun in his lap. Derek had the big bag of potato chips, its contents pretty badly crushed. Derek held the plastic bag tightly. It just occurred to him that they had done an incredibly stupid thing, by robbing a store, or trying to rob a store, in a little valley town with one way in and one way out. The CHP must be waiting for them, eager for the encounter. Where the fuck could they go? They didn't know this town, the roads, anything.

"Where we going?" Derek asked.

"Away," Burns said. His voice sounded tight, too.

"What happened in there?" Kenny asked.

"Total fuckup," Burns said.

"We can't go on the freeway," Derek said. He was really beginning to be scared, now. This was not the kind of fear he had felt going in, that had been almost pleasant. This fear was not. It made him want to throw up. He looked at the faces of Burns and Kenny. They were scared, too. For some reason, that helped Derek with his own fear, and after a few minutes of driving aimlessly around country roads with nothing but fields or trees around them, Derek said, "I wish I'd got that damned Coke. I'm pretty thirsty."

Burns laughed, but it was a tight laugh.

After an hour or so, they found themselves back on the highway, traveling south again. "They'll be looking for us," Derek said.

"They're looking for a lot of people," Burns said. "You think we're the only guys pulling crimes tonight?"

"Yeah," said Kenny. "As long as I drive right, they got no reason to look at us."

Nothing was said about the botched stickup. They finally stopped at a gas station and filled up. It was near dawn. Derek drained three

Coca-Colas for this terrible thirst, while Burns went into the men's room and Kenny talked to the guy at the pump. Derek wondered how he could get away from these guys. He had had enough. Now that he had a chance to think about it, these guys were crazy, on their way back to jail for sure. Kenny seemed like a reasonable guy, but look at the crazy stuff they were doing. Derek felt trapped. He was sure of only one thing. He would take part in no more Mickey Mouse robberies. He had been extremely lucky up to now. Now it was time to be smart.

Burns came out of the toilet, waving his hands to dry them. He came over to the Coke machine and stood next to Derek.

"It's been a long night, you must be pretty tired."

"Yeah," said Derek.

Burns put his hand on Derek's shoulder and gave it a squeeze. "You've been great," Burns said. "You've been through some shit, and you've done really well. I'm really proud of you."

"Me?" Derek said.

"I thought you were a punk, but you've got guts," Burns said.

"Thanks," Derek said.

They stopped for a big breakfast at a truckstop over the mountains near Bakersfield after a long quiet drive on winding two-lane roads. Kenny was amazing. Derek was beginning to like him in spite of his jealousy, which he now admitted to after it was gone. But only to himself, not to the others. Kenny was calm, cool, seemingly more concerned about the new zit on his chin than their narrow escape. Of course Kenny had not been in a gunfight.

After they finished eating and were drinking their coffee and smoking cigarettes, Burns said, "We could rob this dump."

"A truckstop?" Kenny said. He took his glasses off and began polishing them with a paper napkin. "We'd get creamed."

"That's the secret," Burns said. "Nobody robs truckstops. The fucking drivers, right? So nobody is *expecting* a robbery. That's the trouble with that fucking 7-Eleven, they *expect* to be stuck up, so they're prepared. I'll say they were prepared!" He grinned broadly at Derek. "How'd you like that shotgun, huh? Surprised the living shit out of me. I thought I was a dead pussy."

He said no more about robbing the truckstop, and when they got up to leave, Burns said, "Leave a good tip, huh?" Derek left five dollars under his saucer, and Burns paid the check at the counter, joking with the woman behind the cash register.

They got back in the car, Derek once again in the backseat. "What now?" Kenny asked.

"Drive north," Burns said.

Derek had an idea. "Let's go to L.A.," he said.

But they did not go to L.A. just yet. Burns was still the boss, and Derek's idea of dropping in on his father faded. Thinking about his father made him feel empty, anyway, and it was easier to just sit in the back seat and let things whiz past.

For a gang of armed robbers, it was a long hard day. Every place they approached to rob seemed to have its own drawbacks—customers kept coming and going, the store might have too many clerks, or Chinese clerks ("Never fuck with the Chinese," said Burns after they came out of a Fresno corner store with sixpacks of beer and Coca-Cola), or sometimes the little store they entered would have such an air of poverty that they would just turn around and leave. "Why waste bullets?"

All these false starts, all this getting ready for anything, made Derek impatient for action. The money they had was being pissed away, and they were not really having any fun. Derek did not feel like an armed robber, he felt more like a kid who had cut school and now had nothing to do.

They finally scored in a store that had nothing going for it, a store that looked poverty-stricken, with a window full of spotted bananas and a wilted lettuce, a Chinese couple back of the counter by the door, and two Mexican customers, both women. Derek, walking on eggs, thought they would just buy something like a pack of cigarettes and leave, but suddenly Burns pulled out the gun and pointed it straight at the Chinese woman. "GIVE US MONEY! GIVE US MONEY!" Burns screamed like a madman, and then, almost scaring Derek out of his wits, Burns fired a round into the ceiling and pointed the gun back at the woman. "MONEY!!!"

The Chinese man opened the cash register quickly and gave Derek a handful of bills. "The big money, or I'll kill her!" Burns said through his teeth. He looked really fierce, and the Chinese man bent over and came up with a cashbox. The Chinese woman started jabbering at her husband, but Derek and Burns were out of there, into the sunlight. The store was in a quiet shabby neighborhood, and as Derek ran for the car he saw several people looking at them, watching as the car pulled away. But they were all Mexicans.

"They won't turn us in," Burns said with a bubbling laugh. "The fucking cops would put them in jail!"

Even through the numbness, Derek thought that was the funniest thing he had ever heard.

They drove down to the coast and got a motel room on the outskirts of Ventura. The cashbox, which was really an old green tacklebox, had a lot of Chinese papers in it, and down at the bottom, a cache of hundred-dollar bills, eighteen of them, some old and soft, but many crisp as the day they left the mint.

"We're starting to cook," Burns said. While he and Kenny went out looking for some weed, Derek took a shower and then lay down on one of the beds in his underwear. There were only two beds, and Derek wondered who would sleep where. He was really tired.

When he woke up, the other two boys were in the room, eating McDonald's hamburgers and watching television. They had found no weed. Derek got himself a burger out of the big white sack and gratefully ate it, while Burns made funny cracks about the television shows. After they watched the news Burns said, "See? Why would anybody be after us, when there's all this shit going on?"

They made jokes about who would sleep on the floor, but in the end Burns and Kenny slept in the same bed, leaving Derek with a queensize bed all to himself, an almost unbelievable luxury after his time at the Greenleaf Hotel in the Tenderloin.

In the morning they had a big breakfast. "We have enough money for a while," Burns said. "Let's drive down the coast to Malibu and have some fun. It's a great day, there ought to be a lot of great pussy on the beach."

"We all have dirty underwear," Kenny said.

"Always thinking, huh, Kenny? Okay, we'll let old Derek the thief get us fresh undies, fresh socks, anything else?"

"Why don't we just buy the stuff?" Derek asked. He was not going into some store and steal underwear.

"We live off the world, not the other way around," Burns said.

But when Derek went into the store at ten in the morning, it was not to steal but to buy. He didn't tell Kenny or Burns what he was going to do, he just got the two packages of Jockey shorts—they all wore size thirty—and six pair of stretch socks, and paid for them at the counter.

"Thank you, sir," the woman said.

"You're very welcome," Derek said.

"Hey," said Burns. "What's this sales slip, you asshole."

Derek took a lot of kidding, but he didn't care. They were driving south on the Coast Highway, the cliffs and beaches were beautiful, and they were not going to do any stickups, at least not for a while. The plan was that they would check into a Malibu motel, wash up, change underwear, and then do some high-class sightseeing. Derek almost told them his father was down that way, a lawyer, and that Derek now planned to call on his dad, surprise the shit out of him, and he did not know what else. He did not tell the others for fear of what Burns might come up with, like rob his dad or something. Derek didn't want this. In fact, it would be terrible if Burns found out about his dad being rich.

Because of some confusion at the desk, they rented three motel rooms in this big motel north of Malibu, with a sloping garden down to the building with their rooms, down by the beach, a big wide yellow beach. The rooms were big and had fireplaces; they looked out on the beach and the ocean. They cost two hundred dollars apiece a night, but Burns didn't seem bothered as he dealt out hundred-dollar bills to the woman. Derek understood. There was always more where that came from.

"You know what?" Kenny said. They were in Derek's room, looking out at the beach, where there was a handful of people sunbathing, or walking around. "We should have bought some bathing suits."

As it was, they went for a walk on the beach fully dressed, except for jackets.

"I plan to live here some day," Burns said. "And I want my house right on the fucking beach, so the pussy can come and go. You ever hear of the Malibu Colony?"

This beach was not like any beach Derek had ever seen. He was used to the beaches of Northern California, with their grey sand, rocks, seashells and little chunks of shells, and most of all, the piles of kelp, great brown ropy piles of stinking decaying vegetable matter with millions of sand flies rising in a cloud when you came too close. Here the yellow sand gently sloped down to the rich blue water, and the waves came ashore with a gentle slapping hiss. The sand was pure and clean. The beach was at the foot of ochre cliffs and curved out to a point, altogether a perfect beach. The three boys walked toward the point, on the hard sand down by the water's edge, and the game was to walk as close to the hissing water as possible without getting your feet wet. Sometimes they had to jump when an extra-big wave came in, but that was what made it fun.

Then Derek discovered a seashell, the only one any of them had seen in the sand. It was a dull black shell, about six inches across, filled with lovely green and red mother-of-pearl. "This is an abalone," Derek said. "But black. They're supposed to be red on the back."

"What are you, an expert on seashells?" Burns asked.

"No, he's right," Kenny said. "I seen a lot of abalone shells, and they're all red."

"So you found a nigger seashell," Burns said. "So what? Here, give it to me."

"No," Derek said moving away from Burns. "You'll throw it in the water."

"Of course," Burns said, coming after Derek.

"I'm gonna keep this," Derek said. "Souvenir of Malibu!"

Just then two women on horseback came around the point, galloping their horses down the packed wet sand near the water, forcing the boys to move out of the way. One of the women was old, with long grey-white hair, dark tanned skin, wearing a bright red shirt and jeans. The other woman was younger, beautiful, short blonde hair, bright blue eyes that looked down at Derek fiercely as she yelled, "Back!" at him. Derek fell down in the sand, backing up while staring at this incredible pair of women on their horses. Derek got up, and they watched the women ride off south.

"Rich people," Kenny said.

"Let's go back to the motel," Derek said. "This sand makes me tired."

The three of them trudged back down the beach. There were only a few other people out, wandering around, nobody had towels on the sand or anything. It seemed strange. But it was still winter, in spite of the great weather.

"I want to find a gas station where I can clean up the car," Kenny said as they made their way up the bluff to the motel buildings. "I wanna scrape some of the crap off the car. It looks like shit."

"I want it to look like shit," Burns said. "How many dirty old Chevies do you think there are in Southern California? About two hundred thousand?"

"I get it," Kenny said with a small grin. "But I hate to treat my ride that way."

"Your ride," Burns said. "Come on, let's go sightseeing."

They drove down the Coast Highway, all in fresh underwear and socks, Derek, with his washed-off abalone shell, in the back seat. It seemed that they were not yet in Malibu itself. The coast road went on for about four miles with just a few rich-looking houses clinging to the clifftops, and bare open hills on the other side of the road. Then there were lots of houses on both sides of the road, and traffic.

"This is the real Malibu," Burns said. "This is where the smart money lives."

"You been here before?" Derek asked.

"No," said Burns, "but I've been to L.A."

They turned left on Sunset Boulevard, winding up through the canyons toward Los Angeles. Burns was unusually quiet, and Kenny never said anything anyway, so Derek just sat in back looking at all the wealthy homes they were passing. He was from Marin County and had seen his share of wealthy homes, but nothing like this. It amazed him that there were so many rich people in the world. Huge old houses behind great walls, with greenery hiding almost everything but the most tantalizing views into the world of the rich, mansions behind mansions behind mansions, until he felt depressed and intimidated by all this outrageous display of other people's wealth.

"Jesus Christ!" he said at last. "You think there's any rich people around here?"

Burns turned and looked back at him. He looked strained. "You know about Penetrators?"

"No," said Derek.

"They go into houses like this. Middle of the night. They're crazy fuckers. They wake you up by shooting you in the fucking shoulder or something. Then they have their fun. They torture your children, your wife, right in front of you, then they kill them. And you. And there's nothing you can do about it. You can't beg them off or buy them off. They don't want anything. Just to taste that fear. Fear junkies."

"Jesus Christ," Derek said again, but in a different tone. Burns smiled quietly. "There's a lot of crazy shit going on nobody ever hears about. You know why? Because these fuckers never get caught. And the cops don't like to talk about shit they can't do anything about. In fact, some of these Penetrators are probably cops."

Derek did not know whether to believe Burns or not. Penetrators?

"Southern California is the land of crazy crimes," Burns said.

Finally they came to Beverly Hills, and Burns told them this was the worst town in the world to commit crimes in, because the cops would just shoot you.

"They'll take you down in the basement of the police station and shoot you in the head. Then they have this big trash masher they put the bodies in, and then send 'em to the dump. Draws flies but then so does everything else at the fucking dump."

Now Derek was sure Burns was making it up. "Let's go to Hollywood," he said. "You know where Hollywood is?"

"Right up the road," Burns said. "What the hell you want to go to Hollywood for? You want to be discovered?"

Derek laughed. "No, I'd just like to see the place."

"I'm going to be discovered," Burns said.

"Sure you are," Derek joked.

"I mean it," Burns said calmly.

It turned out Burns did not know exactly where Hollywood was. It turned out Burns had only been to Los Angeles once before, on another run with a couple of older guys, right after he had gotten out of Preston. "We ran amok down here," he said. "Tommy liked to stick up car washes, because all the workers are ex-convicts and won't interfere, just look the other way, you know what I mean? We made good money."

"Why don't we do that?" Kenny asked.

Burns laughed. "You're a tough guy, Kenny. No, it's too much work, too scary, man."

But they finally found Hollywood, in the form of Hollywood Boulevard. It was late in the day, and the boulevard was crowded, the sidewalks and streets full. They drove slowly down the boulevard among the traffic, looking at the mobs on both sides of the street. "This don't look so hot to me," Kenny said. "It looks like fuckin' Market Street, only worse."

"That's what it is," Burns said. "Park the fucking car, this is the best place in the world to score dope. All we have to do is find the right-looking people, and they'll turn us on."

"You said that before," Kenny said.

"Shut up," Burns said. "Turn off here."

They parked the car a few blocks below the boulevard and walked back up. They stopped at an open-front orange juice stand and had orange juices filled with sugar.

"Boy, that's good shit," Kenny said, and had another.

They walked along Hollywood Boulevard from Mann's Chinese Theater to Vine Street, looking in store windows, looking at the names inside the brass stars on the sidewalk. There were plenty of people on the street who looked as if they might know where to get drugs, but the boys didn't approach any of them. It was too crude, too much like a police trap or something. Derek did not care. He was not much of a hophead anyway. That was all they needed to do anyway, get hopped up on drugs and run into some store waving the gun and getting killed.

"Look at this shit," Kenny said in wonderment, as they came upon several people on their hands and knees polishing one of the stars.

"What are you guys doing?" Burns asked the man and two women. They were older people, shapeless, with hard faces. They did not answer Burns, and the boys moved along.

"Star-worshippers," Burns said. "Hey, after I'm a star, will you guys come and polish my sidewalk?"

"You bet," Kenny said.

"Right," Derek said.

"You guys don't believe me, but I'm going to be a movie star. I have the looks and the brains. All I need is the contacts. And you know how you get the contacts? First, you get the bucks. Then you come to town in style, right? Big limousine, rent one of those fucking mansions in Beverly Hills and start giving parties. That's the way to break into the movies."

They tried a couple of bars on the boulevard, but nobody would sell to them. "Are we going to have to stick up a grocery store just to get served?" Burns asked.

But they found a little deli that sold them two sixpacks, and they walked back to the car, tired from sightseeing, and sat in the car.

"What now?" Kenny asked. "Anybody want to see a movie?"

"Fuck the movies," Burns said.

"What about the Sunset Strip?" Derek asked.

"Fuck the Sunset Strip."

They drank beer quietly for a while, putting their beers in their laps and looking virtuous when a police car went past them slowly.

"Don't worry about the cops down here," Burns said. "This is fag territory. They're looking for fags to bust."

It was dark now. Kenny started the car and they drove slowly down Santa Monica toward the ocean miles away.

The run ended in Long Beach a little after ten the next morning. They rode around all night, stopping for gas and food, but otherwise roaming the endless streets and freeways of the Los Angeles area. They never went back to Malibu, never spent the night in their $200 individual motel rooms, with fireplaces and marble bathrooms. They stayed awake all night instead, looking for a robbery to commit.

Not just any robbery. Something had happened to Burns in Hollywood. At one point on Santa Monica, when they still thought they were headed back to the beach, Burns said suddenly, "Stop the car, I want to get in back." Burns changed places with Derek, and they kept rolling and kept drinking beer. Burns was quiet in the back, and when Kenny asked him over his shoulder where to go, Burns just said, "Go where the fuck you please."

Kenny found a freeway entrance that looked promising, and they got on the freeway south. Derek saw an exit sign that said VENICE BOULEVARD, but didn't say anything. Finally, Kenny said, "I think we went too far," and got off the freeway, but couldn't find the entrance to get on going the other way.

"This fucking town is nuts," Kenny said. They drove around on city streets for a while, and then found one with a vaguely familiar name, Sepulveda, a long, apparently endless boulevard with shops, liquor stores, cocktail lounges, big supermarkets, used car lots, furniture stores, everything.

"You know what we are?" Burns called out from the back. "We're a bunch of punks."

"What's the matter now?" Kenny asked humorously.

"Fuck you, Kenny," Burns said. "I can't believe what punks we are, robbing little stores and thinking we're such primo guys. God, it makes me sick!"

"I know," Kenny said. "We should get jobs. Tomorrow, okay? We'll all get jobs." To Derek he said, "Sometimes old Burns gets like this."

"Like what?"

"Like I'm about to go crazy," Burns said. "I'm twenty fucking years old, almost twenty-one, I been out of the joint two fucking years, and what have I done with myself? Robbed stores, stuck up a few drunks. Remember our plans?"

"Yeah," said Kenny.

Derek never got to hear the plans, and wasn't sure he wanted to, anyway. "Let's go back to the motel," he suggested.

"Those fucking highway robbers," Burns said, and after a minute Derek could hear him chuckling. "We ought to go back there and stick them up the way they stuck us up. Then we could knock on all the doors, you know, 'Room service!' or some shit like that, and stick up the loving couples. You know what that fucking motel is, don't you? Up there in the middle of nowhere with those luxury rooms?

That's where the Hollywood assholes take their pussy, secret pussy. We could really cash in, find out who's with who, blackmail those fuckers till their assholes bleed."

Burns was funny, but it was frightening to hear him going on and on about it. Derek heard a click and looked back to see Burns fiddling with the pistol. He thought to ask for his gun back, but didn't. He didn't know what Burns would do in this mood. He didn't really know Burns at all, he reminded himself. But Kenny did, and Kenny seemed calm enough. But Kenny was pretty strange himself.

"You know about blackmail?" Burns said. "There's a crime that never gets reported. Who would report it? There are guys who have a whole string of suckers, like a pimp with his girls. They get something on these poor bastards, you know, something really disgusting, like getting caught eating some whore's shit, or butt-fucking little boys, and then they bleed these bastards white, *bleed* them *white* . . ."

Burns lapsed into silence for a while. Kenny had the radio on low, but turned it up now, and they drove aimlessly listening to rock'n'roll. Then Burns said, "Stop the car," and changed places with Derek again.

"You know what's really wrong?"

"Yeah," said Kenny. "I'm hungry, that's what's wrong."

"We'll stop for something after we've done something worthy," Burns said. "That's what's really wrong. We aren't working up to capacity. We got the brains, we got the guts, but we don't have a plan. So we go around stealing hundred-dollar bills, like a bunch of sneak thieves. I need money, I need a lot of money, and I need it now."

"That's the way to talk," Kenny said.

"We should stick up a bar," Burns said.

"Whoa," Kenny said.

"Are you kidding?" Derek said.

Burns' plan was simple. They would wait until nearly closing time, ten till two or something, and then Derek would walk into the bar looking for his father. "You look the most innocent," Burns explained. Then he would ask if he could use the phone, because his father was not in the bar. Then Burns would come in, looking for Derek. Just a couple kids looking for this guy's dad, the old drunk was supposed to be here, damn it all, and when things were perfect, Burns would pull the gun.

"The last few customers will all be drunk," Burns said, "and the guy behind the bar tired, and it's the boss' money, so what the fuck. It only takes a little more than we've been putting out, and the money's so much better. We could walk out with five or six thousand."

But they never found a bar that looked right, and the hour of closing passed without any stickup. They stopped at a place on the corner of Sepulveda and Washington for hamburgers and sat outside in the chill air at one of the picnic tables, eating hamburgers with big hunks of dill pickle. While they ate, Burns talked about a restaurant he wanted to open some day. Burns' eyes were feverish by now, and Derek was very much afraid of him. Drinking beer all night had made Derek wary rather than drunk, which was odd and bothered him. He felt as if he was suffering from jetlag, although he had never had jetlag. It was all this aimless wandering around in a car that was doing it. Once more, Derek suggested they go back to the motel, but Burns was very cold about it.

"Not until we have made a score," he said.

They never made the score. They drove past places and looked in—all-night markets, convenience stores, gas stations—all had a quiet outdoor facade of impregnability, cars in front, lights flooding the parking area, no trees to park under, no way to walk in without being instantly photographed, fingerprinted, and sent away.

So there they were, in this big cafeteria type of place in Long Beach, all sunny, eating breakfast with a lot of midmorning customers, most of them black. Derek was exhausted. He wasn't thinking much, he was just riding along. He stolidly ate his bacon and eggs while Burns and Kenny talked about the possibility of pulling a big stickup, one that would get them real money. The kind of thing the real heavyweights pulled.

Kenny pointed out that they were underarmed. "If we had the guns, we could stick up anybody. A bank."

"It doesn't take guns to rob a bank," Burns said. "It takes guts. You can rob a bank with nothing but a fucking note."

A waitress was going past. "Hey, loan me your pen," Burns said to her. He took a napkin from the dispenser and wrote:

GIVE ME ALL THE FUCKING MONEY OR I'LL BLOW YOUR FUCKING BRAINS OUT

Cocking his head to one side, he thickened the words FUCKING MONEY and FUCKING BRAINS. He showed the napkin to the others. "What do you think? Would you pass over the bucks or not? Some chick makes four an hour? She wouldn't even step on the button."

"What if she does?" Derek asked.

"As I said, it takes guts," Burns said. "Like we could just walk out of here without paying the check, look 'em right in the eye, and they probably wouldn't do anything about it. But that's not guts. That's just being a bully."

Kenny picked up the napkin with the note on it and folded it, putting it into his shirt pocket. "Might come in handy," he said with a little grin.

"Let's roll," Burns said. "You know what? We're so close we ought to head for Tijuana for the fucking bullfights. I never saw a bullfight."

"Do they have them down there?" Derek asked.

Burns paid the check at the counter and they walked out into the sunlight.

"See over there?" Kenny said. They looked across the wide boulevard.

"What's over there?" Burns asked.

Kenny unlocked the door and stood grinning at Burns with the door open. "You like to drive," Kenny said. He tossed his keys to Burns.

"What the fuck is this all about?" Burns asked.

"Give me five minutes," Kenny said. "Then hang a big U and pull into that yellow zone." He pointed again across the wide street to a yellow zone in front of a branch Bank of America.

"Oh, Jesus," Derek said, his heart suddenly in his throat.

"I look like a mad bomber," Kenny said, the light glinting off his rimless glasses, and Derek thought stupidly, yes, he does look like a mad bomber. Numbly, Derek walked around the car and got into the back seat. Outside the car he could hear Burns and Kenny.

Burns said, "Okay, numbnuts, go ahead."

"You think I won't?"

"Five minutes."

"Deal."

Burns got in behind the wheel and put the key in the ignition, as Derek watched Kenny crossing the street, looking no different than ever, kind of slouching along. Kenny disappeared into the bank.

"What a funny asshole," Burns said.

"You better start the car," Derek said. His throat was dry.

Burns turned to him. "You don't think he's going to flash that fucking note, do you? Kenny's kind of slow, but he's not that . . ." Burns stopped for a moment, and then said ". . . uh, gutsy."

Derek wanted to say, "What if he's gone crazy?" but didn't, because Burns started the car. The radio popped on loud, rock'n'roll. Burns yelled over the music, "I'm not going to hang a U. That's an illegal act," but just then Kenny came out of the bank. Even at that distance Derek could see with remarkable clarity. Kenny was holding something to his stomach, and things were falling. They were bundles of what looked like money. Kenny was holding several bundles of money, trying to hurry down the sidewalk. Both hands were busy so he couldn't wave or signal. Behind Kenny, coming up the sidewalk but not from the bank, were two policemen, walking rapidly, their backs straight, their whole attitude eagerness for combat. A police car came from the opposite direction and squealed to a stop in front of Kenny, and outrageously, unbelievably, melodramatically, a helicopter suddenly appeared high overhead, its chopper noises echoing madly from one side of the street to the other.

"Oh, fuck," Burns said in a low voice, and pulled out. They drove slowly away. "Don't look back," Burns said without turning his head. Derek did not look back. The last he had seen of Kenny was his grinning face as he held the bundles of money to his belly. Poor Kenny had forgotten to take anything to carry the money in.

"Get on the floor," Burns said without turning his head. Numbly Derek got on the floor as much as he could, keeping his head below window level. The car made a couple of turns and then speeded up a little. Then abruptly, the car came to a stop. They were at the curb of another wide street, going endlessly nowhere in both directions. Burns opened the righthand door. Derek got out and was about to get into the front seat when Burns said coldly, "We have to split up. I'll meet you back in Frisco."

Derek wanted to ask for his gun, he wanted to ask for his share of the money, but he could see Burns' face and knew it would be useless. Burns pulled the door shut and left Derek standing there.

Derek stood remembering his favorite part of Jack Kerouac's *On the Road*, the part that made him fall in love with the book, the part where Jack decides to hitch-hike from New York to California, and gets quick and easy rides out into the middle of Upstate Nowhere, when it starts raining and sleeting and Jack is wearing sandals and nobody will stop for him. Whiz whiz whiz go the cars, down comes the icy rain and nobody is *ever* going to pick Jack up and take him to sunny California. God, that had been funny, with all the guy's plans and dreams, ending up stuck here with nothing to offer but a wet smile and a moving thumb.

Who had loaned him that book? Al Burke, of course. They had talked for five minutes one day, and then Al brought over the book and left it with his mother. Derek hadn't wanted to read it. It was history. But once he got to that hitch-hiking section he couldn't put the fucker down. Well, Jack, here I am on the Pacific Coast highway, slightly south of Los Angeles. You'll be glad to know, Jack, that the weather couldn't be better. Surf's up, the wind's from the west, it must be at least seventy-five degrees out, I have my jacket over my arm and when a car comes past I put on my best off-to-college smile, but Jack, nothing seems to work for me, either. Where is that friendly grinning truck driver who'll take me where I want to go? Where's that beautiful girl in her little Porsche to take me to heaven? Where the fuck is some Mexican on a mule who will share the ride?

Derek was over being frightened. In the middle of the afternoon, soon after he had been dropped off on the Coast Highway, he had suddenly felt nauseated and threw up at his own feet. The vomiting helped. He had been carrying too heavy a load. He felt terrible about Kenny, whom he barely knew. Kenny was caught robbing a bank, man, they were not going to slap him on the wrist and tell him to go his way. They were going to fuck him around until he gave up some names, cleared up a few crimes, started working for them. How long would it take for Kenny to give up their names?

And Burns. Derek did not like to think about Burns. It made his guts turn over sickeningly to remember how he had trusted that bastard. But why? Burns had never presented himself as trustworthy. If Derek had trusted him, it had been his own fault.

Standing there letting the wind from the passing vehicles cool him off, Derek tried to remember from his Boy Scout days all the things a Boy Scout was supposed to be. Trustworthy first, of course. With his mind floating loose, the words came easily: Trustworthy, loyal, helpful, friendly, courteous, kind, obedient, cheerful, thrifty, brave, clean, and reverent. Wow. He could remember when he had passionately wanted to be all these things. He had gone into the Boy Scouts such an innocent boy, only to find out that at least in Lincoln's Grove the Boy Scouts were every boy's introduction to filth, perversion, and the (to him anyway) heart-shattering realization that adults had been lying about the true nature of the world and were *still* lying, and would probably continue to lie, and worst of all, when you graduated from the Boy Scouts, hopefully an Eagle Scout, with a full sash of Merit Badges, you would then become one of *them*, the adults, and would begin telling lies about everything yourself.

Derek wondered if he took off his sunglasses people might be more likely to pick him up. But no, everybody down here wore them, and besides, Derek felt his little brown eyes looked untrustworthy.

Ha. Also unloyal, etc. The drivers down here were different from Northern California. He and Burns and Kenny had talked about this, the way everybody down here was at least ten pounds heavier, had redder skin, drove better cars much faster, and generally looked like strangers. These strangers did not want to pick him up, obviously, and he had a vision of himself walking slowly backward all the way from Long Beach to Venice. He did not know how far this actually was, but it seemed like hundreds of miles. He had less than forty dollars in his pocket, and did not think that would be enough for a motel room and food, in case he didn't make it to his father's place in time. He held off thinking about what his father would think or do when Derek showed up on his doorstep, all but broke, dirty, and completely without a cover story.

As the cars came along, spaced apart but moving steadily, Derek tried to psych out the drivers and offer an expression designed to appeal. There were a lot of people alone in their cars, and Derek did not understand why none of them would stop for him, or even make eye contact. Some of them seemed to be shouting at him as they passed, waving a fist, or once, giving him the finger, as if by the act of hitch-hiking, Derek was committing some terrible atrocity. Others pointed, jabbing to the right (the ocean was on the left), as if they were going to turn off too soon to be of any help. Like maybe only five or ten miles up the road, you fucking assholes, eat shit . . .

Then a car with a lone guy in it passed, but then slowed down to a stop about fifty yards up the road.

"Yeah," Derek said to himself and started trotting up to the car. But just as he got within ten feet or so, the guy did a rooster and took off, leaving Derek standing there in the kicked-up dust, filled with bitterness.

"Prick," he said quietly.

Some time later he saw a police car coming toward him, and his heart sank into his shoes. He did not know what to do. He was legal, he thought, off the actual roadway, but maybe in this part of the world hitch-hiking was a crime anyway, and if he got picked up by these cops his name and description would be radioed back to Police Central or what the fuck, and they would take him straight to jail. That's if he just stood there. If he turned away or ran or walked fast, they would really come after his ass. If he just boldly held out his thumb, they would think he was a smartass punk and haul him in anyway.

So there was nothing he could do but swallow his fear, smile at the policemen, and wave. They waved back, and went on their way. For a moment, Derek loved them. They were good cops, out doing their real job, and not hassling innocent hitch-hikers. Then Derek had to laugh at himself.

Another hour passed, with two rides, each for only a few blocks. Each time he asked what was the best way to get to Venice, but neither driver, both men, had any idea. "It's right up the road," one of them said, "but I don't know how you'll get past Palos Verdes."

Derek didn't know what that meant, he only knew he was now standing on the Coast Highway between little towns, tired and hungry but too nervous to stop for anything. He was certain that at any minute the police would swarm down on him as they had on Kenny. They must take bankrobbing very seriously down here, he thought stupidly. Ha. Maybe Burns had been right in them splitting up. They would be looking for a couple of boys in Kenny's car. For some reason, Derek hoped Burns had been smart enough to ditch the car. But he had that shock of blond hair, he would be easy to spot. For the first time in his life, Derek was glad he looked dull, blank, uninteresting. It could save him from jail. Of course if they stopped him and looked in his wallet and Kenny had given names . . .

Derek took out his wallet, with its expired driver's license, social security card, pictures, tattered old Student Body Card, a rubber that was at least two years old . . .

He sailed the rubber, still in its packet, into the weeds. He thought about throwing away the wallet itself, after shredding the papers. Then if the cops stopped him, he would have no ID at all. That wouldn't make them suspicious. Shit no. So he had to keep the wallet and hope that he was either not stopped, or if he was stopped, the police wouldn't have his name. Derek somebody. He was not even sure he had told Burns or Kenny his last name. Well, fuck it.

The sun was about an inch from the Pacific when a huge fat man wearing a red tanktop and riding a motorcycle stopped for him.

"Where you headed?"

"Venice," Derek said.

"I'll drop you right off, boy. Climb aboard!" The guy had a wind-burned face, a three-day beard and long wild reddish hair. Derek climbed clumsily onto the bike behind the man, having to grab him on the shoulder to do it.

"Excuse me," he said.

"Hug me around the waist, honey," the guy said, but there was nothing faggy about it, so Derek put his hands on the guy's belly, and off they went.

"Call me Red!" the guy yelled over his shoulder.

"I'm Daaa, uh, Dave!" Derek yelled. Jeez, this was fun!

Red let Derek off at the Venice Pier. It was dark, but there were plenty of people out, dressed for summer, even though there was a little nip in the air. He shook hands with Red, who gave him a grin and said, "Good luck, little bro," and ripped off.

Venice Pier, huh? Restaurants, bars, rollerskate rental places, even people rollerskating around in the semidarkness. Derek felt fine after his motorcycle ride, hungry and thirsty. He wandered up the street away from the ocean, and saw a place that looked friendly, tables with blue-and-white checkered tablecloths. He went in and took a table, a little self-consciously because he was not used to taking a table in a restaurant by himself, but the waitress came right up to him with a nice smile, and pretty soon he was working his way through a big hamburger and sipping from his second Coca-Cola. Everything he had been through now seemed like a dream. He wondered what he would tell his father, when he found him. Several stories occurred to him, but he rejected them all as being too fancy, too involved.

There was a telephone over in the corner back of the cash register, and Derek went over to look up his dad. It took him a while to find the right telephone book from the stack of big thick books. The right one was thin in comparison, just the beach towns. There was no Steven Jeminovski listed. Of course. His father would have an unlisted number, the asshole. Derek's face started heating up. Then he thought to look in the yellow pages, under ATTORNEYS. There he was, 233 Ocean Boulevard, and the number.

"Lawyer's exchange," the sweet female voice said.

"Uh, I'm looking for Steven Jeminovski?"

"Yes, may I inquire as to the nature of your call, sir?"

"I'm his son," Derek said.

"Yes, his son?" The woman's tone had dropped several degrees.

"Yes, his son. I'd like a number to call, please?"

"Is this a legal emergency?"

Derek smiled to himself, even though he was feeling pretty frustrated. "I'm his son Derek. I'm here in Venice. I'd like to contact my father, if you don't mind."

"Mister Jeminovski's office hours are from ten in the morning until five in the evening," the woman said in a mechanical voice. "Unless this is a legal emergency and you would like to talk to the lawyer on call . . ."

"I want to talk to my father. I do not want to talk to a lawyer."

"I'm sorry, sir, I have been given no instructions."

"Okay," Derek said lamely. "I'm sorry to have bothered you."

He left the restaurant after paying for his dinner, and walked up to the corner. Venice Boulevard and Ocean. His father's office was on this street here. He looked at the numbers, and started walking north. At the corner of Ocean and Market he found a two-story building of brown stucco with the right number, and, looking up at the second story, he could see his father's name, in gold letters, curving over the words, ATTORNEY AT LAW. God, it looked so cheap and sleazy. The building itself was not in good repair, but that gilded name on the window really made Derek's heart sink. His father was obviously some cheap shyster, not the bigtime hotshot he pretended to be.

Derek walked back down to Venice Boulevard, and then for lack of anything else to do, walked out onto the pier itself, leaned on the rail and listened to the waves slapping the pilings. Not much smell. The people walking around looked tough, for some reason, with their tank tops and bill caps.

Leaning on the rail, Derek felt a wave of loneliness come over him, a feeling he usually fought. But now he let it fill him, a cold flow of emptiness, like ice cold distilled water, he thought foolishly, I'm being cleaned out, emptied out, poor old Derek, nobody loves him, nobody to care for him, no beautiful girl to love him . . . what was to become of him?

But the slapping of the waves below told him he was full of shit. Slap slap, you asshole, you are the luckiest son of a bitch ever to walk the face of the earth. By all rights you ought to be dead now, or worse, stuck in some tiny jail cell with a bunch of Mexicans and Negroes and Samoans, being fucked in the ass and murdered every ten minutes . . . by all rights you ought to be in terrible pain right now, but instead you are standing here in Southern California, which you've never visited before, you have money, not much, but money, and as soon as you can figure out how, you are going to see your dad, who may not be the nicest guy in the world, but he's at least your dad and he's got to take you in, at least for a while. He's got to. Meanwhile, you have the night to consider. Consider the night, and all its little problems. He could not afford a motel, not at Southern California prices, and he could not find his dad. So he would have to stay up all night. Well, he had done that before. But now he must also avoid the police. Well, he had done that before, too. Hmm. What the fuck. This was life, wasn't it? He was free, white and almost twenty-one, what was he pissing and moaning about?

He walked. He did not go down onto the beach because he didn't want to get sand in his shoes, so he walked up and down Ocean Boulevard. He walked down as far as Marina del Rey, to the man-made channel between the marina and the ocean, and after sitting on a park bench there for over an hour without being disturbed, his ass got sore and he walked back up the path, or whatever it was, between the houses. It was a long straight path, and even late at night he saw other people out walking, bicycling or rollerskating. Several people said hello to him. He saw two police cars, once he was back on Ocean, and both times he just walked along as if he had someplace to go, but was in no real hurry, just moving right along. The police didn't come after him. He found a place up Venice Boulevard that stayed open all night, and he thought with relief that he would stay in there, drinking coffee until morning, but the people who ran the little dump threw him out after three coffees.

"Can't hang out all night, kid," the guy said, not unkindly.

"I was supposed to meet somebody," Derek said as he left.

The waiting room to his father's office was shabby. That was the only word for it. The furniture, two overstuffed chairs and a couch, were all covered in a dull green plastic-leather that was not Naugahyde. The magazines on the coffee table were *Mechanic's Illustrated*, *Time*, *Penthouse*, *Good Housekeeping*. There was a desk blocking the door to the inner office, one of those grey plastic desks with metal rims. It looked like something picked up at an office equipment sale. The woman behind the desk, somewhere between forty and eight hundred years old, looked as if she had been acquired at the same sale. For some reason, Derek had always assumed that his father's secretary would have been one of those L.A. beauties, barely capable of answering the telephone. But this one looked competent, and to Derek's relief, friendly.

"Good morning," she said as he walked in. She looked at him intently, and then smiled a wrinkled old false-teeth smile, and put Derek completely at ease.

"I'm Derek Jeminovski," he said.

"Derek! How nice to meet you!" She gave him an even nicer, more motherly smile. "You called last night, didn't you?"

"Yeah, the woman didn't seem . . ."

"Oh, never mind her. She has her job to do. At any rate, here you are! What brings you to sunny Southern California? Is it spring break already?"

Derek wondered if this woman, ETTA LING according to her wooden nameplate, thought he was a college student. Well, he did not want to blow his father's story, so he said, "Well, sort of. Is Dad around?"

"As a matter of fact, your father has been away for a couple of days on a case, and should be walking through the front door any minute. Why don't you sit down, relax, read a magazine, although I'm sorry about the selection." Etta Ling became busy without seeming to have dismissed Derek. He sat on the couch, which turned out to be pretty uncomfortable, and reached for a copy of *Mechanic's Illustrated*. Now why in hell would his father have *Mechanic's Illustrated* in his office? But Derek's hand strayed to a *Penthouse*, and a minute later he was looking at a somewhat blurry color photograph of a beautiful woman, looking over her shoulder at him, her rear end and private parts gleaming with oil. Derek noticed that someone had placed a small pearl inside her vagina. He wondered why. "Pearl-diving?" Hmm.

As Derek was looking at other, similar photographs, a man came up the stairs and into the office. He was a black man, at least thirty-five, big and bulky, with massive muscles all over his body. He was dressed in striped soccer shirt, white shorts and knee-length white socks with a big green stripe around the tops. He also had on a green eyeshade and white sneakers, and was carrying an old skateboard. He smiled at Derek and limped over to Etta Ling's desk.

"Hello," he said. "My name is Jason Vincent. Is the lawyer in, Mister Jemiskovski?"

"I'm sorry, sir, not at the moment, but I can take your information." Like a sweet old aunt she gestured to the chair beside her desk and Mr. Vincent lowered himself painfully into the chair. "Ouch," he said with a grin.

"Won't you tell me what happened, Mr. Vincent?"

"It just happened," Mr. Vincent said. "Right out on the pier. I can hardly believe the pain."

"Have you seen a doctor yet?"

"No, I thought I would stop in here, seeing as how you're right here and all. The man deliberately pushed me off my wheels. He was not careless or negligent, he was malicious."

"Mister Vincent, I would think you should get to a doctor or to a hospital emergency room, to find out just what has happened to you, in medical terms."

They looked at each other for a few moments, while Derek pretended to be interested in his *Penthouse*.

"Uh, can you give me the name of a *good* local doctor?"

Etta Ling smiled sweetly. "I don't think that would be a good idea," she said. "Don't you have a family doctor, or a medical plan?"

"I just want to get the details of this outrage down on paper with somebody," Mr. Vincent said.

"I'm sure Mister Jeminovski would be glad to see you and listen to your case after you've obtained a medical report." Another smile. "We can't sue if we aren't hurt, can we?"

"Hurt? I'll say I'm hurt."

"Yes, but we'd like somebody else to say it, too," she said jokingly. She took down his name, address, and telephone number. "Is there a number at work where I can reach you?" she asked.

"I'm unemployed at present," he said.

After he was gone, Derek looked at Etta Ling to see if she would smile or laugh or say anything, but she just sat there doing paperwork and answering the telephone, which was starting to ring every two or three minutes. She answered, "Lawyer's office," instead of "Mister Jeminovski's office." It was all pretty strange to Derek.

Then his father came in. He was dressed in a lightweight grey suit, beautifully cut, and carried a tan leather briefcase. He had just gotten a haircut and was wearing air force type sunglasses, which he took off as he entered the room, giving Derek a small smile and saying to his secretary, "Good morning, Etta. For once the plane was on time. I expected to circle LAX for half an hour, but no, we came in like ducks on a pond."

"This is your son Derek," she said to him, pointing.

Steven cocked his head and turned again toward Derek, his face taking on a look of utter disbelief. Derek had never seen such a look before. His father's eyes were really popping.

"*Derek?*"

"Hi, Dad."

"Jesus Christ, what's happened to you?"

Derek felt a stab of guilt. He was still sitting there on the hard lumpy couch holding the *Penthouse*. "What do you mean?" he asked, and got to his feet. Would they hug?

"You look . . ." Steven stopped, his eyes examining Derek's face, as if he had not seen him in years instead of months. "I'll be damned," he said softly, and came to Derek, hugging him hard. "God damn," he said, and Derek's heart melted. He did not think he cared that much about his father, but he wanted to cry anyway. He didn't cry, however.

"Etta," Steven said with pride in his voice, "this is my son."

"I know," she said. "We just met and had a nice chat. Oh, and this came in this morning," she said, and handed Steven some papers.

Steven's inner sanctum was not much better furnished than the waiting room. A big desk littered with papers and junk, a couch in red plastic, a hatrack, some grey filing cabinets. Derek's father's office looked to Derek like the office of a man who was not doing too well.

"All right, young man," Steven said, getting around behind his desk and tilting back in his chair, "what brings you to La-la, and what the hell's happened to you? I know I keep asking that, but I'd really like to know. That last time we saw each other you seemed a little, ah, less mature, let us say."

Derek had had all night to work out his answers, but he was still a little nervous about lying to his father. When Derek had been little and his father living at home, Derek had gotten away with nothing. Not that his father was severe or strict, just that he seemed to *know* everything. Now Derek took his time sitting on the red couch, which was much more comfortable than it looked, and grinned at his dad as if nothing unusual was going on at all.

"Let's see," Steven said. "The last time we talked, you were going to go back to school."

"Yeah," said Derek, remembering with a flush that he had begged his father for ten thousand dollars. "Well, I've been hitch-hiking around the state, you know, doing odd jobs, meeting people, you know, getting out of Marin County, see the real world for a change."

"Odd jobs? What kind of odd jobs?"

"Oh, you know, landscaping, junk like that. Anyway, I'm here, I just sort of found myself near Venice, so I came over to see you."

"Kids," his father said. "I kinda wish I was a kid again. Me and a couple of buddies drove all over the United States when I was a little younger than you, before I went into the army."

"I know," Derek said.

"How's your mother?"

"I haven't seen her since Thanksgiving. I guess she's okay. She's always okay."

"I see you're wearing the Reeboks," Steven said. The shoes had been Steven's Christmas present to Derek.

"Yeah, I took 'em Thanksgiving."

There was a buzz, and Steven picked up the telephone and spoke into it quietly. Derek sat looking out the window at Venice Beach. The beaches down here were so wide, he thought, there seemed to be more beach than ocean.

"Look," Steven said. "I have a pretty light day. I've got a client coming in a few minutes. Why don't you do a little sightseeing and come back here around twelve-thirty. I don't have anybody for lunch, we could eat across the street and then go for a drive or something. Where are you staying?"

"Could I stay at your place? For a day or two?"

Steven looked at him calmly. "I don't see any suitcase, no backpack, not even a paper bag."

Derek shrugged and grinned. "I lost all my shit," he said.

"Well, you may look different, but I guess you're still the same old Derek," his father said indulgently. "Do you have any money?"

"About twenty bucks."

Steven stood up and came around his desk, pulling Derek to his feet. "Okay, scoot, and I'll see you in a couple of hours."

Derek found himself outside, among the rollerskaters and mopheads. Venice was like a resort town, he decided. He walked out onto the pier and watched girls until it was time to meet his father again.

They had big hamburgers and draft beers for lunch, and Steven seemed very happy to have Derek with him. For once he did not haul out the old song about not wanting to disrupt the continuity of Derek's life by having visitations. Instead, he seemed to be taking it for granted that Derek was now an adult and they could be friends. Laughing, animated, charming, he told Derek about the part of the legal profession he had specialized in, the pleasure-related personal injury cases.

"People get hurt having fun, and then some yutz comes along with a thousand dollars and a form to sign. People don't know their rights, especially in pleasure-related injuries. They feel guilty about somebody drowning in their pool. I know a lot about swimming pool accidents."

They went across Ocean to a small private parking lot, where the silver Mercedes sat baking in the sun. After they got in the car, Steven turned to Derek and said, "You've been pretty badly scared recently, haven't you?"

"What do you mean?"

Steven smiled a little sadly. "You smell awful, son. The stink of fear."

"Oh," Derek said.

"Let's get you some fresh underwear, maybe a couple of shirts, some general haberdashery, and then go home, you can shower, shave, brush your teeth, all that shit, okay?"

"Sounds good to me," Derek said, so horribly embarrassed he wanted to kill his father. Even though he knew his father had been diplomatic, had been perfectly wonderful, considering the fact that Derek must have really reeked.

"Instead of using the air-conditioning, let's roll down the windows," Steven said. "It's such a nice spring day."

Derek had to see things from his father's point of view. Here came his kid, dirty, jobless, no particular plan for the future. His dad had his own life here in Southern California. That was why he had moved out in the first place, years ago. Of course he loved his children. He had never failed to send the child-support money, and he was good with presents, almost uncanny, in fact. Derek loved his Reeboks, for example. The perfect shoe for the kid who likes to walk. Derek wondered what his father would have thought if he had known Derek wore his Reeboks while walking all over the city of San Francisco looking for newspaper racks to rob.

But the time for fatherly love, for child support, was long over. Allowing Derek to stay in his house for a few days was not something he had to do, but something he might be doing out of a sense of guilt, you know, for having left in the first place, years ago. Hell, Derek didn't disagree. His parents had fought all the time, and not nicely, either. There was no rough stuff, no hitting, but an endless stream of cutting words and long deadly silences. His folks apparently were incompatible. So his dad's moving to Southern California had been the best thing, all around.

But for now, Derek was terrified of being alone. He was afraid the police would be picking him up any day. He was almost fatalistic about it. But still he wanted to hide, to rest, even to think.

Steven Jeminovski's house was on Spinnaker, off the Pacific Coast highway in Marina del Rey, just south of Venice. The streets were in alphabetical order and all had nautical names, from Albacore to

Zephyr, each little street only a block long, ending at that great wide beach. Steven's house was the third one from the beach. To Derek it looked as if it had been designed by somebody on acid, but so did all the rest of these beach condos, strange angles, lots of windows aiming in all directions.

"Like it?" his dad asked him as they got out of the Mercedes. There wasn't even a garage.

An hour later, Derek came down the narrow open staircase to the living room, dressed in fresh clothes except for his jeans and Reeboks. The stairs were built around a huge chandelier hanging from a brass chain. The part with the light in it was a strange geometric glass and brass object which Steven told him was a star in three dimensions.

Steven was in the living room standing in front of a huge stone fireplace, now dressed in tennis shorts and a dark blue polo shirt. "You want a beer?"

"Sure," Derek said. There was a breakfast bar and a little kitchen behind it. Derek got his own beer. He didn't want to allow himself to think so, but this could be a great time with his dad. The business of offering him a beer, for example. Casual, not like his dad at all. Derek came out of the kitchen and sat on one of the barstools. The furniture was maroon velvet, and all the art was Japanese.

"Well, what do you think?" his father asked.

"It's great," Derek said.

"I'm thinking about getting a bigger place, or maybe moving up the coast a little to Malibu," Steven said. "But for the time being, this place suits me." He grinned widely at his son. "The women seem to like it."

"I'll bet," Derek said. He sipped his beer, a Dos Equis. Wow. "This is great beer," he said.

"Well, I guess we have to have a talk. Let's go out on the patio." Derek followed his father out into a small enclosed garden with spiked century plants and garden furniture.

"Perfect for nude sunbathing," Steven said, and sat on a faded old director's chair, tilting back comfortably. "Nobody can see in or out without really craning their necks."

"That's great," Derek said.

"I'm really ashamed of myself that you've never been here before. But you're here now, and I hope it won't be for the last time. I'm only sorry I don't have a pool," he said and laughed.

"I understand," Derek said, and he and his father had a good laugh together. Derek was beginning to feel almost comfortable.

Then they had their little talk. It was hot in the patio, and both of them took off their shirts. Derek noticed that his father was deeply tanned and well-muscled, while he, Derek, was white and undefined. Steven wanted to know if Derek had any immediate plans. Derek said he didn't, he was just wandering around for a while. Steven explained in a roundabout way that he was not going to give Derek a lot of money and a free pad because it would ruin him, that he was a Jeminovski, and all Jeminovskis were lazy and had to be forced to work, or they would just lay around and be charming and live off others. Derek explained that he understood this, and was not asking for money or even a place to stay, except for a few days, or a couple days, or whatever. Steven explained that he was going out of town in a couple of days, anyway, which sort of put a natural limit to their visit, and that he was subleasing his house here for the time he would be in Tucson, where he would be helping a friend with a case, or of course Derek could stay. Derek said that he did not particularly want to stay that long, and a couple of days would be perfect. Steven fetched them another beer each, and Derek thought about getting a tan. The sun felt really good on his skin.

"God damn, you know what?" Steven said. "I've always regretted that we've never had a chance to talk about women and sex. Knowledge has to be passed on from father to son, you know."

"I think the time passed," Derek said.

"I don't mean the birds and the bees, Derek," Steven said with a wave of his beer bottle. "But I might be able to tell you a few things."

"Like what?" Derek had to say.

But the telephone rang and Steven went inside. Derek could hear him laughing. His father wasn't such a bad guy. In fact, they had a great day together. They went for a walk on the beach, and Steven told Derek all about women, how to attract them, how to make friends with them, how to get them into bed. Derek didn't know whether to be embarrassed or to take notes. His father was apparently quite a ladies' man. The secret of his success, he told Derek, was his rationality.

"Women are not objects," he said. "But it pays to think of them that way. Like a boat that has to be sailed. Since the Stone Age they've been looking for the same things, and if you want to get anywhere with a woman, you have to give her the illusion that she is going to get what she wants. Mostly, it is money or security, although there are plenty of women who want only to destroy you. So you have to watch for that. When you put a bone in front of a dog and the dog turns its head, you know that dog isn't hungry, huh?"

"I guess so," Derek said. "My problem is I can't even get their attention."

Steven laughed. "Yeah, I know what you mean. I guess I could sum it up by saying, never put them uptight. Relax them. Don't be on the prod. Act like you've had so many fucks you don't care if you ever fuck again."

"Gee, Dad, watch your language, huh?"

They both had a great laugh.

After dinner at a big seafood restaurant on the beach, where Steven pointed out two movie stars Derek had never heard of, they drove up Sunset Boulevard to Westwood. On the long, winding drive Steven named the famous communities they were passing through, Pacific Palisades, Brentwood, Holmby Hills, Bel Air, driving down through Beverly Hills and turning back west on Wilshire. "This is the home of UCLA," he said. They had also been talking on the long drive about Derek's future, although Steven had done most of the talking. It was clear to Derek that his father did not think he had much of a future. There was no talk of law school, following in the old man's footsteps, or any of that. What his father really seemed to be talking about was the dignity of labor. It would be okay, he pointed out, if Derek never went back to school, if he got some kind of job that did not require a suit and tie. Steven even railed against the new world of computers that was dividing humanity into those who Could and those who Couldn't.

Derek did not mention that he had been up Sunset Boulevard before. But as they wound along he began to realize that one of the reasons he had such a low opinion of himself was that his father had a fairly low opinion of him, too. Maybe even lower than Derek's. Steven did not seem to think that Derek would be good at anything requiring manual skills or brain power. He did not seem to think Derek would make a good salesman, lacking the skill of persuasion. What was left? Well, gosh, there was lots of stuff. There was the civil service, for example. Steven himself had once contemplated entering federal civil service, until he was accepted at law school.

The trick with civil service was to hang on. They never fired you, but you could be moved around until you ended up nowhere, so there were certain political gifts necessary, but Derek could develop those.

"Or, you could go in the army. I was in the army. It's not a bad career. When there's a war on, you can make rank fast."

"I hate the army," Derek said.

"Of course," Steven said smoothly. "Everybody hates the army, even the guys in it. You don't have to love the army, but they pay on time, and the pay isn't bad these days. You know, if we finally disarm the nuclear, we'll have to go to a ground army, and there you'd be, on the ground, so to speak."

They went to a movie in Westwood, and Derek fell asleep five minutes after they sat down. When his father shook him awake, he grinned and said, "Sorry. It wasn't the movie. I guess I like to sleep a lot."

"Where'd you sleep last night?" Steven asked.

"Oh, you know," Derek said.

When they were back in the car, Steven turned to Derek before starting the engine, his face serious. "You're on the bum, aren't you."

"Yeah," Derek said. He could feel his face tightening into his old fuck-you-don't-lecture-me expression, and he slid down in the seat, staring straight ahead.

"Son, you can't keep it up. You have to find a place for yourself. You know that, though, don't you?"

"Yeah," Derek said.

"You must have had stuff. Somebody ripped you off, didn't they?"

"Yeah," Derek said.

"I thought so," Steven said with satisfaction. "I thought I recognized the symptoms. Was it somebody down here? Is there any way I can help you get your stuff back?"

"It wasn't much," Derek said.

"You don't even have a shaving kit," Steven said.

Derek made up a story about losing all his stuff by leaving it in the backseat of a car and not remembering until too late.

"All right," Steven said. "I'll accept that story because you want me to. But I'm no fool, Derek."

"I know," Derek said.

"I hate to just give you money," Steven said. "I mean, sure, I'll bail you out, get you on a bus back north. Why don't you stay at your mother's house while you get a job? She's got that big house all to herself."

"Maybe I will," Derek said.

Back at home at last, Derek only wanted to go to bed. "Where do I sleep?" he asked. Steven showed him the guest room, a little corner upstairs room with a slanting wall and a big skylight.

"Have a brandy with me," Steven said, and Derek followed him down to the living room. They drank brandy for an hour, while Steven told Derek about his last important love affair, which had been devastating, at least for Steven. "I should never fall in love," he said late in the evening. The brandy seemed to have no effect on him except to make him talkative, but Derek was getting drunk, as well as sleepy. He was already tired of his father. They were never going to be honest with each other, why should they? And this shit of being friends wasn't going to work.

"I'm going to bed, Dad," Derek said finally.

"I think I'll give the bitch a call," Steven said, staring into his empty fireplace. "I hope she's not alone."

Derek trudged up the stairs, took off all his clothes except his brand new Jockey shorts and fell into bed. He was so tired. But he could not fall asleep. He could hear his father murmuring into the telephone below, and then silence. He must have gone to bed. Derek expected to fall asleep at any moment, but he did not. He wondered what was keeping him awake. He had not slept much lately. The couple of hours in the movie theater wasn't enough to keep him awake. Maybe it was something else.

He remembered the story of *The Princess and the Pea*. His mother had told him this story as a child, and it had stuck with him, for some reason. No matter how many mattresses under the princess, she could feel this one hard little pea underneath, and it kept her awake and complaining. Derek liked her for that. Now he felt the same, only it was not a pea under the mattress that was keeping him awake. It was something else. What? Usually, he could fall asleep anywhere, anytime. But not now. Why?

He got up some time later to take a piss, and was standing over the toilet blinking down into the blue water, watching it turn green as he pissed into it, thinking, gee, the water's actually turning green, when something inside him turned bright red with anger, and he knew what was keeping him awake. *Burns*. He had given his trust and his friendship to Burns, even handed over the fucking pistol, and what had Burns done? Dumped him. Fucked him over like a dead dog. Burns had dumped him. Dumped him. Dumped him.

"Dirty motherfucker!" Derek said through his teeth, and looked up to see himself reflected in the mirror over the toilet, his face twisted in emotion. "Dirty motherfucking son of a bitch!" He could see from looking at his face that he wanted to cry, cry about Burns deserting him, and he was terribly afraid his father would come upstairs from his big bedroom with the kingsize bed and find him crying in the bathroom. Derek went back and threw himself into the little bed under the slanting skylight, the tears streaming down his face as he saw the face of Burns in his mind, the face cold and friendless, shutting the car door on Derek. *Bastard! Bastard! Bastard!*

Then a sweet calm descended on Derek. Ahh, he had gotten that out. It had been like a splinter in his guts, and now it was gone. He wasn't sleepy; instead, he felt energetic. It was time to do something. Get up, build a model airplane, enlist in the marines. Run downstairs and set fire to his dad. Derek giggled. Ransack the place. Steal all the Jap art. Hmm. Next thing he knew, he was in the shower. Next thing he knew he was shaved and dressed. He brushed his teeth with his new toothbrush. He had good little teeth. He should take better care of them. He put the new toothbrush back into its plastic tube, capped the tube. Back in the little bedroom with the bedside light on, Derek picked up his tweed jacket and sniffed it. He couldn't smell anything. This old coat had been through some shit, that was for sure. He put the toothbrush tube, his new comb and his new Gillette razor into the jacket's pocket. Into the Reeboks and down the stairs. Sneakers, he thought, were for sneaking. He sneaked into his father's bedroom, which was not quite pitch dark because it was getting light out, and his father's bedroom window looked out over his patio, the big patio, the tanning cell, you might call it.

"Dad?" he said softly. He could hear his father's steady heavy breathing, and decided he was pretending to be asleep. He must have heard Derek banging around upstairs. But this was fine, this was perfect.

Derek went out into the little kitchen-bar, turned on the flickering lights and made breakfast for himself, not bothering to be too quiet. He could trust his father not to get up and come in sleepily to ask him what the hell he was doing at five in the morning. No, six—there was a little digital clock on the bar. Derek scrambled three eggs in butter, using a big orange frying pan. The stove was electric, which Derek wasn't used to. He had to work fast with the eggs because the pan got hot too fast, but finally there was a big pile of steaming yellow scrambled eggs on the plate, ahh, yum yum, he batted catsup all over the eggs, smelling the sharp tomato flavor, his mouth watering madly as he gobbled his first bites. Derek hadn't felt so good in days, months, maybe years. This was life, eating breakfast at the start of a day that belonged to him.

Before he left, he looked in again on his sleeping father. No, he was not faking. He was asleep, lying on his back, his mouth open. "Goodbye," Derek said. He did not leave a note. He did not do the dishes or make his bed. He did make a salami and cheese sandwich with mayonnaise, put it in a jiffy bag and slipped the bag into his jacket pocket, not the one with his toiletries in it, and headed out into the dawn.

Sometimes you know from the beginning that a day is going to work out well, and this was one of those days. There was no traffic on Pacific at that hour, so for fun he walked over a couple of hundred yards of sand to the wet part by the ocean and turned north along the water until he came to the Venice Pier. The surf was only a foot or so, the water dark blue against the almost white-blue of the sky. There was a slight breeze in from the ocean and the air smelled delicately of the sea.

At Venice he started hitch-hiking, and the first ride took him to Ventura, a Japanese man in a pickup truck who said almost nothing and seemed to be enjoying the morning as much as Derek. Derek was so happy to be away from his father he could have almost screamed. His father was not at fault. He was what he was, and Derek still admired him greatly.

It took ten minutes for Derek to get the right ride in Ventura. He rejected the first two cars who stopped for him because he didn't like the look of the people, but the third was a salesman type who said, "I'm going to San Francisco."

"Me, too," said Derek, and off they went.

The salesman type must have been looking for somebody to talk to, because he started talking right away. The radio was on low, and the man burbled on, and Derek fell asleep. When he woke up they were in a gas station in San Luis Obispo. Derek went to the bathroom, drank two Coca-Colas rapidly, belched, apologized to the man for sleeping all the time, and went right back to sleep. The next time he woke up they were on the big freeway through San Jose, traffic-bound.

"You must have needed your sleep," the guy said kindly.

"Geez, yes," Derek said. "Sorry . . ."

"It's okay, you don't snore or talk in your sleep."

"Hey," Derek said. "Aren't we in the wrong lane?" They seemed headed for OAKLAND rather than SAN FRANCISCO.

"I'm going to Hayward," the guy said. "You want to get off here and head straight up, or go on up with me to the East Bay?"

Derek looked out at the busy freeway and did not see any good places to stand. Anyway, he hated San Jose on principle. But what really made up his mind was that his sister lived in the East Bay, and it might not be a bad idea to stop at his sister's place first, then call his mother and see if the police had been around asking for him. That was just elementary caution. He could do it from any phone booth, he knew, but it would be fun to drop in on Diedre. He did not even know where she lived. Just some little house in Oakland. He did not really think the police were after him. If they had been, he reasoned, then his mother would have called his father and screamed her head off. Or the cops would have come around to his father's place. So Kenny had kept his mouth shut. Derek should have known. And that fuckhead Burns had not been caught. Or if he had, he had kept his mouth shut, too. Burns was right; the cops had a lot of people to look for.

But still he wanted to see his sister, if only to tell her all about their dad, and his Southern California pad.

Diedre and Jerry Ledbetter lived in East Oakland, out MacArthur Boulevard. Derek found them in the telephone book, of course, since they both worked for the telephone company. They had been at dinner when he called from downtown. Jerry answered the phone, his mouth full.

"Hi, Jerry," Derek said. They had known each other, if you could call it that, for about three years. "Uh, is my sister there?"

"She sure is," Jerry said. Chomp, chomp. "You want to talk to her?"

"Yeah, if it's not too much trouble."

"No trouble at all," Jerry said, still chewing his dinner.

"Great," Derek said.

"I'll see if I can't pull her away from the table," Jerry said.

Derek was already beginning to think this wasn't such a good idea, but when Diedre came to the telephone she seemed very glad to hear from him, and when he asked her if he could come over "for a while" she seemed very happy about it.

"I'll have Jerry come down and pick you up," she said, when she found out where he was.

"I can take a bus or something," Derek said.

She gave him instructions, when he insisted on taking the bus, and in forty minutes he was walking up a dark street at the foot of the Oakland hills, a street of small houses with cars, trucks and motorcycles in the driveways, yellow light coming from picture windows, and a bunch of little kids, mostly black, playing some kind of catch in the dark. Out in front of 389 Robbins was a sign on the mailbox: THE LEDBETTERS. There was no vehicle in the driveway, and the double garage door was shut. The lawn was neat and trimmed, unlike several on the block, and the place looked recently painted, just as the mailbox sign looked brand new. Diedre was almost nineteen, and Jerry was in his middle twenties. There was a little brass knocker on the front door, and a bell. Derek tapped the knocker.

Diedre opened the front door and threw her arms around Derek. She had not seemed that glad to see him at Thanksgiving, but what difference did that make? Derek hugged her back and saw big Jerry grinning at him over her shoulder. Jerry was still chewing on something, his cowlick up, his expression as dumb as ever. Yet Derek was glad to see him, too, and after he disentangled himself from his sister he shook hands with Jerry, a hard, almost crushing grip.

"God damn, boy," Jerry said. "Let me look at you. Nope, no cuts or bruises. Looks like you made it through the neighborhood pretty well."

They went into the tiny neat living room and with great formality sat down; Jerry in what was obviously his favorite chair, with his bridge light and his newspapers on the rug, and Derek and Diedre sat beside each other on the small couch. Everything was neat and clean and comfortable. The smells lingering in the air made Derek dizzy with hunger, but he didn't say anything. He could smell roast pork, and, what was that? Brussel sprouts? Yes.

"Are you hungry?" Diedre asked him.

"No," Derek said.

"Make him a sandwich," Jerry said, and Diedre got up with a quick smile for Derek and went into the kitchen through the dining room, taking some stuff from off the table with her. Derek was a little confused. He had expected to be made welcome, but not this welcome.

"Well, Jerry, how goes it at the phone company?" he asked, just for something to say. Jerry grinned and rubbed his knees with his big hands.

"Be fine if it wasn't for the public," he said. "We could have this whole country wired down and whippin' out products like the goddamn Japanese if it wasn't for the public. You folks want too much. You know, I've listened in on about ten million private conversations, and I have yet to hear one worth two farts in a windstorm. Why don't you people just pay your bill and shut up? That's what I want to know," Jerry said.

Derek hadn't realized his brother-in-law could be so funny, with his drawling hillbilly voice. There were a lot of things Derek had not suspected about Jerry and about his own sister. In just a few days he came to like them both very much, and to be grateful for their hospitality. The basic thing he learned was that his baby sister and her goof husband really had things together, knew what they wanted, knew what they were doing, and from the look of it, were going to get ahead in life in ways Derek had never thought about, or if he had thought about them, thought they were boring and not worth doing. Like working for the telephone company.

Jerry had started coming around when Diedre was fifteen. Jerry was then working for the company over in Marin, and although their mother argued against it, Diedre started dating Jerry openly, defying her high school friends, who all had their eyes on higher things. Derek, having his own problems at the time, merely ignored them whenever possible.

Now they all seemed to have matured nicely, and got along very well. At first, Derek told some lies about where he had been and what he had been doing, telling the truth only about their father, and making both Jerry and Diedre laugh wildly as he exaggerated the scene in Venice and Marina del Rey. They drank beer and talked until nearly eleven-thirty, and then Jerry said, "Well, old Derek, time for beddy-bye."

"You don't mind the couch, do you?" Diedre asked. "We have the extra bedroom but it's furnished for the baby."

"The baby?" But there was no baby on the way, just planned for and the room waiting. Jerry shut the door separating the front and back parts of the house, and Diedre took Derek's hands in hers and said in a low voice, "Okay, Derek, what's cooking?"

She was his baby sister, but she seemed so mature.

"I've been doing some terrible shit," Derek admitted.

"It's okay," she said. "I sort of knew."

"Robbing stores, shit like that. I'm on the run, sort of."

"I thought so," she said gently.

"But I've been *terrible*," Derek said, just now realizing it was true.

"You're safe here," Diedre said.

Even though he had slept most of the day, Derek slept like a rock that night, the couch wonderfully comfortable, the sheet fresh and soft, the quilt warm. In all, Derek stayed with Diedre and Jerry for three days. It was long enough to see what their lives were like, but not so long as to overstay his welcome. And he was welcome, he knew that, even welcome to stay indefinitely while looking for a job, or making plans, or whatever he wanted to do. Jerry made that clear. Jerry thought it was wonderful that Derek had been out robbing stores and getting shot at. He eagerly asked Derek for details over dinner, and, getting into the spirit of the thing, Derek gave wildly exaggerated accounts of their criminal run through the middle of the state.

"I know it sounds awfully stupid," he said more than once.

"No, no," Jerry would insist, his eyes alight. And Derek would continue to romanticize Burns and Kenny and himself as young predators running wild on the landscape. He had to keep reminding himself that it hadn't been like that at all, it had been *really stupid*, but for the life of him, he could not tell it that way.

Then Jerry said something interesting. "Well, I guess your life of crime is over. Pretty lucky guy."

Derek knew by now that his sister and Jerry were anything but outlaw types. They went to church regularly, went to night school nearly every night, and the time they spent at home not studying was spent working around the house or cheerfully talking company politics. They both planned to get ahead in the company.

"We're never gonna leave the phone company," Jerry said cheerfully, after night school and a couple of beers. The three of them were sitting at the dining room table—the center of the household—and it was always the best time of the day. "We're just so goddamn grateful," Jerry said without a trace of guile on his big simple face.

There was no petty moralizing, no suggestion that they thought Derek ought to pay for his crimes. "Hell, if I did time for all my own crimes, I'd be in jail about a thousand years," Jerry said cheerfully.

"Your crimes? What crimes?" Derek asked.

Jerry and Diedre smiled at each other. "Well, aside from the little shit, like stealing from the company, I've committed probably about three or four hundred separate acts of statutory rape with your baby sister here. I know. It's stupid, I could have screwed any adult woman I wanted in those days, but I chose your baby sister, molested her with my attentions, and here we are."

All day long Derek was alone in the house. His sister got up early and was always at work in the little kitchen when Derek awakened. They always had a good breakfast without much talk, and the beds were made and the dishes done before Diedre left for work. Derek offered to do these things for her, but she smiled and said, "I don't want to start any bad habits," and continued doing the work herself. Jerry was always gone by this time. This left Derek in a clean empty house all day, to think. He often sat looking out the picture window at the seedy street they lived on. There were very few people out in the daytime. Most of them black. Derek took a couple of walks in the neighborhood, not looking for anything, just walking around, but although he ran into no overt hostility, he could feel it zeroing in on the back of his neck, it seemed, telling him to get the hell off the streets before his very whiteness infuriated some unemployed Negro beyond his ability to resist, and Derek would be laying there in the street with a knife sticking through him. Well, that didn't happen, did it? But he stopped going out for walks. He tried the television, he had not watched daytime television in a long time, but there was nothing for him to watch. The news was the same old shit, and he had no reasonable expectation of finding himself featured: "Fugitive criminal Derek Jeminovski, twenty, of Lincoln's Grove, is still at large after a daring three-day criminal spree that left no known dead and not much stolen . . ." No. And the rest of the programming was just shit as far as he was concerned.

So, finally, the truth was that the life he thought would be boring and lonely was actually boring and lonely. If he had been able to share Jerry and Diedre's dream of a happy life with the telephone company, maybe it would have been different. Jerry, just for fun, had told him that there were ways of getting jobs. Not necessarily with the company, but a job that would mean hard physical labor for a few years, and then, if you applied yourself, movement up and away from dirty hands. Security for the babies.

"But it's not like it used to be," Jerry said darkly one night. "It used to be a white boy could just go out there and gather in the shekels. You could get your own house in a nice neighborhood, pick up a boat and a summer place, two cars *at least*, and still be lookin' ahead at your thirtieth birthday. But not no more. Now you have to fight for every fucking quarter. You have to fight the government, mostly. They take all your fucking money and give it to the niggers."

Derek had come from a county whose idea of integration was to have its own black city, Marin City, which Derek visited only when he had to change buses. He did not know anything about black people except what he had heard. His own personal experience was that black kids let you alone if you outnumbered them. Otherwise, watch out. He laughed at Jerry's version of history, but noticed that Jerry had cordial relations with the people on his block, who were mostly black.

Anyway, none of that mattered. Derek didn't leave because he was afraid of black people, and he didn't really leave because he was bored. He left because he was itchy. He could not think of another word to describe it. He had been going to call his mother and find out if it would be all right for him to stay with her while he found a job and laid low, but he never did call her, and by the time he put all his stuff in his pockets and left Jerry and Diedre's, he still didn't know whether he was headed for Marin County, or back to San Francisco.

Derek was on Market Street between Fifth and Sixth, heading for the Tivoli Billiards, when Burns appeared, walking beside him as if they had never been apart.

"What's doing, Dude?" Burns said.

Derek's immediate feeling was a gush of pleasure. He had missed Burns in spite of everything, and had been going up to the Tivoli to look for him, although Derek had never quite allowed himself to think so.

"Tracking pretty well," Derek said.

"Heading for the poolroom?"

"I was thinking about it."

"Feel like a beer somewhere? My buy."

"I'd be delighted," Derek said. The old run feeling was coming over him whether he liked it or not. Actually, he liked it. He and Burns crossed Market, Derek holding in the flow of words that boiled around inside him, cool as Burns as they went into the hofbrau on the corner of Turk and Jones.

"Just grab a place to sit, I'll get the beers," Burns said. In the middle of the afternoon three-quarters of the long tables in the room were empty. Derek chose a seat where he could look out the window at the flow of Tenderloin foot traffic. It was almost nostalgic.

Burns arrived with a tray with two Coors on it and two grey-looking tumblers upside down on the tray. While Derek took a pull from his beer bottle, Burns lit a Pall Mall with a goodlooking gold lighter, laying the pack and the lighter on the table.

"You don't smoke much, do you?" he said to Derek, who grinned and took one of the cigarettes.

"I see you got your lighter out of hock," he said.

"That's a new one. Dunhill, the best." Burns looked no different. His blond hair a little longer, the roots a little darker. In his eyes Derek could see nothing.

"How'd you get back up here?" Burns finally asked, when Derek just sat there looking out the window and sipping his beer.

"Hitch-hiked," Derek said. He was not going to mention his family to Burns. "How about you?"

Burns grinned impishly. "You steal anything from your rides? Anything good?"

Derek grinned. "No," he said. With a prickle of excitement, he realized that he was here in San Francisco to steal. With less than twenty bucks in his pocket, he intended to attack the helpless city before him. He laughed.

"What's funny?"

"Oh, I am, Man. Here I am again, broke out at the ass and sitting in the middle of one of the most expensive, well-guarded cities in America."

"You want to go rob a store?"

"No, man, that scares me too much. I still wake up in the night. I'm a thief, you had it right. We could go stealing, though. Know any good places to steal?"

"You know me," Burns said, sitting back. "I blew all our money on some of that Persian heroin. I'm just coming out of it. I feel like something the dog did on the sidewalk. Sure, I'll go stealing with you. Hey, I still got your seashell, remember that?"

"Yeah," said Derek with some surprise. The last he had seen of his black abalone shell it had been in the corner of the backseat of Kenny's car. He would like to have that shell. He would like to give it to Jerry and Diedre, he thought, a memorial of his run, and a good ashtray.

Burns' long fingers played with the cigarette pack and the gold lighter. "I couldn't sell it. I gave the gun to my T-man."

"What's a T-man?" Derek asked.

"T for tenth," Burns said. "Tenth of a gram, smoke that, get real high for a day. I've done it a few times, and man, I can see how you can get hooked. It's sweet. You ever smoke smack?"

"I'm not much of a smoker," Derek admitted. He did not want to go somewhere and zone out on some drug, and he didn't want to think that Burns, crazy Burns, was just nothing but a smackhead after all. Derek wanted to do some stealing.

"It takes a while to get the Jones. I got a little left, if you want to just see what it smells like. We can go out to my crib and get your seashell, too. I still got Kenny's car. I wonder what happened to Kenny. I got to thinking, you know, that he could get out of that rap pretty easy, if he has a good lawyer."

"Are you nuts?" Derek said. "He was caught walking out of the bank with a double handful of money. How the fuck could he get off?"

"Listen to this," Burns said happily. "They get to court, every-thing goes like clockwork, it's like watching Perry Mason. And then they get to the note, which, naturally, they assume was written by Kenny. But it wasn't. I wrote that note."

"So what? They still caught him with all the money, walking out of the fucking bank."

"Yeah, so what yourself. Kenny comes in, he comes up to the win-dow, and some asshole has left a note there, which Kenny had noth-ing to do with. So the fool behind the counter gives Kenny a bunch of money. Kenny doesn't know, hell, it might be an inducement to bank there. So he takes the money and is on his way out when the shit hits the fan. See? Kenny won't talk, you can count on that. And they got absolutely no physical evidence against him. Case dis-missed!" Burns laughed happily.

"You still got his car?"

"I still got his car. Come on, my crib's out in the Mission. We'll get your seashell, smoke the last of the brown stuff, maybe smoke a little of my precious Hawaiian boo, and then do a little career planning. Sound good?"

Burns was on his feet, draining the last of his beer. There was really nothing for Derek to do but stand up and finish off his own beer.

At ten that night Derek found himself sitting behind the wheel of Kenny's car, now dirty and undistinguished, the motor running. There had been no heroin. There had been no marijuana. In fact, there had been no crib, and of course a search of the car had not turned up any seashell. Instead, they had spent the time driving around drinking beer and looking for a perfect place to rob. Derek had had to pay for gas as well as a sixpack, and he was almost broke. Burns had promised him he could stay at Burns' place, but Derek no longer believed Burns had a place, since they never seemed to turn the right corner to find it. Now they were out in the avenues, with Derek in the car parked on 15th Avenue, just around the corner from California Street, next to a small grocery store where Burns said there could be a lot of money.

"I read in the paper a while ago this place got robbed and the guy got away with fifteen hundred bucks," he said. "They're ready for another hit."

"Doesn't it take three of us?"

"Naw, I can handle inside. I need you behind the wheel, like good old Kenny. Only take a minute, okay?" And Burns was gone.

Derek was sitting with his hands on the wheel, the engine running quietly, when he heard the two distant snapping sounds he knew were gunshots, close together, just the two of them, and he knew it was all over. His mind told him desperately that sitting on the side of the building like that he could not possibly have heard what he thought he heard, and any second now Burns would come around the corner grinning like a monkey, and off they would go. But this did not happen, and Derek was still sitting at the wheel with the engine running when the police got there.

OLD PEOPLE

She was at least sixty years old. She liked to say, "I'm the same age as Marilyn Monroe—you figure it out." Her name was Kitty Brown, and she worked the graveyard shift at the Buttermilk Corner in Lincoln's Grove, the last 24-hour greasy spoon in South Marin, unless you counted Denny's across the freeway in Corte Madera. The Buttermilk Corner was a long low building above the freeway with a parking lot in front, its entrance in the middle of the building. There was a long counter and a row of stools covered in red plastic, booths on both sides of the entrance. Kitty's shift was from midnight to six A.M., but there were two other waitresses and two frycooks on until three, because the place got its big bulge of late-night business after the bars closed.

But after three things quieted down, and Kitty was alone out front, with Elizaldo the Filipino cook behind the service slot in the kitchen, his white greasecap always at a jaunty angle. Kitty had to wear a uniform dress of green and yellow starched to the texture of plywood, but by three the uniform would be comfortably wilted, over what everybody admitted was a spectacular figure, especially for a woman so old. This is what she had in common with Jackie Jeminovski, or Jackie Jay, as everybody called her. Kitty liked Jackie, and was worried about her. Jackie used to come in all the time after the bars closed, always the life of the party, always with at least one man but usually with a group of ladies and gentlemen who had been out drinking in San Francisco or Marin, winding up their evening with big plates of breakfast and mugs of coffee.

The thing about Jackie was that she never seemed to gain any weight, even though she drank like a fish and ate everything in sight. It couldn't all be exercise. She must have inherited one of those bodies like Kitty's own, which just seemed to stay thin and attractive no matter what kind of terrible stuff she put into herself, as Kitty had for so many years. But of course Kitty worked all night on her feet, and on her nights off went dancing or whatever the hell there was to do.

But these days Jackie was coming in alone and sitting over in the corner by the south window, coming in at odd hours, like eleven at night or three in the morning. She would talk to people if they came up to her, but she didn't join any parties and she seemed to want to be alone. She seemed preoccupied. Sometimes she was drunk, sometimes not. Lately, she was more drunk than not, but Jackie Jay was not a sloppy drunk or a messy drunk. Kitty thought she recognized the signs.

Kitty herself drank with care. You don't get to her age without a certain amount of care. If you liked to party—and Kitty did like to party—you had to watch your step. In her time, she had seen a lot of people just party themselves right over the edge, and where were they now? Sometimes she thought about her sister-in-age, Marilyn. There was a girl who did not know how to party, Kitty guessed. There was a girl who put her life in the hands of men, and look what it got her. Kicked in the ass by everybody, and finally left to die. Kitty had never liked that guy anyway, and even suspected that he talked her into killing herself over the phone. Why not? Nobody could tell Kitty these people wouldn't just get rid of somebody they thought was going to mess things up for them. Kitty had been around too long. She could not count the number of men who had tried to fuck her over. And where were they now? Dead, most of them. Dead or put away. Kitty liked men. They had their uses. But in her opinion, there were damned few of them who weren't just braggarts and liars. Especially the goodlooking ones.

So it wasn't hard to figure that Jackie Jay was in some kind of man trouble, or men trouble. If Kitty had been less polite she might have asked, but instead she left Jackie to herself, fed her coffee—she wasn't eating much anymore—and left her alone. But one morning about four o'clock, when the place was empty except for Kitty and Elizaldo and Jackie Jay at the south end of the counter, Kitty poured herself a mug of coffee and came around the counter and sat beside Jackie. They sat there with their coffee looking out the window down at the lights passing on the freeway, not many at this time of night, trucks rolling by, a few late drunks on the way home.

Then, after a few little comments about nothing, Jackie opened up, and told Kitty that she was worried about her son, who was in jail.

"Oh, God," Kitty said. "What'd they get him for?"

Jackie smiled tiredly. She seemed a little drunk, but not so much that she couldn't talk properly. "Oh, he went hitch-hiking around the state, went down to L.A. to see his father, and the police caught him with this other boy who was robbing a store."

"Uh-oh," Kitty said. It was not her place to say more.

"He's been in jail for days. I don't know what to do."

"What about his father?"

Jackie frowned. "Well, you know how it is," she said.

"Yes, I do," Kitty said. That was all the conversation they had on that matter, and Jackie left and went home. But before she left, a couple of policemen came in and sat at the counter, and the two women exchanged looks. Cops, huh? The cops had her son. Kitty noticed both cops turning on their stools to watch Jackie leave.

At 6:00 A.M. when Kitty's shift ended, the place was a third full, early morning regulars, all behind their newspapers. It was a chilly morning, and she wished she had brought her sweater along. The car heater in her Toyota worked, but it worked too well, blasting heat from every direction. It was easier to wear a sweater and leave the damned thing off. She was getting old, forgetting her sweater. It was the middle of winter around here, and usually was except in September. She laughed to herself. She'd forgotten all about Jackie Jay.

Having her son in jail was the most humiliating thing that had ever happened to Jackie. Losing her husband had not been bad; in fact, she had thrown him out, been depressed for a few weeks, and that had been that. She had been too busy raising her children to care much. No, that wasn't true. She hadn't been that busy. Memory was strange. In her memory the marriage seemed to have lasted only a few weeks, and yet it had been years, years and years, of what must have been boredom. She could not remember making school lunches, but she must have made thousands, standing there over the cutting board, slicing sandwiches in half, folding each half into a plastic bag . . .

One thing she did remember was watching through the venetian blinds as Derek and Diedre waited for the school bus with the other kids. The bus stopped right in front of her place, still did, and even now children gathered there. They would climb aboard the bus, little flowers, and she would pull her finger out of the blind and let it fall back into place, the rest of the day hers, until of course they came home in the afternoon. What had she done all day? She could not remember.

Now she lay on her living room couch, which would have been a shabby old thing if she hadn't kept it clean all these years. It was late in the afternoon of Derek's fifth day in jail, and her stomach wrenched tightly at the thought. Five days! My God, what was happening to Derek in there? Everything she knew about jails was terribly frightening. Derek was young, and if not handsome—even his mother did not think he was goodlooking—at least young and fresh-faced. Terrible men would be after him, and the jailors did not care. He could be knifed or raped or beaten to death, and she knew she wasn't just being a frightened mother, these things really did happen, and her son really was in terrible danger.

She lifted her bottle of ale from the floor and took a swig. The stuff was getting warm, and tasted bitter in her mouth. Her tongue was a little thick, too, and tasted bad. Maybe she should swallow it, or spit it out. Instead, she picked up the green bottle again and took the last of the ale into her mouth, rinsing it around before swallowing, trying to get rid of the taste of her tongue. It didn't work. She sighed. Her tongue felt big in her mouth. She swung herself upright. She was still in underpants and tee shirt, and it was the middle of the afternoon. She had a lot to do today. She absolutely had to get Derek a lawyer today. But, my God, getting a lawyer just started the trouble. The lawyer would have to be paid, bail would have to be found, or at least money to get a bond. Ten percent, it would be. The charge against Derek was felony murder, and bail would be high. But she could not leave him in there. She got up and went into the kitchen for another ale. She threw the empty bottle into the garbage sack, but there was no room for it, and it bounced off and went rolling across the floor under the kitchen table. She had a terrible temptation to just let the bottle lie there, but instead bent over grunting and stuck a finger into the neck of the bottle. Should I start another garbage sack?

The whole kitchen needed cleaning. The stove and back of the stove were getting a thick layer of grease. She liked bacon too much. You can't live on bacon. She opened the refrigerator, took out a bottle of ale and unscrewed the top. Leaning against the stove she had a sip of the icy ale. It tasted remarkably good after the warm stuff. She should clean up the kitchen, think about her problems, then take a nice long shower, dress in fresh clothes, and get out of here. She would not find a lawyer sitting around the house. Having been married to a lawyer, she knew finding a good one would be hard. Steven had been no help and would be no help in the future, she knew. When she called him he hadn't even wanted to send her any money. He was such a bastard, with his murmuring voice and his evasive answers to her questions. She had to swallow the fact that Steven wasn't going to be any help.

Derek had to have a lawyer just to get bail set. She did not know much, but she knew enough not to get a public defender. Derek was being smart and sitting there in jail without talking to anybody. He was not a lawyer's son for nothing. But it was horrible in there, and if he was arraigned, he would be sent down to the county jail in San Bruno, a real madhouse. So Jackie's problems were simple—she had to get money, she had to get a good lawyer.

She had already thought about selling her Jag, but that wouldn't really help. It would not be enough. With a sinking heart, she realized again that there was no way she could do what she had to do, and once again the terrible thought that she might just let Derek rot in jail . . . No. Don't even think it.

She was so mad at herself that she started in on the kitchen. First she washed the dishes, then wiped the kitchen table clean, put away the mayonnaise jar and the catsup bottle, and, still mad at herself and trying not to think, attacked the stove and the stovepipe and the wall. Sweat ran down her sides underneath her tee shirt, and it was pleasant to think that soon she would be in the shower getting clean herself. Derek, Derek, Derek, she scrubbed and scrubbed. Finally she rinsed the soap out of the sponge pad, squeezed it dry and put it by the hot water handle. There. She opened another ale and went into the bathroom, turning on the water and waiting for it to reach the right temperature. She put her hand into the stream, feeling the hard slap of hot water against her palm. It was just right, and she stepped into the stall. It felt so good on the back of her neck. But she had forgotten to take off her tee shirt and pants. She went hot with shame, and then laughed at herself. This was not the first time she had showered in her clothes. But it was the first time she had done it by mistake. She was getting absent-minded!

After she had properly showered, naked, that is, she stepped out of the stall leaving her wet clothes on the tiles. She avoided the long mirror over the twin sinks as she dried herself. Were these the last of the fresh towels? She would have to do a load of laundry, maybe two loads. There was a memory, tons of laundry every week. Not any more.

Jackie combed out her hair, still not looking in the mirror. She had spent so much of her life looking in the mirror. Vanity. Now she was afraid to look. She did not know what she expected to see, just that she did not wish to see it. Her face. How many people have told her she had a lovely face? A classic face, a face that would always be beautiful. She always thought her face was plain. Now she looked at herself, the dryer howling as she held it to her hair. As she had known, the eyes were bloodshot from booze.

"Hello," she said to herself over the dryer. She pulled back her lips in a snarl, to examine her teeth. Perfect, except for the one eye-tooth that slanted a little inward. An imperfection that had devastated her as a girl, yet in her entire life nobody had ever said anything about it. And the one chipped tooth. Had she brushed her teeth that day? Of course not. She wished her hair would dry quicker. She wanted to brush her teeth. She stuck her tongue out. Ahh! It was white, an ugly pink-greenie white, coated thick with white stuff. She could hardly bear to let it back into her mouth. But of course she couldn't go around all day with her tongue out. People would notice. Now she was terribly impatient with her hair. She wanted to brush her teeth and her tongue. Anything to get rid of that taste.

Getting dressed was a problem, too, because she had so much laundry piled up to do. But she could not be bothered with that. She found clean panties in the back of the drawer, behind a tangle of bras.

There was a clean man's shirt in the closet, and her favorite jeans were still clean enough to wear. Tuck the shirt into the jeans, put on her old faded red leather jacket, and she was ready to seek out a lawyer for her son. Did she need gas? Yes, and the oil should be checked. She would have to look in her wallet, which she dreaded. She was sure there was money in there. If not, she would have to go to the bank and try the machine. She hated to use her credit card because of the bill. She was afraid of the banking machine, oh, not really the banking machine but the thought that she mightn't have enough money in the bank and the machine would spit at her or make loud noises, proving to everybody she was broke.

But she had over fifty dollars in her wallet, enough to get some gas, a quart of oil, and have money left over, so she wouldn't have to face the machine until at least tomorrow. Or she could look in her checkbook, do all the math she hadn't done, and find out that way if she had any money in the bank. Instead, she went into the kitchen and poured herself a nice cold shot of vodka, killed it, and then poured herself another.

"Let's not throw up," she said. But she felt fine, and the vodka hadn't even hit yet. Okay, time to go out and get into the Jag and get looking for a lawyer. She sat down at the clean kitchen table with her shot. The sunlight was starting to come in the kitchen window. It was getting late. But she could not just sit here and let Derek spend another night in jail. He must be wondering, he must be desperate for her to get him out. Her stomach was warm from the vodka, but there was a coldness in her chest. Maybe it was resentment. Her children had grown up and gone away. Why couldn't they stay away? Why did she have to be the one?

"Ah!" she said. She turned around and got the telephone and the Marin County phone book off the counter and put them before her on the table. Before opening the book she sipped a little of her vodka, and then threw back the rest of it. It burned coldly going down, but made her stomach even warmer. She knew it wouldn't really kick in for about fifteen minutes, and that made her feel good. Certainly her life was fucked up, but what difference did that make? It would have been fucked up anyway.

She opened the telephone book to ATTORNEYS. Good God, there were a lot of them. Almost eleven pages of lawyers, in this little tiny county. Of course a lot of these were actually in San Francisco, but there was a lot of money in Marin. Money means lawyers. They were advertising now, too. Jackie had seen the ads on television, and here were a few display ads in the book.

But wait a minute. She didn't have the money yet. She couldn't call a lawyer until she had the money. That much about lawyers she knew. It had not been that way with Steven, because Steven did P.I. work, and what he looked for was a good juicy accident rather than a solvent client. Sometimes Steven's clients were very poor. But thinking about Steven was not getting her the money. Although it should have. She did not know how much money Steven had, and the time to have found out was long past. But she knew he had plenty. Without even thinking, she punched up Steven's number in Venice.

"Etta, is Steven there? I need to talk to him about Derek."

"Oh, yes," said Etta Ling. "Is he out of jail yet?"

"That's what I'd like to talk to Steven about."

"He's out doing a reconstruction," Etta said, "but I'll have him call you the minute he gets in. Are you at home?"

"Etta," Jackie said, "I can't get him out of jail without money. Do you understand?"

"How much is his bail?"

"I don't want to sit around gossiping about it," Jackie said, to her surprise. "My kid's in jail, can you understand that?"

"I'm not your enemy, Jackie," Etta said in a kindly voice. "When Steven gets in I'll have him call."

"If he comes in," Jackie said.

"I'm sure he wants to talk to you," Etta said.

"Oh, shit," Jackie said, and hung up. Immediately she felt bad about it. All she had done was make an enemy of Etta Ling, who was, as far as Jackie knew, a perfectly nice person and somebody Jackie could have used on her side. Her side? What side was that? Steven wasn't going to give her any money. She was lucky he was letting the rent slide, or she would be out on her ass.

She poured herself another shot of the nearly frozen vodka, and leaned against the sink. Running out of vodka. Must stop at store. Gas station, banking machine, Grove Market. No, no bank machine, she had the money. For what? Gas and vodka? Then what? Go visit Derek and tell him one more night in jail, maybe more? Maybe life in jail? Life in prison? For Derek? Because he had gotten picked up hitch-hiking? Jackie began to cry for Derek, when the door chimes sounded from the living room, DING-DONG!

Oh, Jesus Christ, tears running down her face, unfit to answer the door to anybody, Jackie froze, begging God to make whoever it was go away. Who could it be? It could be the paper boy, wanting to be paid. No. She had dropped the paper long ago. She wanted to peek out the window to see whose car was parked outside, but she couldn't, because whoever was out there would see her. Maybe the best thing was to just sit still and let them go away. She threw back the rest of her vodka. It burned in her throat. Shit, all she needed to do was cover her eyes. She had her sunglasses in her purse in the bedroom. She could put on the sunglasses. DING-DONG! Oh shit, shit shit shit, she would put on her sunglasses, throw open the front door and blast whoever it was clear back to the street. *No dice! Get it?*

Jackie opened the front door as far as the chain would let her. There was nobody there. No car, nobody. The lawn needed mowing. She liked mowing the lawn. But the lawnmower was out of gas, she remembered. She closed the door. Had the chimes rung? She turned around, leaning against the door. There was a noise in the back of the house, but instead of frightening her it excited her. So somebody was trying to break in! Ha, she could take care of that!

"Who's back there?" she called out. She made her hands into fists.

"Mom?" The kitchen door swung open, and there was Derek.

She tried to understand later why she had done what she did. Maybe there was too much adrenalin in her system. Maybe the chimes had frightened her more than she thought at the time. Maybe, though, she was really mad at Derek, mad at him for a lot more than just scaring her, mad at him for being Derek, for not turning out right, for not being the sweet boy he had been, for growing up into . . . *this*. Anyway, he came into the room, sort of grinning, and she screamed at him and hit him a hard slap on the face. "God damn you!" she screeched, and hit him again.

"Hey, Jesus, Mom!" he yelled, and put up his arms in self-defense. Then she was sobbing and hugging him.

"I'm home," he muttered.

"I guess I better get control over myself," Jackie said. They walked into the living room, and Derek plopped down on the couch. "I never thought I'd be so happy to see this old place," he said. He looked terrible, pale and shrunken inside his clothes.

Jackie sat in her armchair and looked at her son. He looked back at her, and finally grinned. "Thank you," he said.

"For what?" Her mouth was dry as cotton. She wanted very badly to have an ale.

"Oh, for everything. I don't know how you did it, I'm just glad you did."

"I didn't do anything," Jackie said.

"Can I have a beer?" he asked. "I didn't eat much in there, but I'd rather have a beer than eat."

They went into the kitchen and Jackie got them each a bottle of Green Death. She got glasses out of the cupboard and they sat at the kitchen table. Sunlight came in through the window and lit Derek's hair as he slowly poured the ale into his glass. She poured her own and waited until Derek formally raised his glass to her.

"Thanks," he said.

"How did you get out?" Jackie asked. "Tell me all about it."

"Well, you probably know more than I do," he said.

"What do you mean?"

"Well, I guess they listened to you. Anyway, the guy came and got me, and I had to go downstairs and sit in some guy's office for more than an hour, then I signed a release and they let me out, no charges, no nothing. I guess they really didn't have a case. I don't know. Anyway, I have to thank you. I'll never really be able to thank you enough."

This was driving Jackie crazy. "For what?"

"You know, for going down there, for talking to them." Derek grinned, the first real grin since he had been home. "I guess you scared 'em."

"Are you being sarcastic?" She had meant to go down there, to visit her son, but somehow she had never quite made it. She had been hoping to go down there with a lawyer and get him out on bail, instead of just visiting him in some horrible visiting room with telephones or something. She deserved his sarcasm. But he didn't really sound sarcastic.

"If you're drunk, Mom, I don't blame you," Derek said.

"I am a little drunk," Jackie said. "How did you get home?"

"I hitched," Derek said. He drained his ale and went to the refrigerator for another. "Maybe I'll get drunk, too," he said.

"You went hitch-hiking? After all the trouble it got you into?" she said, and immediately felt foolish.

"Look, Mom," Derek said seriously. "I didn't get into trouble hitch-hiking. I lied." He sat down with his fresh ale, poured some for her, some for himself. "I was really with that guy. We were robbing the store."

"What do you mean?" she asked, but she knew.

"I did some really bad things. We went all over. I did some criminal things. But being in jail got me over that. I'll never steal again," he said.

"That's good," she said. She would think about it later. Right now it was good to have Derek home. Her big problem of the day had been solved without effort. She did not want to pry the truth out of him. She didn't really care. She felt too good, just having him back. None of it made any sense anyway. Just like the rest of her life.

Derek wished there was a magic potion he could take that would put his life in order. He knew what the problem was. He had let puberty and then high school knock him off and leave him by the side of the road. Twenty-one was three times seven, and for the last seven years of his life he had been off-balance, his brain going one way, his body another, his heart another, and on and on until he was all over the landscape.

He gave himself a week, after getting out of jail, to get on the right track. For once he appreciated being home. It had been humiliating to have to ask his mother if he could move back in, after having been independent, but that was a joke. Some independence. Working at ever shittier jobs until he found himself nothing but a thief. His picture hadn't been in *The Grover*, because he hadn't really graduated, but if he had, what would have been printed underneath? He remembered his semi-friend Sandy Cole had been listed as most likely to succeed, after a string of student body offices held, team positions, honor societies, and all that shit. For Derek it would have been: Stage Hands Club, Junior Play, and that was it. Maybe it would have said, "Thief of Baghdad." But Sandy Cole, ha. Sandy had gone off in a cloud of cheers and kisses to Dartmouth College

back East, and everybody who knew him thought he would be a
United States Senator at least. But Sandy came back that first year
for summer vacation, worked as a busboy at Horizons in Sausalito,
swam a lot, played tennis and spent his nights with a woman at least
twenty-five, and when fall came, refused to go back to Dartmouth.
Nobody asked him about it, at least Derek didn't, when he would
wave to him on the street or run into him at the Grove Market. Sandy
had been the hottest of the hot in high school. Maybe he hadn't been
so hot at Dartmouth.

Derek had at one time planned to attend Harvard. What a joke.
Harvard because it was the best, even better than the University of
California, where most of the brainy types from his high school as-
pired to go. Harvard, because with a Harvard degree he could get
into any law school he wanted, and for years he had assumed he
would be an attorney, like his dad. What a crock of shit that had been.
Even as he cut classes and let his grades fall apart he daydreamed of
Harvard, of meeting the girl of his dreams, getting a house in Pacific
Heights and practicing the general practice of law in San Francisco
with his father, Jeminovski & Jeminovski.

But he hadn't wanted to become a lawyer because his father was
one. No, it was for the protection he thought lawyers had. When he
had been a kid in high school he had assumed that no policeman
would ever dare arrest a lawyer. Ha ha. What a joke. He had always
been terrified of the police. Maybe it was natural, being afraid of the
police.

One time when they had all been about fifteen they got caught
parking about halfway up the mountain drinking beer, four of them
in one of the guy's father's car, and they were just drunk enough and
just cocky enough to give the two cops a bad time. Derek cringed in
remembrance. It had seemed so hip, so right, at the time, to insult
the cops, to jeer at them that their fathers made a lot more money,
that the cops were employees and would not get away with this, etc.
And for some reason, the cops let them go. Derek could not figure
out why, thinking back on it. But at the time he had believed in his

heart that the cops had been afraid of them, afraid of their fathers who made so much money and had so much power in the community. Derek had even yelled, "My father's a lawyer!" at the cops. He wondered now why the cops hadn't just pulled him out of the backseat of the car, punched him out, handcuffed him painfully and thrown him in the back of the police car. But they hadn't.

Thinking about it, Derek thought maybe the cops had been amused, and had seen themselves at a younger age. Or maybe, he thought tiredly, they *had* been afraid. You never know.

So dreams of Harvard faded, and he knew he had needed that dream to protect him from the knowledge that he was a cipher in high school. A boy who could not get a date. Not, he remembered with hot embarrassment, that there weren't any girls who would go out with him, only that he set his sights too high. He wanted to date the popular, beautiful girls, not just any girls. And so he dated nobody. No dates, and damned few friends.

But that was feeling sorry for himself, which would not accomplish anything. Now he was home again, ready for a fresh start on life. Derek considered himself one of the luckiest guys in the world, because he had gotten out of stealing without terrible consequences. Except for Burns. He hadn't even seen the body. They left him handcuffed in the back of a police car that smelled of stale wine while the meat wagon came and went. And then terribly lucky in jail. There were twelve guys in his part of the jail, all dressed in orange jumpsuits, and most of their time was spent playing poker on the floor between bunks. The bunks were four-high, and Derek would lie on his bottom bunk and watch. There were some scuffles in the night and some homo stuff he tried not to hear, but nobody seemed interested in him. There were no bullies or psychos in their part of the jail. Derek was broke, and so they left him alone.

He wished he had not been broke. You could buy better food and you could get into the poker game. Derek was amazed at the low quality of the play. He felt he could have won a fortune, and when he daydreamed in jail it was often of a career as a gambler. But usually he was too depressed to daydream, and in his depression he could see reality very clearly. In reality, there was no career as a gambler. That was bullshit. Reality told him he was a little guy with no particular talent, the kind of guy the world didn't give a shit about. He could see no special destiny for himself. In fact, he was a cowardly ignorant punk. And if he wanted to get anywhere, he would have to work harder than most, to make up for his lack of skill or brains or talent.

Sitting at his own kitchen table, drinking hot coffee sweetened just right and with real milk in it, he could hardly remember what it had been like in jail. He could remember the physical parts, the faces of his cellmates, mostly black, but his mental state had faded and was nearly gone from memory. He had to remind himself that most of the time he was in jail he expected to be tried, found guilty of homicide, and sent to prison for he did not know how long. He only knew that other inmates talked glibly of nickels and dimes, which they boasted they could do standing on their ear. Bravado. Derek himself often dreamed of suicide, but decided to put it off until the time between sentencing and going to prison, where it would be hard to kill yourself. Prison had frightened every other thought out of his mind until he made himself watch the poker game.

A four-day college education. Didn't some people call prison college? Not the guys he met, but people who had never been there. Four days of it had been enough for Derek, and when he had been told he would get out soon, he went nearly crazy. One thing jail was full of was rumors, and Derek heard many stories of administrative fuckups, how guys about to get out found themselves instead transferred down to County Jail in San Bruno. Cages inside cages, and a fresh young punk like Derek would be bought and sold openly. You were only supposed to go to County for a year or under, but there were stories of guys who had been left in there by administrative fuckups for years and years. A lot of them liked it, a lot of them had found a home, but they were the institutional types, and Derek was not one of them by a long shot.

After a couple of days in the city lockup, Derek began to delude himself with thoughts of getting out, and once out, finding something to do with his life that wouldn't end him up back in jail. Because of his low self-esteem, which he acknowledged almost cheerfully, he had counted himself out for any respectable profession. Once the Harvard Law School dream faded, he just assumed he would be fit for nothing respectable. No degree, no profession. He had gone through the list of available jobs many times. In high school he had briefly flirted with the notion of going into show business. But that had only been to get girls. He had been a stagehand to get near the girls. It hadn't worked, because the girls he wanted to get next to were all busy with star athletes or rich kids. Well, why not be a star athlete? Easy. He did not have the strength, the coordination, or the father, to make him into a star athlete. He caught like a girl, wrists together, hands in a butterfly, arms stiffly extended. The ball would bounce off before he could think to close his fingers around it. Some star athlete.

And being a rich kid was out of the question.

But sitting there in jail watching a poker game he was morally certain he could dominate, he seriously gave thought to a career as a crossroader, a loner, moving from town to town, playing cards, pool, bowling, betting the horses, like that. The only drawback was that he was not good at pool or bowling or any of that stuff. Reality again. In jail, reality was a definite factor in your thinking. The reality of jail was that you had to get out before you could do anything else.

Now that he was out, and thinking back on it, he realized that he hadn't been able to get even slight control over his mind until his mother visited him. Before that his mind had been frozen on the idea of life in prison. Then he was told he had a visitor, and was taken down to the visiting room, where you could talk to your visitor by telephone and look at them through bulletproof glass.

There was his mother, her eyes a burning shade of blue he had never seen before. His mother actually frightened him with her eyes, and he forgot all the things he had meant to say to her. She talked through the whole visit. She would see whoever was in charge, she would get him out of there, it was horrible, etc. The old principal's office guilt and embarrassment came over him, and he was taken back to the cells full of embarrassment, but also with the unreasonable feeling that his mother would get him out of this, if it was at all possible.

Then he began to think of what he would do when he got out. And the conclusion he came to was that there was nothing out there for him unless he made it himself. If he could not become a regular worker because he was too slight and regular work terrified him with its boredom, and if he could not become a professional because it took too much college, then he would become a salesman. It would not be easy, because he had so little confidence in himself, but it was all that was open to him. He would have to develop the confidence. He would have to learn to sell himself. That was the secret.

So he thought a lot about being a salesman while he waited for his mother to get him out of jail. The only point of being a salesman was to get rich and retire. You could sell anything, once you got the confidence, so the trick was to get into a field that paid big. But of course that would be where the competition was, so you had to be good. He could get a job selling from door-to-door, train himself, and work up to selling . . . what? Munitions? Steel? The sky was the limit.

Derek was astonished when word came down that his mother had scared the DA into letting him go and it was only a matter of time until the paperwork came down. Into the DA's office she had gone, the story went. Let him go! she had yelled. You don't have a thing on him! she had yelled. And when he talked it over with some of the guys in his cell, they agreed. The DA didn't have a thing on him; hell, he ought to sue for false arrest. He had been sitting there in the car trying to get the radio to work. Then the cops showed up. No gun, no evidence of any kind, they really didn't have a thing. Derek had been smart not to talk. Anything he said would have hanged his ass, they told him. And as if to prove it, the DA's office made him sign a release so he *wouldn't* sue them.

Derek was glad to sign. The cold of the San Francisco air as he came down the steps of the Hall of Justice made him want to laugh. But he did not laugh, for fear of being thrown back in jail. Instead, he walked over to the freeway ramp and stuck out his thumb.

He made more coffee for himself. Ha, free coffee! His mother was still asleep. They had both gotten pretty drunk the night before. After she had taken a nap they went to the Grove Market and bought a bunch of stuff and then sat in the kitchen, making dinner, drinking vodka and talking. God, he had not talked to his mother like that in years. He felt a warmth of love for her. She was really the greatest. He could not get over it. The funny part was, she did not seem able to remember having gone down to the Hall of Justice at all. She must have blanked out. She was very sensitive about it, so they talked about other things, about Diedre and Jerry and their life in East Oakland, about how Steven lived. His mother had never seen either house. When she saw Diedre they came over here, not vice-versa.

"I know why," Derek said. "They're afraid your car'll get ripped off!"

"Don't talk like that," Jackie said, and giggled.

Derek had no hangover. He felt great. If being a salesman was his only chance at life, God damn it, he was going to become a salesman!

The romance between Richard Kreach and Jackie Jay probably started right there at the Buttermilk Corner, early on a Sunday morning after a big Saturday night. Kitty was there, but she didn't hover, she didn't snoop, she didn't listen in. You couldn't miss what was going on. Kitty knew them both, but hadn't known they knew each other. Kitty liked romance but hated seduction, drawing a fine distinction between the two entirely by intuition. Kitty believed strongly in her intuitive powers, since they had gotten her out of many a scrape. Intuition was the women's edge over men, to make up for the fact that most men were stronger than most women. Kitty was not much of a theorist, but she knew an advantage when she saw one. Thus she felt the romance between Jackie and Richard Kreach before either of them knew about it.

Jackie's son had been home from jail about two weeks when Jackie came in after bar-closing with a couple of men Kitty had never seen before. They were all three drunk as hell, laughing, cutting up, having a fine old time. The place was jammed, and it took a while for Jackie's party to get a booth. The floor waitress took care of them, while Kitty had her hands full with the customers at the counter. She liked it when things were this busy; it made the time go faster. Richard Kreach was at the counter, alone for a change. He was a nice man, a heavy tipper who never got arrogant or upset. Usually he would be with a group of people, and Kitty knew he was a heavyweight rock and roll lawyer. There were a lot of rock musicians living in Marin County and they would come in from time to time, and Richard knew them all. They would sit in the last booth on the left, by the window and the jukebox, and other people would always be looking at them or trying to sit near them and listen.

But this night Kreach was alone, sitting there in his leather jacket, still there at three-thirty when everybody else had gone home except Jackie and the two men she was with. Then at one point Jackie got up from her booth and came over to the counter and sat next to Richard Kreach. For a while Kitty thought there might be trouble, because the two men Jackie left behind sat whispering to each other and looking over at the counter, as if they were trying to decide what to do, how to get Jackie back with them. One of them even called out to Jackie, but she didn't even turn her head. After a while, they left, and Jackie and Kreach were the only customers in the place. Kitty stayed at the other end of the counter and had a much-needed cup of coffee, leaning against the service counter. There was no music, unless you counted Elizaldo's humming from the kitchen. Elizaldo was such a nice man, hardworking, cheerful, a perfect mystery about his private life. Kitty wondered about his life outside the Buttermilk Corner. Was he in the bosom of his family, sitting there reading the papers in his easy chair? Or was he one of those overdressed Filipino guys down in North Beach, standing around on the street corners looking for white women? Kitty smiled to herself. She had never dated a Filipino man. Generally, they were too short for her. She was a tall woman, slim and blonde, just what they were looking for, but no thanks. Nothing racial here, just no thanks. Kitty liked her men tall, although from time to time throughout her life she had dated men shorter than herself, and they had been all right.

This Richard Kreach, now. He was about her size, a little plump for her taste, but she could tell it was muscular fat rather than lazy fat. He seemed about fifty and had a kind face that could probably turn hard in a split second. That was why Kitty had sort of hoped the two guys in the corner booth had been a little more forthcoming. But they hadn't been. They left, full of some secret between themselves, which turned out to be that they stuck Jackie with the check. Revenge!

Kitty wondered if Richard would pay. But he did not seem to be romancing Jackie. When they ordered refills, Kitty overheard them talking about fishing. Kreach liked to go out on the bay and fish for sturgeon, and Jackie liked to go out and sit on the rocks and fish for striped bass. Well, they had something in common, Kitty thought. Could marriage be far off?

"You ever go fishing, Kitty?" Jackie asked her.

"You know the great quote from Jesus," Kitty said.

"Which one?" Jackie asked. She looked good tonight, her eyes clear, the tension gone from her jaws.

Kreach said, "I think I know the one. 'I am a fisher of men.' Right?"

"That's the one," Kitty said.

As she walked away from them to put the coffee back on the heat she heard Kreach say, "Can I give you a lift home?"

"Oh," Jackie said. "I don't have my car, that's right, yes, thank you." When they left, he held the door open for her politely but not romantically, and both of them said goodnight to her. Everyone had forgotten the check on Jackie's table, which came to twenty-two dollars and some change. Usually when this happened, Kitty would put the check in a glass next to the cash register and lay it on Jackie when she came back in, but this time, for no reason at all, Kitty dropped the unpaid check into the wastebasket. Stiffed again, Boss.

Kitty always parked her car down the hill from the Buttermilk Corner, in the commuter lot next to the freeway. It was a cold foggy morning, and the iron railing next to the steps was wet with the fog. She held on anyway. As usual, her legs were like fire at this time of the morning, especially from the knees down. Through the cyclone fence she could see, hear and smell the commuter traffic. Once again she was glad she was not going their way. That year she lived in San Rafael, out Fourth Street, in a little apartment over a television store. It was a nice apartment, gas stove, a quiet refrigerator, but no view, and she could hear the Fourth Street traffic all day when she was trying to sleep. The refrigerator was a nice break, even though she had to defrost with a pickaxe. Her last apartment had been a horror show, even though on paper it was more than a girl could hope for. SAUSALITO VIEW APT, yes, but. It was somebody's basement, turned into an illegal mother-in-law, and you could hear everything from upstairs, especially when the landlady wore high-heeled shoes. Kitty could swear she could tell the woman's mood from the way she walked. And the refrigerator, my God. It was the kind that defrosted itself, which meant in this case it would give out a huge sigh every now and then. The damned thing breathed, and it had lung trouble. HUU-HAA, *HUU-HAA*, all night long. And the woman upstairs, who was about Kitty's age but had nothing to do all day, played classical music when she got moody, and Kitty would wake up with a start to hear Beethoven chasing wood nymphs across a field. And as for the view, yes, she had a view, a few masts in the yacht harbor, a slice of water about this thick, and two inches of sky.

The San Rafael place was much smaller, but Kitty could stand up in it, and the daytime sounds from the TV store were never disturbing. At night she had the building to herself, but of course she was seldom home at night. This morning, when she got home, she was still thinking about Jackie and her chance meeting with the lawyer. Some people were always meeting the high-income types. Kitty parked in her little slot beside the store, climbed the stairs holding onto the railing. Her new landlord was a sweet guy to let her park right there. He was a sweet guy anyway, a little roly-poly balding guy about fifty, Lebanese, nice smile, good teeth. She unlocked her front door and opened it, looking around her tiny furnished living room. Nobody had broken in during the night and stolen everything, thank

God for minor blessings. It was good to be home. It always was. It was never stuffy in here because she kept the window over the sink and the window over the toilet both open while she was gone, both with nails toed into the sash so nobody on the outside could open them wider. Kitty sat down on the big blue overstuffed chair and put her purse on the rug.

"Home again," she said. She wasn't at all sleepy. She almost never was at this hour. She liked working graveyard, but didn't like sleeping all day. People didn't go to bed after work, they went out and played for a while first. She could pretend she had been out partying all night, but that didn't work very well. She had eaten breakfast at the joint, so that wasn't something she could do. She thought about making a cup of tea. For some reason, tea made her relax sometimes. But she didn't feel like going to all the work of boiling water. She sat with her fingers laced under her chin, staring at nothing, staring at the wallpaper opposite, faded ribbons and grapes in bunches. The place could use a coat of paint. But she was not going to bother her landlord over a little matter like that. It would probably cost a thousand dollars. Everything cost so horribly now. Well, scream about it. She remembered the Great Depression, and it hadn't been so great. Things were better now, much better, even if she couldn't afford anything. She remembered some old jackass telling her things had been better back in the old days, much better, and she laughed at him.

"Oh, yeah?" she said. "When?"

That stuck him, whoever he was, she couldn't even remember his face. Maybe it had been one of her husbands. She had been married five times, six if you count Mexican marriages, which she didn't, not really, not in this case, because they had only been together three weeks and then she saw him no more. Bill Phillips he had called himself on the marriage license, chief petty officer in the navy, and they had to run to Mexico to get married because he had a wife and child living in San Diego at the time. Bill had been a dreamer, a drinker and a dreamer. She wondered what ever happened to Bill Phillips.

Bill had been a lot of fun, although not much else. She had been selling tickets at the Star Burlesque at the time, they liked having a looker in the box, and Bill hung around day after day, never buying a ticket, never going inside to see the girls, just flattering her with his attentions until she gave up and ran off to Ensenada with him. They stayed one night at the Rosarita down at Rosarita Beach, that used to be a big gambling spot for the Hollywood hotshots, but Bill acted up and they were thrown out. Did they sleep on the beach one night, or was that another memory, of another guy?

It did not matter. She was going to fall asleep right in her chair if she didn't look out. But she wasn't sleepy. She knew what she should do. She should start the water for the tea, undress, take a little shower, put on her pajamas, have the tea and slip into bed. She would be asleep in minutes. She never really suffered from sleeplessness unless there was a racket outside. But she didn't want to slip into bed. She was wide awake and wanted something to do. What time was it, almost seven in the morning. She could drive out to Stinson Beach and walk along the water's edge. It might still be foggy out there, but fog didn't ruin the beach. There was something mystical about beaches, day or night. She had gone out to Stinson at night with some guy once, and they had walked along under a full moon looking at the eerie green fire in the surf. It was the plankton, she knew, making the water light up, nothing to hurt you, and so she had waded out into it, leaving a wake of the green fire. Out a few yards the water was like glass, yet she could feel the pull of the undertow. Never lose your respect for Mother Nature. She could kill you with her gentle undertow, have you out there around the Farallones in about five seconds if you didn't look out. And there were Great White sharks here too, cruising the shallows, no place to play in the water on a dreamy night.

She found she had actually fallen asleep in the chair. Now she could go to bed without any cup of tea. That was fine with her.

Jackie was amazed at herself. Why hadn't she thought of Richard Kreach? When she had been so desperate for a lawyer? Now they were parked in front of her house, and she didn't have the heart to tell him that her own car was parked in the little alley between the Happy Hour and the drugstore. It was no problem, she could walk downtown later in the day. Right now it was like high school, they were sitting there in the car talking when they could have just gone into the house and been comfortable. But this was comfortable too, and pleasantly nostalgic. Jackie had never really talked to Richard before. He was not one of those men who turn on the fascinating charm. Instead he seemed gruff and shy. If it was an act, it was a good one.

"My mother had a tavern out on Eighty-Second," he told her. "Do you know Portland at all?"

"I've never been there," Jackie said. "I hear it's nice."

"Oh, Portland is great. Totally different from down here. Back in the old days it was really a rough town. A real frontier town. My mother's place was an Irish tavern, the kind where they serve you green beer on Saint Pat's Day. Not real green beer, beer with green dye in it. You know what a tavern is?"

"It's a bar, isn't it?" All this bar talk.

"Not a real bar. Back then they had real strict liquor laws. You had to buy your booze in a state liquor store and you had to belong to a private club and bring your own bottle. They would serve you setups, ice, soda water, that kind of shit. The taverns served beer. Oregon is the original home of the grand old beer bust. My mother's place was out where the used-car lots were, and all the salesmen used to hang out. But it was Irish, see, so everybody in the joint had these thick Irish brogues. I thought we lived in an Irish neighborhood until I woke up to the fact that everybody faked the accent when they came in through the front door. *"Good evenin' to yah, Lad!"* they'd say to me. And I'd see them out on the street, same guys, and they'd talk like normal people."

"Is your mother still alive?" Jackie asked him. It was getting light out.

"Yeah, she's fine. I'm talking too much."

"No, it's okay," Jackie said. "Would you like to come in for a nightcap?"

"Nightcap? Thanks, but I have a long day. I better go home and get some sleep."

"What do you do?" she asked. "I know you're a lawyer, and you work with musicians."

"That's about it," he said. She waited for him to brag, but he didn't.

She told him about her son, Derek, and he listened carefully and finally laughed and said, "They didn't have anything on him. Or they would have deep-sixed him." Then he sighed and said, "You've been through it, haven't you."

"Oh, it was worse for Derek," she started to say, but Richard took her hand.

"He's a kid. You're the one who suffered," he said, and she thought he was throwing a pass, and suddenly, at this moment, she didn't want him to.

"Let me walk you to your door," he said. At the door, she expected him to try to kiss her, try to come in, but he didn't, just shook her hand and said what a nice time they'd had and how glad he was to get to know her better, and then he was gone.

The next time she saw Richard Kreach was at the Happy Hour, a few nights later. Jackie had been staying away from the place, but here she was. Derek had gone out with friends and she had been about to make dinner for herself. There was a chicken in the refrigerator, all cut up for frying and wrapped in butcher paper, but while she was unwrapping it she remembered there wasn't enough oil to do the thing right. The trick with frying chicken was the oil. The oil had to be deep, very hot, and fresh. She could go to the store for more oil, or she could open a can of soup, but this decision was put off by a couple of vodkas, and the next thing she knew she was at the Happy Hour, looking for somebody to take her to dinner.

Thank God her money worries were over, at least for the time being. Two days before, she had gone to the mailbox and found a letter from her sister in Hong Kong. Apparently this was a reply to a letter Jackie couldn't remember having sent. But her memory was getting terrible anyway. The letter from Joey contained a check on the Hong Kong–Shanghai Bank for $2500, and a note saying things were rough these days and Joey was getting out of hair. She was sorry but this would be all she could spare. Jackie felt humiliated and pleased all at the same time, paid her outstanding bills, except for the rent, and still had plenty of cash left over, cash that should hold her until she got a job. She wondered if she had written to Jill, too. She could imagine her drunken scrawl. Begging letters. What next?

Jackie sat at the bar and drank her Ramos Fizz. She had meant to order a glass of white wine, but Dick Stoffel brought her the Ramos and said cheerfully, "First one's on the house!" The place was pretty crowded, and Jackie felt cosy and at home. So much of her life had been spent in bars. She remembered that Richard Kreach had been raised in a bar. She wondered what it had been like for him, underfoot among the barstools and spittoons of an Irish pub in Portland, Oregon.

Even as she was thinking about him, Richard came into the place, waved to a couple of people, and sat down next to Jackie.

"That stool's taken," she said, flirting with him.

"Hi, beautiful," he said.

She laughed. This guy was always funny.

"Where's your boyfriend?" Richard asked her, after ordering a beer.

"I don't have a boyfriend," she said. And it was true. She and Al Burke had had a terrible argument. They had gone into the city for a seafood dinner and both gotten terribly drunk. On the way home Jackie screamed at him and begged to be let out of the car in the middle of the Golden Gate Bridge. "I WANNA JUMP!" she had screamed at him, and he had screamed back something, and then later she heard he had been seeing this woman in Larkspur. Apparently he didn't come into the bars anymore, at least not the Happy Hour.

"Have you eaten yet?" Richard asked her, and she felt a guilty little thrill. She cocked her head and gave him her biggest smile.

"Dinner?" she asked brightly.

She did not want to wake up. Waking up meant facing the pain. It was easier to slip back down into the dream. Or was it memory? She did not know. They were in a bowling alley. She was with Richard. He was a wild man. He looked so funny, standing there holding the ball up to his belly, a boozy grin on his face. She was laughing and then she was running across the alleys. Everybody was after her. Richard stood there grinning, a little pixie grin, an Irish grin, holding the ball up to his belly.

"What happened to your fingers?" she asked him in the dream.

"What fingers?" he said. It looked like his fingers were gone at the second joint, but they were just stuck in the ball. "I got no fingers," he said in the dream, and she laughed and ran across the alleys. Everybody ran after her. She was laughing.

"What fingers?" he said. She could feel him behind her, trying to show her how to throw the ball.

"I know how to do it," she said. "You don't have to show me how."

"But I want to," he said, and she laughed and ran across the alleys. She could feel his stubby fingers against her waist. Was he in bed with her? Was she in her own bed? She sniffed without opening her eyes. It smelled like her bed. Her own arms were under the pillow. She ran across the alleys laughing. Were his fingers on her waist? Was she naked? No. She was not naked. She could feel the elastic of her panties, the neck of her tee shirt. So she was home in her own bed, not naked, alone. He could not be in the bed with her. If he had been, she would have been naked. Unless they just came home and went to bed like married people, no sex. She tried to remember, but it was easier to fall back asleep, back into the dream. The noise of the bowling alley. Running across the alleys, pissing everybody off, had she done that? Where was the bowling alley? San Rafael?

"Let's go bowling!" Loud laughter.

Something uncomfortable was keeping her awake. It was her tongue, filling her mouth. Too much tongue. She knew if she opened her eyes, the feeling would go away. Reality would set in. Her headache would start. She knew from experience. This was going to be a monumental hangover. She must have gotten drunk. Ha ha. Yes, she must have gotten drunk. It was like holding a big moist hunk of meat in her mouth. Too much tongue. But she would not open her eyes. The dream receded. She tried to remember what had really happened the night before. They had gone to dinner. Where had they gone? She could not remember. Scott's, in the city. They had gone to Scott's. Or had that been a couple of weeks ago? She had gone to Scott's a couple of weeks ago, she remembered, with some man. *Sole almondine*. She remembered that clearly, although she could not remember who the man had been. Had she gone back for more *sole almondine*? She loved it, but she couldn't taste any fish in her mouth. Ugh, better not to try. Her damned tongue.

They must have gone to dinner somewhere. Unless they had skipped dinner and gone bowling. She did not much like to bowl. She was not very good at it. The kind of men who took you bowling.

But that had been long ago. Now things were different. He was behind her, holding her wrist with his stubby fingers. His fingers on her waist. Was he in the bed with her? She could move her leg, as if in sleep, and find out. What if he was lying there on his back, wide awake, waiting for her to wake up, waiting for the morning? Or had morning already come? With her eyes tightly shut she could not tell. The drapes could be open, flooding the room with light. But she always pulled the drapes, even when she was drunk.

The headache was beginning anyway. First a mild throbbing in her temple, like one blood vessel thumping away, unmindful of the pain it caused. Then spreading. A vague feeling of nausea. The only escape lay in retreat. She would have to fall back down into the dream. There was no escape from that damned dream, just tattered fragments of a dream, running across the alleys with everybody after her. Okay. Here's what must have happened. They must have sat there in the Happy Hour and gotten pretty drunk. Then they decided to go to dinner together. She could almost remember sitting there trying to decide where to eat. Maybe they went over to the city, maybe not. Were there any bowling alleys in San Francisco? There had to be, but somehow she thought the one in San Rafael must have been the one. They must have gone bowling, she couldn't imagine why. Maybe Richard was a good bowler. Men liked to show you things they were good at. So they would go bowling, and being drunk, she would get crazy and go running across the alleys. Everybody chasing her. Angry faces. Everybody in an outrage. Or were they all laughing? Never mind, it was just a dream. But remember the dream where she scraped the door of her Jag? Remember that? She had lain in bed all morning, half-asleep, half-awake, trying to think if she had dreamed wrecking the car or she had really creamed that concrete post and screamed with laughter. She remembered all she had to do was go out to the garage and look at the car. The thought had put her to sleep, but when she did get up and go out, the car had a big scrape down the side. Which cost her a lot of money. Back when she had the money.

Without thinking, she rolled over and opened her eyes. The room was grey with morning light. She was alone in the bed. Well, that was something. She felt guilty, but hangovers always made her feel guilty. She hadn't done anything. Unless the bowling dream was true. She realized she had to pee, very badly. She threw back the covers and got upright and stood up and walked halfway across the bedroom floor toward her bathroom before the hangover came up behind her and sacked her. She grabbed the bathroom doorframe and shuddered with nausea. Oh, she was going to have to puke, oh she didn't want to, but she staggered forward and fell with a low cry to her knees on the thick bathroom rug and just managed to get the toilet seat up before the nausea overcame her and she began coughing hot bitter liquid into the toilet. Thinking: Ah, yes, better. Puking with her eyes shut against the sight of it. She wet her pants and the rug before it was done, and then pulled down the panties and dizzily turned and sat on the toilet, jumping up because there was no seat, cursing, putting down the seat, sitting, pissing, angry, kicking the wet panties into the little wastebasket, feeling the pain burrow into her forehead.

"Ugh," she said aloud. Thank God for private bathrooms. At least Derek hadn't seen her in her degradation. Oh, Derek was old enough. He knew about hangovers. Mother has a hangover, dear. Walk softly. Humor on the toilet. Her mouth tasted awful. Cut to the breakfast table. But no, this wasn't a movie. Cut to back in bed, the taste out of her mouth, sleep, sweet sleep, saving her from herself. But no. This was no movie. She was really sick, really sitting on the toilet, really savagely hung over. Ha ha, you have a hangover! Ha ha, you're sick as a dog! Yes, woof, oh God. Sick. Thank God Richard had not spent the night. How humiliating if he had. Maybe he was asleep somewhere, avoiding his own hangover. Maybe he was awake, suffering. Maybe he was sitting on a toilet somewhere, suffering as she was suffering. But you could not call it suffering, could you? Since it was your own fault. Suffering was noble. This was a joke.

Jackie knew a lot about hangovers. She had flown all over the free world with hangovers. Those had been happy days, before she picked the most promising of the men she dated, married him and settled down in Lincoln's Grove. Working with a splitting headache had been a badge of honor in those days. Every major city around the world had apartment buildings that were nearly all airline personnel, and because people were always coming and going, there was always a party in somebody's suite or out by the pool, and it was considered hip to be able to fly from San Francisco to Hawaii to Tokyo, party for twenty hours or so, getting only the sleep that came after sex, and then jump on your turnaround flight back to the States, everybody working the flight hung over, killing their hangovers with bennies or amps while the passengers got whacked out themselves.

Jackie had not been known as a party girl, even though she had flown in the days before married stewardesses, when they were all supposed to be party girls. But getting bombed and sleeping around was nearly all she could remember about her life in the air. Skiing in Colorado or Switzerland, she remembered that, and she remembered her pride in her ability to do things physical, to ski, to swim well, to be able to pick up snorkeling in only a couple of days (yet she

also remembered her mask leaking and the terrible panic she felt until she broke the surface, a mile from the boat); she remembered the
week she had spent with Charlie O'Donnell in Key West, out on the
flats in his flatbottomed boat, the heat and glare unbelievable, checking his crab traps, clawing the crabs and watching them scuttle off
into the shallow glare clawless, the hangovers burned away by the
terrible sun. She remembered Charlie O'Donnell's relentless search
for his manhood, that got him in fights and made him fiercely pro-
tective of his own section of flats, where no man dare put down a crab
trap or face Charlie, either right there out on the flats or in one of the
many bars in Key West. She might have stayed with Charlie, she
thought now, except for that look in his eye if he felt somebody had
taken something of his, a look that meant sanity was out of the
question, and somebody was going to get hurt. Charlie drank and
brooded, building himself up to his fights, because those were not
fistfights, where one man would knock the other one down, and they
would shake hands and have a drink together. No, these fights sometimes lasted for years, grudge fights, and Charlie never went into one
without his fishknife. She wondered if Charlie was still alive. He
would be about fifty now, the same age as Richard Kreach. Why had
Richard not spent the night? She wished she could remember.

If her hangover was going to be a normal one, she would be sick all
day, unable to eat. Coffee would make her nauseated, but she would
have to drink a couple of cups of it, just to stay awake. But she also
knew she couldn't just lie there in bed and wait for the pain to go
away. It was just too awful. She thought about putting on her running clothes and running on the mountain until the hangover
sweated itself out of her body. But she was too tired. She sat at the
table in the kitchen and put both hands on her belly. Was she finally
getting fat? Running would be the best thing for her. Run and sweat.
But a wave of nausea put an end to such thoughts.

The headache, the helpless feeling, the guilt, the dread of going
outside, should last all day. By night, she would feel a lot better,

enough to eat something, a peanut butter and jelly sandwich or a bowl of vegetable soup, and she could sit in front of the television watching anything, blowing her nose and wiping her eyes, because when she had a hangover everything made her cry, even television. It was really very funny. She would go to bed early, get a good night's sleep, and wake up as if nothing had happened. Just a day cut out of her life.

Or she could kill the hangover by getting drunk again. Quite early in the day she decided she did not want to. It was just putting off the inevitable. She did not thirst for booze, not even a bottle of ale. She preferred to go ahead and go through the agony, so that she would be sober, clean and clear by tomorrow morning. That would be justice, balance, the proper thing to do. The house was dirty. She could spend the day slowly, agonizingly, cleaning house.

By one in the afternoon, when Derek got up and came into the kitchen, she had managed to do nothing but have a third cup of coffee. The dishes were in the sink, in grey soapy cold water. She had tried, but standing there at the sink she had been wracked by headache pains, THUM, THUM, THUM, until she lurched back to her chair and sat, her hands between her legs, panting like a dog.

Derek was in a cheerful mood and had a cup of coffee with her.

"Did you have a nice time last night?" she asked him. He was dressed in jeans and one of her black tee shirts. They could wear a lot of the same clothes.

"Sure. I had a good time. Thanks for the use of the wheels."

Jackie had forgotten she had lent him the Jag.

"Don't we get the paper anymore?" he asked her.

"I got tired of it," she said. "You can drive down and pick up the *I-J*, if you want to look for a job."

"I don't want to," he said with his shy little smile. "I figure I have to."

"What kind of a job are you looking for?" she asked him. She had asked him that before, and he had told her, and she had forgotten.

"Selling," he said.

"Oh, yes," she said, feeling a momentary contempt for her own son.

Derek grinned. "You got a hangover, don't you?" Obviously, he thought it was funny.

"If you're going after a paper, you can do the shopping, too," she said. Soon Derek was gone, taking the car and leaving her helpless. But that was just her mood; she wasn't really helpless, and he would be home soon anyway. She hoped by that time to be fully engaged in housework. It was nice having Derek home again, but it made a lot of work for her. He was a good kid, though, and pitched in a little bit. Well, not much, but he was twenty, almost twenty-one. She passed her twenty-first birthday in Lisbon. Kids were older these days. Less opportunities. Derek might have to live at home a long time before he got it together enough to move out on his own. He had been so insistent on leaving home before. And here he was back, after a narrow escape from the law.

She remembered his earnest desire to go to Harvard, and it made tears come to her eyes. Such ambition, all gone to hell. She never told him he didn't have a chance at Harvard, it would have crushed him. Maybe it had crushed him. Men want so badly to be the best. She felt once again the sadness of being unable to protect her child. Derek really didn't stand a chance, she knew. She had been out in the world long enough to see the kind of men who succeeded, and Derek was not one of them. He seemed just slightly out of step. Not out of step enough to be a rebel, just sort of missing the beat all the time. It made her so sad sometimes. Tears ran down her face, and she cursed herself for being a hung-over sentimental idiot. She could not help Derek, and agonizing over him was not going to do anything for either of them. But the pain was so deep.

She never felt pain over Diedre. Funny. She began to kick herself for not feeling enough for her daughter, who was so unlike any of the rest of the family, a quiet girl who never seemed interested in anything, got along well in school until she abruptly quit and got married. Derek tore up her painting, and she cried and clung to Jackie's legs. Then her dog died and she said, "Good, now we can get a cat." Strange child. Sweet child, knew what she wanted, had her life all figured out, married to that lunk. At least she was out of here and on her own, which brought Jackie back to her son Derek. She wondered with a start if Derek was stealing again. No. Because he didn't have any money except what she gave him. She even had to give him money for clothes, because all he had was what he was wearing plus two extra pairs of underwear. Maybe the underwear helped get him off. You don't go robbing stores with your pockets full of underwear. Or do you?

The dishes sat coldly in the sink, reproaching her. She could not sit there any longer. She got to her feet, made her way over to the sink, stuck her hand down into the cold grey water, and turned the stopper. By the time Derek got back with two sacks of groceries, she had finished the dishes and was on her knees, scrubbing the floor before giving it a good waxing. Her head was pounding.

"Uh, I'll be in my room, looking for a job," Derek said when she looked up.

"Like hell you will," she said coldly. "You go out into that garage and fix the lawnmower and get the lawn mowed!"

"Huh?" said her son.

But Jackie was wrong about the hangover. True, she had been able to work all day, finish off the kitchen, vacuum the rest of the house, vacuum the drapes in the living room and her bedroom, hearing with some satisfaction the roar of the lawnmower outside as Derek did the front and back yards and then at her insistence trimmed around the trees and flower beds, even though the beds themselves were too much for him. One day soon Jackie would have to make some decisions about the flower beds. And other things. The house didn't just sit there, it went to pieces. Although she dreaded it, she was going to have to call Steven about getting landscapers out, and maybe even having the house painted. If she knew Steven he would be surprised over the phone that she and Derek couldn't take care of the place by themselves, forgetting that when he lived here they had a landscaper come in every month.

Finally, with sundown, she allowed herself to stop working. Derek had long since walked off down the street, saying he would be back "soon." He tried to borrow the Jag, but Jackie said no, she might want to use it herself. Even though she was sure she was going to stay in that night, she didn't like the helpless feeling of having no car, and besides, Derek needed to know the car wasn't his to use any time he wanted. Well. She had cleaned the kitchen, although the ceiling still needed degreasing. She had vacuumed, changed the beds, straightened out the magazines on the coffee table, even though they were all out of date. She hated the look of the coffee table without them. She felt all right, tired but virtuous. Derek had not said whether he would be back for dinner, so she fixed herself a can of Campbell's vegetable soup, two pieces of buttered toast, and sat herself down in front of the television. Once again, the empty house seemed such a luxury. Growing up with two younger sisters had kept her busy, always something going on in the house, and solitude had been pure luxury. Jackie wondered if her life had gone the way it had because she secretly wanted to be alone. It was certainly possible.

The first time the telephone rang it was Richard Kreach, wondering how she was. "I'm hung over," she said with a little laugh. "How are you?"

"Never mind me," he said. "I just wanted to make sure you were okay."

Jackie hesitated, and then said, "Did we go bowling?"

Richard chuckled. There seemed to be a lot of static on the line. "Did we go bowling! Nobody ever went bowling like we went bowling. What's the matter, did you black out?"

"I must have," she said, and her chest went cold.

"How about having dinner with me, one of these nights?"

"Sure," she said. "Where are you?"

"I'm in L.A.," he said. "I'll be back soon. I just wanted to make sure you were okay."

"I'm just fine," she said. After they hung up, she wondered why he had called. But while she was still thinking about it, the telephone rang again. It was her sister Jill, calling from Arlington. It was Jackie's night for long-distance calls. Jill had gotten her letter and wondered what her circumstances were. "You didn't say in your letter," she said.

Jackie explained that she was looking for a job, and needed a few dollars to last until she could find work.

"What kind of work are you looking for?" Jill asked. The hangover was returning full force now, headache, sweat running down from her armpits, her stomach heavy.

"I don't really know," she said, being more honest than she wanted to be. "Maybe waitressing."

"Did you ever think of going into real estate?" Jill asked. She talked about the real estate business, and Jackie barely listened. She was afraid she was going to lose her dinner. It could have been funny, Jill trying to talk her into moving to Texas and her sitting there trying not to throw up, but it was serious, and the sweat popped out on her forehead and she wished her sister would shut up, and finally she interrupted Jill, sweet Jill who only wanted to help, by saying, "I can't think about moving. Not now. And I don't know anything about real estate."

Jill apologized and said she would see what she could do about sending money, although she did not mention an amount. Jackie was very glad to be off the telephone. The nausea went down, and she decided to take her shower and go to bed. Thank God this day was over at last. As she showered she thought about Jill, who was getting a Texas accent. Real estate. She knew a hooker who had gone into real estate, platinum blonde. She made a killing in the real estate boom. She and Jackie had talked at the No Name bar in Sausalito. Years ago. And Jackie knew a former chief stewardess who had gone to college in her spare time instead of partying, and she now owned some buildings in the East Bay, lived in her own little house in Point Richmond. Jackie went to bed realizing she had probably thrown her life away. But she hadn't done anything wrong. She had, in fact, done everything right, or so she had believed at the time. Oh, fresh sheets, how nice. And the room clean, no dust behind the drapes, the drapes themselves clean, so there was a last feeling of comfort and snugness before she passed into sleep.

But when she woke up in the morning the hangover was still there. She could not believe it. The headache was back, the queasy stomach, the vague guilt and dread, all there. No. It was a dream. She could not be having a hangover. She knew very well she had drunk nothing the night before. Therefore, she could not be having a hangover. She was dreaming. If she opened her eyes, it would go away. She opened her eyes. It did not go away.

"Oh, shit," she said, but she was frightened. She sat up. Her head vibrated with pain.

He wanted to talk to his mother about what had happened to him. He just couldn't. She would not understand. Why should she? It had been like war. Seven days of combat, and then here he was, back in civilized Marin, driving a Jag, eating free food, sleeping in a free bed. It was insane. Derek was certain nothing like it had ever happened to his mother. What made Derek wake up in the middle of the night sweating was how close he had come to killing somebody. That gun in his hand. He had been like a zombie. Burns. He would turn on his bedside gooseneck lamp, which his father had given him years ago, a million years ago, saying it had come from his office. Then he would light a cigarette, using the metal base of the lamp as an ashtray. He was a real smoker now. He couldn't understand the way he had been, smoking and not smoking. It was like his whole life up to now, Derek Jeminovski, not quite in, not quite out. A smoker, but not really. A thief, but not really. An armed robber, but come on, not really. He could not believe that Burns had been shot and killed. Shot and killed! And Kenny was in prison by now. Kenny was too much of a dink to be in prison. He wondered how Kenny was getting along. Maybe he should find out where Kenny was, and pay him a visit. Maybe Kenny didn't know Burns was dead. Then he sneered at himself. There was no way he was going to visit anybody in prison. The very thought scared the shit out of him. Just seeing San Quentin across Richardson Bay frightened him. Maybe Kenny was in San Quentin. Even so, Derek was not going to visit him. It was probably impossible anyway. Relatives only, probably. But it did not make Derek feel any better about himself. Not even enough guts to visit his fellow robber.

So he sat at the dinner table and said almost nothing. His mother did not want to seem to pry, he guessed, and thank God for that. They talked about little things, nothing important, and in a way it was comforting and in a way it was very discomforting.

But one thing had changed. For so long he had feared he had no place in life, that he was a complete misfit. Now he knew better. The value of going to jail. He didn't know much, but he knew he belonged outside jail. Nothing bad happened to him in jail. It was like being dangled over the pit, getting your feet scorched, and then being pulled back at the last minute. He had been so lucky, both with Burns and Kenny, and in jail. Lucky guilty happy sad. He knew why he had gone back. Because he had loved it. There was clearly something wrong with his mind.

But no more. With jail in his memory he would *impel* himself into a career in sales. So what if it was a joke? The paper was full of sales jobs. In fact, sales jobs were all the paper was full of that required no experience. NO EXPERIENCE, in fact, meant sales job. Derek actually tried out for a couple of jobs before he decided more thought would be necessary. Once for the traditional door-to-door job of selling encyclopedias. But all he needed to see were his fellow applicants to know he was in the wrong place. They sat there, six or seven of them in the little office waiting room in Novato, all of them badly dressed in suits or sports outfits, sweating failure from every pore. Most of them had really bad faces, red faces filled with what Derek decided was unexploded rage. You could smell the failure coming off these guys. There was one woman, but she looked like the men, fat, bulging out-of-date blue suit, floppy bow at her throat, angry red face,

and drenched in a cheap perfume that fought with the smells of co-
logne and cigars that seemed to have soaked into the walls. A young
guy, not much older than Derek, came in to give them their group
talk and pass around application forms. He frowned at Derek when
he came in. Then later after they were all sitting there with their paperwork on their laps, he asked Derek if he owned a suit.

"Not yet," Derek said, and blushed. They all laughed at him. He
was dressed in shirt and tie, sports jacket, jeans and his black Reeboks. At that, he looked better than most of them. He could not wait
for the end of the session, so he could leave, throw his paperwork into
the nearest trash can, and drive back south to Lincoln's Grove.

The other sales job he looked into was pure surrealism. Selling
siding. He got involved through a friend from high school, Dave
Beltz, whose dad was an "inside man" with the siding company. Derek ran into Dave one afternoon and they sat out in front of the Grove
Market talking about the future. Dave had plans to go in the navy,
but first he had to try working for his dad.

"My dad's sold everything," Dave said. "Sometimes we live high
on the hog, sometimes not. Sales is like that."

The three of them went over to Richmond, their "territory," one
Monday morning. The old man let them off at the end of a street of
former housing project buildings, surrounded by worn-out lawns,
play areas and clothes lines, and told them to meet him an hour later
at a bar three blocks away. At first they divided the street, but then
when they saw that they were the only white people around, they
started going up to doors together. Their pitch was simple: the
homeowner had been picked to have his house resided. They found
nobody who would listen to them, and at the end of the two hours
Derek was ready to quit, and so was Dave. The old man told them
jokes, bought them lunch, called them a couple of quitters, and
drove them back to Marin.

"I guess I'll go in the navy," Dave said gloomily. "How about it?
Wanna come along?"

"No," said Derek.

Dave's father depressed him, and reminded him of the time they put on *The Death of a Salesman* at high school. Derek had been backstage helping work the lights, and he got to know the play pretty well. It was depressing. His favorite line was, "A man is not a piece of fruit!" Dave's father reminded him so much of Willy Loman that he wanted to laugh out loud, but of course did not. Mr. Beltz was a tall thin man with bloodshot blue eyes, stained teeth and a hard little pot belly. He really made Derek want to reconsider his plan to become a salesman. To end up like this? No, thanks. Dave's father, as they drove across the almost empty Richmond–San Rafael Bridge, talked about "milking the niggers." Kids talked like that, but it was embarrassing to hear it from a man of fifty.

In spite of his misgivings, Derek did become a sales person. It happened like this: A few days after the abortive siding adventure, Derek borrowed a hundred dollars from his mother, walked down the hill and under the freeway to the shopping center, and went into the shoe store on the mall. He didn't even know the name of the store. He had come in to buy some regular brown leather shoes to complete his sports outfit, and the shoe salesman turned out to be a guy he had gone to high school with, Billy Clodfelter. Derek had hated Billy, a big chunky kid with stiff blond hair and rabbit's teeth. He was a bully and a total prick, as far as Derek was concerned. Now here he was in a sports jacket and bow tie, grinning and wanting to shake hands.

The store was empty except for another salesman and a woman behind the counter. Derek sat down in one of the row of chairs, and Billy Clodfelter pulled up a stool and sat at his feet.

"Well, Derek old man, what's happening with you these days?" Billy asked, slipping off Derek's right Reebok. Derek remembered a school dance where he had been dancing with a girl, he couldn't remember her name, but she had been nice and Derek had been deep in erotic fantasies when Billy didn't so much cut in as just bump Derek out of the way and dance off with the girl. Kicked sand in his face. Maybe that was where Derek got the idea that Billy was a bully.

Maybe he was a nice guy. He certainly was friendly now, as he brought out several boxes of shoes.

"There," Billy said. "Now walk around in those." Derek walked around in the new shoes, perforated wingtips, although he did not know this at the time. "How do they feel?" Billy asked hopefully.

"Pretty stiff," Derek said.

"That'll work out," Billy said. He looked critical and stroked his chin. "They look nice on you."

"They're heavy," Derek said.

"You're used to those Reeboks," Billy said.

Derek was tempted to make Billy Clodfelter show him a dozen pair of shoes, just to keep him on his knees. But he didn't. It would have been stupid. These shoes were just fine. "I'll take these," he said.

Derek started to put his Reeboks on again, but Billy got down on his stool and said, "Here, let me," and Derek let him.

"Where you been, Derek?" he asked. "School? Working?"

"Over in San Francisco," Derek said.

"Oh, yeah? What kind of work you doing?"

"Oh, you know. I'm looking for a job now," Derek said. He stood up and they walked over to the counter, Billy carrying the new shoes in their box. Derek wanted to ask him what had happened to his career in professional football, but didn't. He could guess at the tumbling of ambitions that led from high school football player to shoe salesman.

"You need any socks?" Billy asked. There were racks of stockings beside the counter and on top of the counter. Derek pretended to look at the socks and then shook his head. As he was paying the woman she said, "Just the one pair?"

"Uh huh," Derek said. She was goodlooking, about twenty-five, and Derek was suddenly embarrassed about buying only one pair of shoes.

"No socks or anything?" she asked him sweetly.

"No," Derek said, almost blushing. The shoes had been forty-nine dollars plus tax. She gave him his change.

"What kind of work are you looking for?" Billy asked. "We could use another salesman-trainee. That's what I am."

"You mean work here?" Derek asked dumbly.

"Yeah," Billy said, grinning. "We could have a ball."

Derek could not think of a reason why not. It was within walking distance of his mother's house. It was a sales job. Derek had never imagined himself on his knees selling shoes, but what the hell. Without wanting to, he remembered how Burns had put him on his knees and taken his money. The thought made him go cold.

"What's the matter?" Billy asked. "Somebody walk on your grave?"

"No, I was just thinking," Derek said. They walked to the entrance together. On either side of the door were big windows full of shoes. Sure enough, in the window was a sign: SALESPERSON-TRAINEE WANTED.

"What's the pay?" Derek asked.

Billy grinned his old bully grin. "Six and commish," he said.

"Commish?"

"Commission. I make good money, but I have to admit, the first few weeks can be kinda light. You have to learn how to do it. Then the money's good."

"I don't know," Derek said.

"Come and meet the boss," Billy said. "But be careful, he might sell you another pair of shoes!"

It would be something to do while he looked for a better job. And he could practice selling himself. He smiled at Billy as if he liked him. "Take me to your leader," he said, and Billy laughed as if it had been the funniest thing he ever heard.

Standing in front of Rotterdam Footwear, Derek could look out over the vast parking lot to the edge of the bay, and see beyond it San Quentin, pale yellow in the haze. He often did this in the morning, after opening the store, smoking a cigarette and waiting for the day to begin. As soon as they felt they could trust him with the keys they gave him the job of opening up. Derek was fresh blood, low man on the totem pole, the new kid, and so it was his job to get there by 9:00 A.M., punch in on the time clock in the stockroom, check the store over to see that the janitors had done their work, start the coffee in the Bunn coffeemaker, and handle any earlybird customers who might come in before the rest of the employees got there. Derek liked opening up. He liked being trusted with the keys, and he liked having that first coffee and cigarette by himself.

The mall was covered by a shingled roof and every so often there was a potted wisteria. It was part of Derek's job to sweep the mall in front of the store, and although he wasn't told to, he watered the wisteria climbing the post in front of the store. Then, if no customers came along to bother him, he would go back into the stockroom and memorize numbers and models. Knowing the stock was the second-hardest part of working in a shoe store. The hardest part was selling the shoes. But it wasn't long before Derek learned he had the touch. Some people had it and some didn't. Most didn't. You probably had to be born with it.

It was funny, he had been prepared to hate getting almost literally on his knees in front of people. He thought he would feel humiliated, but he didn't. He liked it. After the first few days of inexperience, clumsiness and embarrassment, Derek fell in love with the act of selling shoes. It was wonderful to discover something he was good at. He liked the feel and smell of fresh leather. He liked the very act of fitting shoes. There was nothing sexual about it. They kidded about shoe fetishism all the time. No, he did not get a thrill from touching milady's foot, he seemed to be getting his thrill from the work itself. This was not something he could talk about, especially to a clod like Clodfelter. In a matter of a few weeks, Derek was outselling Billy.

"You have the touch," their boss told him. The boss was a man of about forty-five who seldom came into the store until afternoon, and then spent his time in his tiny office with the door shut. "My door is always open," he told Derek. "Don't you believe it," said Billy Clodfelter. Billy also told Derek that Old Man Glidden was a drug addict.

"What kind of drug?" Derek asked. His boss didn't seem like a drug addict to him, just sort of reclusive.

"My guess would be speed," Billy said.

Rotterdam Footwear had been part of a chain of stores in shopping centers all over California, but then the chain went bust and Bob Glidden bought the store. Before that he had been regional manager for the chain. He was a good shoe salesman, but not as good as Derek.

"You got the touch," he told Derek one day about two weeks after Derek had come to work. He was signing Derek's paycheck, commission and salary, over $500 for the week.

Billy was more direct. "You are a natural-born shoe salesman," he told Derek one late afternoon, as they came out of Baskin-Robbins licking ice cream cones: "You'll probably get rich selling shoes. I can't compete with you. Besides, I have bigger ambitions." It turned out Billy's ambitions were identical to Derek's—make a lot of money and retire young enough to enjoy it. Billy had been a big help in getting Derek into the game. So had Denny Wolff, one of the other salesmen. They laughed and kidded when there were no customers in the store, trying to outdo each other in making outrageous proposals to the woman behind the counter, but when a customer would walk in, they were all business, and at first, Derek merely watched and listened. Denny sold more shoes than anybody. If a woman came in for a pair of deck shoes, Denny would sell her the deck shoes, a couple of pair of heels, and eight or ten pair of panty hose. If the woman came in just to have her feet fondled, as so many of them did, Denny would end up selling her a couple pair anyway. "If they got feet and plastic," Denny said to Derek, "I can make 'em buy."

"How?" asked Derek.

Denny grinned. He was a fairly goodlooking guy, about thirty, who worked in the store days and drove a cab nights. He went to school at San Francisco State between jobs, and hoped some day to be one of those freewheeling entrepreneurs who buy and sell, fly all over the world, and marry into society. Denny was already married, but he knew how to fix that. "If I ever met the right rich woman, I'd dump my old lady like that," he told Derek.

But he would never tell Derek his secret, and eventually Derek learned it on his own. It was nothing he could put into words. Derek learned that people came into shoestores for attention as much as shoes, and so he paid attention to them. He looked them in the eye when he talked to them, he acted sincere and he listened carefully, and he tried to fit people with what they wanted. But beyond that, he made himself appear to care greatly about the customer.

"I know you have the ones you want," he might say. "But indulge me," and he would go into the stockroom and come out in a few seconds with a couple of boxes of shoes. "I just want to satisfy myself about something," he might say, and slip a shoe on the customer's foot. "I knew it," he might say, and slip on the mate. "Walk around in those," he might say. "No, don't buy them, it's just when they came in I knew only a few women could wear them." And the customer might walk out with two or even three more pair.

But "the touch"—that was something else, that was the way you handled people's feet, and it could not be taught. Derek had it, the gentle firmness that sold shoes.

"People coming into a shoestore want the same thing they get in a barbershop or a beauty parlor," the boss told him on his first day. "They want to be pampered, to be touched and fussed over. But not attacked by a sex maniac, if you see what I mean."

"Yes," said Derek, but he did not understand until he actually got down on his knees and started feeling people's feet. You couldn't be rough about it, but you couldn't be too smooth, either, or the people would get self-conscious. It had to be like a doctor's touch, a faith-healer's touch.

And Derek had it. How gratifying, to know at the end of the day that your hands had brought you thus-much money. Really, you could talk your head off and people wouldn't buy. You could flatter them, threaten them, and they still wouldn't buy, not if you didn't have the touch.

After two months at Rotterdam Footwear, Derek was the top sales-man, beating out Denny Wolff. This changed everything. He had more money to spend than he had ever had in his life, and to his great surprise, he did not just go out and spend foolishly. It had the op-posite effect, of making him money-conscious, a careful spender al-though not miserly. Making money filled a need in his soul, he de-cided. It wasn't the things he could buy, it was the money itself. For example, he could have rushed out and bought an expensive car and a lot of expensive clothes. He didn't. On his time off he looked for a good used car for himself, not letting the salesmen talk him into any-thing, and passing up several cars that would have been okay, but only okay. He wanted that special car that would reflect his new-found personality. And besides, it was fun going into mortal combat with the used-car salesmen. They were such rats it was good training.

The only really expensive thing he bought for himself was a gold watch, a Taiwan Rolex Denny Wolff sold him for two hundred dollars. It never hurt to have some good metal on your wrist. And he bought a slightly cheaper watch as a present for his mother, who had, after all, gotten him out of jail. He had long since repaid all the money he owed her, and it had been wonderful to see the surprise on her face. "You must be making good money at that shoestore!" Jackie exclaimed. Derek knew his mother didn't think much of selling shoes. It was not a respectable profession. He would show her that it could be pretty goddamn lucrative, however, and it amused him that she could not say "shoestore" without twisting her mouth.

Derek didn't care, and he didn't care when former classmates would come into the store and be patronizing. Let them. He would grin and look shy and sell them shoes. And for him, he knew, selling shoes was only the beginning.

His fellow employees tried everything to put the blocks to him. They would stick him with the people who came into the store all the time but never bought anything, just sat there trying on shoe after shoe, always displeased with one thing or another. Derek would plop down on the fitting stool looking earnest, slip them out of their own shoes and into something they couldn't live without. Even Denny Wolff had to comment:

"That old lady's never bought anything since I been working here. What did you do, promise her a date?"

Derek laughed. It was really a lot of fun to take the worst and do the best. "She's my aunt," he said.

"Your aunt my ass," Denny said.

Billy Clodfelter was patriotic. He was now claiming to be Derek's mentor. "Things are really perking up around here, since I brought Derek into the store," he said to Pam Jenks, who worked behind the counter four days a week. Pam was twenty-five, with long dark hair and deep dark eyes. She was just another of the exciting but out-of-reach women in Derek's life. When he was not busy he thought about her a lot, feverish daydreams of stockroom sex, or taking her out in his mother's Jag and seducing her on the mountain, with millions of lights winking below them. All the salesmen kidded around with her, and she kidded back, but she never dated them. Derek did not ask her for a date because he felt she was too old for him. Not that he didn't want her, just that she probably would have laughed at him. Even though he was top salesman, he was still just a kid in her eyes. Probably.

Bob Glidden was certainly happy with him. Bob got a piece of Derek's sales, and Derek's repeat customers were starting to take up all the chairs. They would sit there and wait for Derek, brushing aside the other salesmen. Derek would have to modestly ask his customers to let the other salesmen wait on them. This made commissions go up, and so nobody was mad at Derek. "He brings them into the store," Bob Glidden said to Pam one day. "The least we can do is strip them bare." Everybody was having a good time.

Then Derek turned twenty-one. His mother invited him out to dinner, but surprisingly enough, so did Pam Jenks. She took him to a Mexican restaurant in San Rafael and fed him chicken enchiladas and then took him home to her apartment in Greenbrae and kept him all night. It was Derek's happiest birthday. Early in the morning when it was time for him to go, Pam said to him shyly, "Please don't tell anybody about this."

"I won't," he said, but he did. He couldn't keep it to himself. Denny and Billy were all over him for news of the date. Derek grinned and blushed and tried to be a gentleman, but finally had to admit he had been to her apartment. They were standing in front of the store smoking cigarettes. Denny laughed and stuck his head into the store, shouting to Pam, "Hey, you really robbed the cradle!" But Pam did not seem angry, and all throughout the day she and Derek kept exchanging looks, and he began to dream about an endless cornucopia of sexual delights. Was this love? Derek didn't have a chance to find out, because about four in the afternoon Pam told him to regard their date as "just a birthday present, do you understand?"

"Yeah, sure," Derek said, his face reddening. He was upset for a few days, but he got over it and became friends with Pam. He felt he was maturing.

By now he had gotten over his infatuation with the act of selling shoes. It was kind of embarrassing to look back on how he had sold himself. "The touch." My God. But it had gotten him through those first weeks, and by the time he came to his senses he was making too much money to care. The job was really boring and stupid most of the time, but so what?

It was time for Derek to move out of his mother's house, to stop using her car, to make himself independent.

"How about splitting my place with me?" Billy asked him. Billy lived in a former motel that had been turned into tiny apartments, out on 101 north of the Civic Center. Derek had visited Billy's place, and silently marveled at Billy paying four-fifty for such a dump.

"I'd rather get a place all by myself," Derek said. "You know . . ."

"Yeah," Billy grinned. "Pussy."

"Well, other things, too," Derek said.

Derek looked back on his time at the shoestore with great fondness. There are a lot worse things than selling shoes. And the friends he made were the first real friends of his adult life. Billy Clodfelter, who seemed like a bully and a jerk in high school, turned out to be a pretty nice guy. Billy had been snobbish in high school, but he had a right to be—he was on the football team, big and strong, with a good personality. But two years out of school and one year in the shoestore turned him friendly as a puppy, and he and Derek did a lot of things together. They double-dated, they went to dinner together, they would often spend evenings at either Billy's or Derek's apartment, ordering out for pizza and watching television, drinking beer and making salty remarks at the stupidity on the tube. Billy could be very funny.

Denny Wolff was older, nearly thirty. Derek and Billy almost never saw him outside working hours. Denny drove a cab in San Francisco, had an apartment south of Market somewhere. He was always asking the other two to come to the city some weekend night, and Denny would show them around. Derek kept his San Francisco past to himself, at first because he was shy about it, and then later because it was nobody's business. He would listen to Denny's tales of the Tenderloin, nod and click his tongue and say, "Wow," but he wasn't much impressed. Denny Wolff seemed to be running off in all directions at once. He was taking courses in business administration, driving cab, selling shoes, dating a couple of different women, including one who was married to a really mean guy, according to Denny. He was trying to get a franchise to sell hearing aids, and of course he was a prime source of stolen goods. He claimed that if Derek wanted to get a suit of clothes or a television set, or really, anything at all, Denny knew guys who would steal the stuff on order. As an ex-thief, Derek shied away from this kind of a deal, after the one-time purchase of his and his mother's watches, which he didn't think were stolen anyway.

But there was something wrong with Denny Wolff, something missing, Derek did not know what. He only knew he did not trust Denny, and deep down, did not like him. It hardened one day when Denny told Derek and Billy about slapping one of his girlfriends.

"It's not that he beat the shit out of a harmless woman," Billy said later. "I mean, hell. It's that he had such a good time."

"You think so?" Derek asked. They were in his new apartment in Sausalito, looking out at the bay. Derek had searched everywhere for a cheap apartment, but in Marin County cheap places were so scarce you really had to be on the inside to get one. The story was that people would wait around outside the office of the *Independent-Journal*, to be first at the want ads.

"But that don't work," Billy told Derek, "because there's guys working at the *I-J* who read the ads in *proof*, and call their buddies."

Derek finally had to make a decision. He could either raise his standards and pay through the nose, or keep on staying at his mother's house, which had a couple of drawbacks. Especially since he bought himself a really cherry 1974 Alfa-Romeo Berliner sedan. He got the car cheap through a deal with a friend of Bob Glidden's, who, it was said, wanted to get the car away from his wife before she wrecked it. Derek gulped a little at signing the papers for the car, but he sure wasn't going to drive any piece of shit. Good stuff costs.

So he didn't need the Jag anymore, not even to impress people. The other problem with living at home was that he was working and making good money, and his mother was looking for a job and not finding anything. He tried to talk her into getting a sales job. In his mind she would be great working in the department store right there in the Bay Shopping Center, but Jackie refused to even look into it. She would not say why. Derek knew why. She was too much of a snob. He could guess that the transition from casual shopper to salesgirl might be tough on her, but what the hell, he did it, and it didn't make him break out or anything. But he could excuse her. She had been pampered all her life, because she was beautiful.

Then Derek had a really good week and found himself with a pocketful of money and no apartment. That was stupid. He went down to Sausalito to a rental agency and treated himself to a studio apartment right on Bridgeway, overlooking the bay, the yacht harbor, and, if you stood on the toilet and craned your neck, the city of San Francisco glittering across the water. The place cost one thousand dollars a month, but it had some great advantages. The walls and floor were thick—it was an old building—and he could play his music as loud as he wanted and nobody would complain. And, most important, the place impressed everybody—girls, friends, potential customers.

"Hey, you must be doing real well, huh?"

Derek was not doing quite that well, but he reasoned that paying off a car, various household junk and an Alfa-Romeo would put some real energy behind him.

Which meant, of course, that he would have to leave the shoestore and go out where the real money was. He did not jump into anything, and he did not bother much with the classified ads. Instead he kept his eyes open for something he would like to sell, something non-glamorous but highly profitable. One thought he had was to sell industrial cleaning solvent. You build up a list of customers and pretty soon the stuff is moving itself, and all you do is go around picking up new customers. Denny knew a guy who did this, and he drove a

Mercedes 450 SEL. But, looking into it only a little, Derek could see
that the business was glutted. Every store he checked was up to its ass
in industrial cleaner. He also thought about selling cars, but the sales
were too few and the profits too little for an outsider like Derek.
Those car salesmen were a tough bunch, and a new kid would be
chewed right up.

Meanwhile, there was the shoestore, and Derek was very careful
not to get cocky or arrogant about being top salesman. But discon-
tent was swelling within him. One day he looked around and saw he
was working seven days a week, eight or ten hours a day, and he was
only making enough money to pay his bills and feed himself. Gradually he came to feel that the shoestore was some kind of hell, where
he was condemned to go in there and be charming every waking hour
of his life. He would get up on a Sunday morning, swear to himself
he would take the day off to hang around Sausalito, maybe go out on
his little deck and get some suntan, or meet a pretty girl on Bridgeway and fall in love. But then he would take a shower, dress, and find
his mind wandering to the store, which of course was open from ten
to six on Sundays. Sundays were good days to sell shoes. And he
really didn't have anything else to do.

One day his mother finally came into the store. She looked around
and said, "So this is where you spend all your time." Derek sold her
three pair of shoes. After all, she had the use of his discount. After
she left, Denny said, "Who the hell was that?"

"My mother," Derek said proudly. She was still pretty damned
goodlooking.

"Why didn't you introduce me?" Denny demanded to know.

"Sorry," Derek said, and laughed. But now that his mother had
come in and seen the place, he truly lost interest in selling shoes.
Now it was almost torture for him to come in to work. He cut his
hours back and spent a lot more time at home being lazy, but the dis-
content would not go away. Nor could he find anything he really
wanted to do. It was beginning to be obvious to him that the upper
echelons, the highest ranks of selling, were beyond his reach, at least

for the time being. Because he had not gone to the right schools. You had to be at least a college graduate, and preferably a Harvard MBA, to get into the higher ranks, selling bulk steel or computer systems. He didn't want to eke his life out working in a store, not even if he got slowly rich at it.

Finally he was recruited out of Rotterdam Footwear. A small older man with round-rimmed glasses came into the store one evening when business was slow and sat down as if to be fitted for a pair of shoes. When Derek sat on the fitting stool and smiled up at the man, he said, "You work pretty hard, don't you?"

"I guess so," Derek said. Maybe the guy was a nut. He didn't look like a nut, though. He was dressed too well. His shoes were old but beautifully cared-for cordovan wingtips, polished to a glow.

"My name is Potter," the man said, and held out his hand. Derek shook it, wondering what the hell he wanted.

"I have a lot up the freeway. I sell motor homes."

"Gee, that's great," Derek said cautiously.

"I've heard you're a hell of a salesman," Potter said.

"Thank you," said Derek.

The trouble with living too long is that the past starts throwing ghosts at you. Kitty Brown was always running into people from the past, and it was not always pleasant. Watching old boyfriends wither into old men wasn't so much fun. Of course some withered less than others, but she didn't see much of those. The ones who made good money, good marriages, the ones who could afford to keep trim and tan, the ones with manicured hands and deep smooth voices, they disappeared, maybe into a world where everybody was like that, Kitty didn't know. She only knew they didn't come into where she worked.

Except this one, and when it was all over, she could have wished he had never walked into the Buttermilk Corner. She did not recognize him at first. His hair had been grizzled like a grizzly bear when she had known him in L.A. twenty years ago. He had been selling cars then, up on Sunset Boulevard, and she had been waitressing cocktails on Santa Monica at Teddy's, half a block from the Troubadour. Those had been great days, and Kitty remembered them and Dakin LeFevre very fondly. Dakin had been her boyfriend for nearly a year. He had been a big soft man with milky skin and a sweetness of disposition he tried to hide from everybody but her. Teddy's was a little bar next to the Trixie Motel, and the crowd was a mixture of sales-men from the motel and overflow from the Troubadour. It was a bad mix, because the salesmen and their girlfriends were more conser-vative, hard drinkers who dressed up to go out, even to a place like Teddy's, and the Troubadour leftovers were more hippie-like, dressed in bright-colored rags, with wild hair. Neither group took any trouble to hide their feelings about the other group. Kitty had to bust up a lot of fights or almost-fights. She got pretty good at spot-ting trouble before it really got going, and putting her body between combatants. "Come on, fellas," she might say, and smile prettily.

Dakin liked to sit where he could look out the window. He would have a couple of drinks before dinner, play a little liar's dice with friends, and then leave early in the evenings. He would not be part of the hostilities, if any, later on. But when he started being interested in Kitty he moved to the number one booth, and began staying later and later. He had the usual old lines she heard so often, and it was amazing that men couldn't come up with anything new. With Dakin it was, "You remind me of somebody. Really. Just give me time, I'll remember." Of course the person she reminded him of had been a raving beauty who had been terribly in love with him.

The first time he took her out they went to Pink's for chili dogs and beer, and then went walking up on Sunset. It had been a Saturday night, and so Sunset was jammed with kids from all over the Los An-geles basin, who dressed up as hippies and flocked to Hollywood. They were going to take over the world, they thought. What struck her about Dakin was that he was so tolerant. He was dressed in a glen plaid suit, she remembered, with a little skinny necktie, and kids would point at them and call them squares. He would laugh and point back, yelling, "Hey, got any spare change?" Quite a guy. They spent the night together at the motel, because he had a wife some-where, although he didn't actually admit this, and he had been very loving and affectionate without pretending to be in love with her.

Later in their affair he took her to better and better places, Dino's, the Imperial Gardens, and all up and down La Cienega, and they would hold hands and gaze into each other's eyes, and he would tell her his big plans for the future. He was not always going to be a car salesman. He was well over forty but his ambitions hadn't been squashed yet. He was going to start his own corporation some day, and make a fortune. He was going to be smart, bide his time, and not rush into anything. The field he was going to go into was the recreation field. That was where the future was, once they got over this war.

She hadn't thought anything of it at the time. Most of the men she knew had ambitions, foolish ambitions, but something to talk about, to plan on. Daydreams, mostly. Then he disappeared one day and she didn't see him again until twenty years later and four hundred miles north. He walked into the Buttermilk Corner at one in the morning, after the theater crowd had thinned out, but before the bar-closing crowd started coming in. The place was almost empty, and Kitty watched this distinguished-looking man come in and sit at the counter. She didn't recognize him. She only saw a tall, silver-haired, well-kept gentleman wearing a dark brown cashmere sweater over a button-down shirt, open at the throat. He put on heavy horn-rimmed glasses to look at the menu, and when he put it down and she came over to him for his order, he looked up at her, his face calm and relaxed until their eyes met, and then he like to jumped a foot.

"Kitty? Kitty Brown?"

"Do I know you?" Kitty said, but the hairs at the back of her neck were standing on end.

He grinned beautifully, and she could not help noticing some gold in his otherwise perfect teeth. "It's me!" he said. "Don't you recognize me?"

"Not Dakin," she said.

"Dakin," he said, still grinning. "My God, Kitty Brown! I never thought I'd ever see you again!" He reached out a soft manicured paw, and she shook it, noticing a big gold ring with a topaz on his next-to-little finger.

"New ring?" she asked with a grin of her own.

"Had it about six years," he said. "My God, you look the same, exactly the same . . ."

"You don't," she said. "You look about ten times better."

"I feel about ten times better," he said. "What was I doing then, selling cars? Yeah, I was working for Greasy Louie. Well, things are a bit better now."

"So it would appear," she said. She waited for him to point out she was still working as a waitress, or that she seemed to have come down in the world, but he didn't. He just sat looking at her and smiling.

"You better order," she said. "I hate to see a man go hungry."

"Same old Kitty," he said. "God, I remember you. I see you finally got out of L.A."

"You know me," she said. "Basically, I'm on my way to Alaska."

He laughed, picking up the menu.

The place was fairly quiet, so she sat next to him while he ate his hamburger. He lived in Belvedere now, had for four years. This was not the first time he had come into the Buttermilk Corner, but it was the first time he had come in on Kitty's shift. He owned a company that manufactured electronic parts. "I just fell into it," he said to her, but she knew better. He had dreamed, worked hard, and now here he was, a big success, living with the rich people.

"What drove you out of the house tonight?" Kitty asked.

He blinked and then smiled. "You know," he said. "The usual."

"Yeah," she said, and went to take somebody else's order. She was not sure how she felt about seeing him after all these years. Maybe she should just ask him bluntly, "Hey, what the hell happened to you?" But when she came back to him, all she said was, "It's nice seeing you again."

He told her anyway. "I'm sorry I ran out on you" is the way he put it.

"Oh, you didn't run out on me," she said at almost the same time.

"My wife caught me," he said. "I guess I talk in my sleep."

"Calling out my name in your sleep?" she said. "I'm flattered."

"It's funny, when you stop and think about it," he said.

"Yeah. 'Kitty kitty!'"

A couple of carloads of teenagers came in, keeping her and Elizaldo and the busboy busy for a while. Dakin sat quietly eating his hamburger, and when she refilled his coffee cup they exchanged smiles. He certainly looked dignified and respectable, even in a sweater and shirt. Those had been tough days for her, the late sixties. When she met Dakin she was just back in the work force after three years of marriage. Three years not working, living high off the hog but pretty unhappy about it. She had been Mrs. Charles Weeberkit, living way the hell out in the Valley, with the San Gabriel mountains staring down at her backyard, with its flagstone patio and its tile-bottomed pool. Chuck had been a nice guy when they met, but as soon as the bed cooled on their honeymoon he became a jealous asshole. There just simply wasn't any other word for it. He owned a small upholstering company, doing custom work on cars and vans. She hadn't really thought about him until they caught those Hillside Stranglers, and one of them had done custom upholstery work, too.

It took her three whole years to get herself together enough to leave the man. He was so jealous he wouldn't take her anywhere unless she threw a fit, and even then he was suspicious of every man who as much as said hello to her. She was perfectly faithful to him, if you could call it that. He was not much in bed, after they got married. Sometimes she would get up in the middle of the night to find him roaming around the house or the yard. Sometimes he heard things outside the window, or in the bushes. He never found anybody, but they had a small dog, Brando had been his name, a cute little mixed breed, and one night somebody threw a ball of poisoned meat into their yard. The dog got well, but Chuck went crazy. He took it personally, even though several other pets in the neighborhood had been poisoned. "That's just a coverup," Chuck told her bluntly.

She hated to go back to work, but just as soon as she could locate an old friend to take her in for a few days, she took off. No regrets. No divorce problems. Chuckie already had himself another tall blonde, no doubt hypnotized by the money he liked to flash. As Kitty had been.

"What time do you get off work?"

This was Dakin, not Chuck. God, they didn't look anything alike. Here was Dakin, tall, no longer plump, tanned, swathed in cashmere. Chuck had been short, bald, and rubber-lipped. What time did she get off? What was he going to do, ask her for a date? Or maybe he was just curious.

"Dawn," she said.

But he stood up and pulled a thick wad of bills out of his pants pocket. She gave him his check and stood behind the cash register, waiting for him to pay. The jukebox was blaring away and the kids were making a lot of noise in their booths, so he had to speak right up. "Maybe I'll see you again!" he all but yelled. "Now that I know where to find you!"

He went out the door and before she could think to move, came back in again. "You aren't, uh, living with anybody?" This came in one of those funny silences that happen, the record came to an end and the kids weren't yelling, so the whole room heard him say it. The whole room sat there waiting for her answer.

All she could think of to say was, "I'll check it out when I get home."

Everybody laughed, Dakin gave a little crooked grin and saluted her, going out the door again. He left her a twenty-dollar tip.

"You're pretty tough," Elizaldo said through the slot.

"You bet I am," she said.

"You ought to take a bath in papaya juice," he said with a little smile.

"Why?"

"Make you tender," he said.

"We could all use a little of that," she said.

Later on, nearly five in the morning, Jackie Jay came in alone. Jackie had been coming in a lot, then she disappeared for a while, and now here she was again.

"Long time no see," Kitty said.

Jackie looked up. Her eyes were bad.

"Couldn't sleep," she said. "I'll just have coffee for now."

"You want to look at the paper?" Kitty asked. But Jackie shook her head, sadly, Kitty thought, and so she came around the counter and sat down and told Jackie all about running into her old boyfriend from the late sixties. But Jackie seemed preoccupied by something. Kitty wanted to pry but didn't. Instead, she went to the storeroom and woke up the busboy and made him come out and refill all the shakers. He was a Vietnamese kid who was studying electronics somewhere, she could not keep track of all the busboys and their various schemes. Jackie sat over her coffee staring at the wall for almost an hour, and then left without saying good-bye. Kitty was worried about her, but she put it out of her mind. You couldn't live other people's lives for them. She had known a bartender once, nice little man in the white jacket they made him wear in that bar, polishing glasses and listening to everybody's troubles, until one fine day he put a pistol to his head and blew his brains out. No note, but everybody was sure it was because he took everything too seriously.

This would not be Kitty's fate, she was certain. She could not even remember the little bartender's name.

So they finally all got together and went out on a double date. They shouldn't have, but they did. Kitty, for all her experience, didn't see this one coming. But there you are. Dakin LeFevre began coming in once or twice a week for hamburgers and coffee, always late at night. He became known around the Buttermilk Corner as "Kitty's rich boyfriend," and he always sat on the same stool right next to the cash register. They even had their little running joke:

"Can't get a hamburger in Belvedere."

"How about Tiburon?"

Tiburon and Belvedere were two rich little towns right next to each other.

Kitty wondered what Dakin wanted of her. She hoped he wasn't trying to recapture the past. As far as she was concerned, the past was over. But maybe all he wanted was a good hamburger and some conversation. If so, he was certainly welcome to that.

Then one night when Dakin was sitting there over his third or fourth cup of coffee, Jackie Jeminovski came in with her own rich boyfriend, the rock lawyer. Kitty hadn't seen Jackie with Richard Kreach for quite a while. Kitty performed the introductions and her three friends sat next to each other at the counter and seemed to hit it off right away. Kitty noticed that all three were wearing leather jackets. "What's this?" she asked. "Some kind of overage motorcycle gang?" This got a good laugh, and later on, while Dakin was standing at the cash register paying his check, he said, "I like your friends. Not the kind of people you run into in Belvedere."

She smiled and gave him his change. "How about Tiburon?" He laughed and went back and put a bill under his plate. Kitty knew it would be a twenty.

After Dakin left, Jackie and Richard Kreach went over and sat in the corner booth, talking far into the morning, cup after cup of coffee. It couldn't have been a very private conversation, because once Jackie smiled up at her and said, "Why don't you take a minute to sit down with us?"

"Too tempting," she said, and went back behind the counter. She was glad Jackie had a boyfriend, or at least a friend, but she knew this wasn't having any effect on Jackie's insomnia, because she kept seeing her come in alone in the early morning hours. By now she knew a lot about Jackie from their conversations, and she didn't wonder at the sleeplessness. Jackie was at a tough place in her life. She was going to have to hustle up a job somewhere pretty soon or things were going to fall apart.

"Everybody thinks I've got it made," Jackie said one morning. "But I have to eat and pay the rent, like everybody else."

"Sure you got it made," Kitty said. "All us beautiful girls got it made."

"Do you know what I did when my son left home the first time? And I found myself living alone? With nobody to take care of?"

"Tell me."

Jackie looked a little embarrassed, now that she had brought it up. "I hid in my closet," she said.

"What, just sat there on the floor, on top of all the old shoes?"

"Exactly."

"I'd call that a return to the womb," Kitty said. "Except for the old shoes."

Jackie liked that one.

"Didn't you tell me he was gone again?" Kitty said.

"Yes," said Jackie. "But this time I celebrated. I'm too old to have a kid around the house."

"I'm sure they get in the way," Kitty said. She had never had any children, although she had taken care of mobs of kids at one time or another. She had twice married men who wanted her as a babysitter and housemaid. Those had not been happy or successful marriages. Come to think of it, she had had only one happy marriage, and she hated to think about it, because it made her sad.

Then she ran into Jackie on one of her nights off. Dakin had been after her for a date, delicately sliding over the fact that he was married. Kitty didn't even know if his present wife was the same one he had been married to twenty years ago. For some reason, she didn't think so. But she didn't ask; it was none of her business. If she went out with the guy, she went out with him. His private life was his own.

"I can pick you up at home," he said, but a long caution made her want to meet him on neutral ground.

"Let's meet at the Happy Hour," she said. "Do you know the place?" If the date didn't work out she would have her own car and could get the hell out of there without too much fuss.

She wondered what to wear. She went out on dates all the time, but usually just to local places, the movies or bars. She knew Dakin planned to take her into the city, and now that he was president of his own company he might want to take her someplace good. As she stood looking into her closet, dressed in her terrycloth bathrobe and blowdrying her hair, her wardrobe seemed either too dressy or not dressy enough: the old complaint, nothing to wear. The two men who regularly took her out were nice guys but neither of them had any money to spend on her. Freddy Lowenstein worked as a foreman at the suitcase factory up the road, and Vern Trotter was retired from the PG&E. They were her friends rather than her boyfriends, though. Freddy liked to drink beer and talk about life at the plant, and Vern was all caught up in marijuana, which he had been smoking for thirty years and now grew in his little backyard over in Hercules. She would drink with Freddy or smoke with Vern, go to dinner with one or the other, movies, or sit home with them and watch television; really, she had been leading a pretty quiet life since moving to Marin.

She tried to remember what kind of clothes Dakin liked. Oh hell, she thought, what difference does it make? She had a nice black dress that wasn't worn through yet, she could wear that, and some heels, and her sunburst diamond pin. Everybody who gave her a look would be looking at her hair, anyway. Her hair was her best feature these days, long and wavy and a shade, or shades, of grey that made women demand to know what kind of dye she was using. "If I dyed my hair, it sure wouldn't be grey," she would tell them. Shoes. She could wear her black ones or she could wear her turquoise ones or she could wear her Wicked-Witch-of-the-West red sparklers. There they all were, sitting there on the floor of the closet. It made her think of Jackie, all curled up on her shoes, with the closet door shut on her misery. Sure, she could understand that. In fact, she felt like that herself, from time to time.

She ended up wearing the red sparklers. You only live once, if that. She had not started to wither or shrink or bend yet, thank God, and she still had really good legs. After she finished dressing she looked at herself in the mirror, thinking once again that she did not want to get old. She had visited a friend, what the hell was her name? Anyway, this woman had had a stroke. Half her face was drooping and she was in a wheelchair at this public hospital in Glendale. But what had been so terrible were all the old people in the hallways of the hospital, in their wheelchairs or on their gurneys, thin, tiny, almost transparent people, whose mouths were loose and whose eyes seemed to be looking into nowhere. She did not want to be one of those. No, no, she did not want to be one of those. Yet she would never kill herself, ha, fat chance! So she hoped for the big one, a nice heart attack, the kind that just knocks you dead.

She remembered that her friend had beaten the system, wheel-chair, walker, crutches, cane, and away on her own. The last time Kitty had seen her, ha, her name was Lillian, the last time she had seen Lillian had been at the all-night market on Vine, pushing a cart full of groceries. Still, Kitty hoped if she ever had a stroke it would kill her like a sword.

Why had she left Los Angeles? If there was an L.A. person it was Kitty Brown. She remembered the occasion, an ordinary Los Angeles October, burning heat, fires surrounding the city, earthquakes underfoot, people going mad on the freeways, and her with a heat rash. That was why she left L.A. After a while you get tired of living in hell.

She smiled at her memories and looked at her rose gold Bulova watch. She was late. That was fine, she had no desire to sit around the Happy Hour by herself. She pinned on her diamond sunburst pin, a gift from herself to herself, admiring the flash of the stones in the mirror. Then she grabbed her purse and left.

Dakin LeFevre was late himself, or wasn't going to show up at all, and Kitty felt that old left-out-in-the-rain feeling, until Jackie Jeminovski and her boyfriend Richard came into the Happy Hour.

"My God, you look wonderful!" Jackie said to her. Jackie's face was alive with friendliness, and Kitty couldn't help feeling good.

To make her feel even better, Richard Kreach pretended he did not recognize her. He was in his same old leather jacket, but Jackie was wearing a skirt and sweater and looked very nice.

"Where are you guys heading?" she asked Jackie.

"Just a quiet evening," Richard said. "Are you out on a pub crawl?"

"I'm waiting for Dakin," she said. "Remember him?" And just at that moment Dakin came in the door, dressed in a dark blue three-piece suit that made him look prosperous and handsome.

"Well, here we all are," Jackie said. "Let's have a drink together and then decide what to do."

"They might have tickets to the ballet," Richard said.

"We have no tickets I know of," Kitty said. She looked up into the kindly handsome face of Dakin LeFevre. "Have we?"

"No," he said fondly. "Let's make it a party."

And so it was all settled.

Out in the parking lot Kitty asked Dakin which car was his. He pointed to a little maroon BMW sedan. It turned out they were all parked next to each other: Dakin's BMW, then Richard's two-tone grey Cadillac, then Jackie's shiny green Jaguar, and finally Kitty's own rusty little Toyota.

"We could go in my car," she said. But no, the men had to have a little macho contest right there, to see who drove.

"Plenty of room in my car," Dakin said. "I just bought the thing. The backseat's pretty comfortable."

"I just gassed up," Richard said.

"How come you brought both cars?" Kitty asked Jackie.

"I like to have my own car," Jackie said. "Anyway, if I get too drunk to drive, I can always walk home from here."

"I always wanted a Caddie when I was a kid," Richard was saying to Dakin.

"Me, too," Dakin said. "But my car would be easier on the girls; I've got four doors."

"I'll bet there's more room in the back of the Caddie," Richard said, and he had his door open and the seat forward. Just to stop the game, Kitty smiled at Richard and bent herself into the back of his car. "Come on," she called to Dakin. She much preferred Cadillacs to BMWs. Dakin got in beside her, and then Jackie and Richard got in, and off they went.

"San Francisco?" Richard asked at the freeway.

"San Francisco!" everybody yelled, and they headed south.

They tried to decide where to eat as they drove along, but it was too hard, shouting back and forth, so they decided to stop at a bar first, have a nice quiet drink and then decide. Kitty sat back and watched the view. Dakin took her hand. He had nice big soft dry hands, and it was comforting to feel his confident grip, but she did not want to hold hands in the car. As they were going through the Waldo Tunnel she took her hand back and leaned forward. "Aren't you going to honk the horn?" she asked Richard.

He laughed. "I haven't done that in years."

They broke out of the tunnel and there it was, the Golden Gate Bridge, glittering below them, with San Francisco behind it, impossibly beautiful, with a gigantic moon rising over the East Bay. Kitty was thrilled by it. She loved the moon, and she loved San Francisco.

"Look," she said, "the moon's coming up out of my old home town."

"Your home town? Oakland?"

"East Oakland, Spring Street, out in the Diamond district, out MacArthur Boulevard, only they didn't call it that then."

"What did they call it?"

"I don't remember. I don't remember hardly anything about East Oakland except playing on the playground while there was a big forest fire in the hills, and we were too little to go fight the fire."

"My daughter and her husband live in East Oakland," Jackie said.

"Now?" Dakin said. "That's kind of a tough neighborhood."

Jackie smiled back at them. "I've never been over there. But it couldn't be so bad, could it?"

"It's a jungle," Dakin said, and chuckled.

"That's all NEGROES out there," Richard said loudly.

"Not my kid!" Jackie said loudly.

Everybody laughed.

"I think," she said, and everybody laughed again.

They stopped on Lombard Street for a drink. The bar was part of a Mexican restaurant, all dark Mexican tiles, bandoleras, bullfight posters and a big crowd of San Francisco types. They took a booth in front, and the waitress told them it would be at least forty minutes before they could get seated in the dining room. They looked at each other.

"Do we want to eat here?" Richard asked the group.

"Let's have them hold a table in case," Dakin said, and they did. The other three had margaritas, but Kitty just had a bottle of Tecate beer. It looked like a long night.

"I like Mexican food," Richard said, starting another macho contest. "But you can't get the really good, downhome shitty-gritty Mex chow here on Lombard Street. You have to go down into the Mission District. I know a little dump down on twenty-fourth with the best tostadas I ever ate, but you have to fight your way through some pretty nasty-looking people to get in."

"I used to go to a place out in East L.A. for huevos rancheros when I had a bad hangover," Dakin said. He patted Kitty on the hand. "Did I ever take you out to the Quatro Habeneros? Like on a Sunday morning?"

"No," Kitty said. "You used to take me to the El Coyote, though. They had good food."

"I've been there," Richard said. "But that's not a grungy place. The place I'm talking about, down in the Mission, is really grungy. There might even be bodies on the floor. Depends on the time of night."

"You couldn't go out to the Quatro Habeneros at night, not a white guy, or they'd just kill you." Dakin laughed wickedly. "You'd be on the menu by the next day."

"Sounds pretty tough," Richard said. "Pretty tough. I've hardly spent any time in East L.A. Usually when I go down there I'm on too tight a schedule."

"What do you do?" Dakin asked. Jackie looked at Kitty and winked. "I mean, I know you're a lawyer and you represent musicians."

"That's it," Richard said and shut his mouth.

"As for that," Kitty said to Dakin, "what do *you* do?"

Dakin grinned and looked down at the table. "I don't do anything. I'm president now."

"What do you make?" Richard asked, and the women exchanged looks.

"We make software," Dakin said. "But don't ask me to explain it."

"Please don't," Jackie said.

"I'm not sure I could," Dakin said. "Let's get another round and then decide if we want to eat here."

Kitty didn't want another beer, and she would have been perfectly content to eat here, but she just sat back and let events carry themselves. The conversation was about electronics, which she didn't know or care anything about, and pretty soon there were two conversations, she and Jackie talking about Jackie's son, who couldn't seem to hold a job but kept a big expensive apartment in Sausalito, and the two men trying to top each other without giving away too much about themselves, or so it seemed.

"Don't you have computers in your office?" Dakin said.

"I don't have an office," Richard said.

"Oh," Dakin said.

"The IRS is always after him," Jackie said.

"I just haven't settled down," Richard said.

"Where shall we eat?" Kitty asked. "My stomach keeps sending me messages. Like, 'Pass the food!'"

"What kind of food?" Dakin asked Kitty. "Anything you want, anywhere you want. We could call in reservations from here." Apparently, Mexican food was out. Fine with Kitty.

"Why don't you pick a place?" she said. "I don't really know San Francisco that well."

"We could go to Trader Vic's, or Vanessi's or some place like that," Dakin said.

"I'm a little tired of those places," Richard said, starting another macho contest.

"Me, too," Dakin said. "San Francisco's got six thousand restaurants. Every kind of food you could imagine. Some of the greatest restaurants in the world."

"Yeah," said Richard, "and some of the scummiest."

"Oh, let's go to one of those," Kitty said.

"Don't you have a favorite?" Dakin asked her.

An hour and two drinks later they were all piled into the car and crawling up and down the hills of North Beach, looking for a parking place.

"I always find a place," Dakin said. "Don't worry."

"I used to park in the alley between City Lights and Vesuvio," Richard said. "But I guess that was a long time ago."

"Must have been," Dakin said. He was sitting forward, with his head between the bucket seats, craning his neck, looking for a spot. "Look, there's one," he would say, but it would be a red zone or a driveway.

"North Beach is a shithole," Richard said finally, after they had crawled around for what seemed like hours. Kitty was not even hungry anymore. They had decided on Italian food family style, at either the Green Valley or the Golden Spike, depending on which was less crowded, but they couldn't even park.

"In L.A. all the good restaurants have valet parking," Kitty said to Jackie.

"Should we go to L.A.?" Richard asked. "It would probably be faster."

Finally they found a place, but it was miles from anywhere. "Let's take it anyway," Richard said. "Fucking lots are all full, streets are packed, what the fuck is going on?" He jackknifed the big car into the parking place neatly, throwing Kitty and Dakin together in the backseat. Dakin kissed her, his fingers on her arms.

"You taste good," he said in a low voice.

"We're here," Kitty said.

They were among the tall buildings of downtown. The streets were almost empty as they walked toward the hill that would lead them back up into North Beach.

"It's eerie down here at night," Jackie said. She was clinging to Richard's arm. Kitty was not in that great a mood. She was wearing heels and they were facing a long uphill walk in a chilly, windswept canyon. But they had come to the city to have a good time, and she was determined to enjoy herself.

"If we were from the Argentine," she said to Dakin, "we would dance our way up the hill," and he grabbed her and they did a swooping tango past the other two. Jackie laughed a long wild loopy laugh.

"Here's a restaurant!" Richard yelled. They were in front of a place called D'Oro. Kitty had never heard of it, but it promised warmth, food, and a place to sit.

"I vote yes," Kitty said, and before you could say "Jack Robinson" they were inside and seated at a nice banquette with tall menus in front of them and drinks on the way. It was amazing how going from cold walking to warm sitting could liven up the party mood.

"I remember eating a steak in here once," Richard said. "I'm still alive. Steaks around?"

"Why not?" said Kitty. "And I want a martini."

"A martini? You *are* old-fashioned," said Jackie. "But I'll have one, too."

So they had four big rare steaks with baked potatoes and green salad. "Jesus Christ," Jackie said. "We came all the way to San Francisco for this? I could have fixed us steaks at my place for half the money!"

"This is good meat," Richard said. "And besides, no dishes to do afterward."

"And," said Dakin, "after dinner we have the city at our feet."

"We could go dancing," Kitty said. "I wore my dancing shoes."

"Where is a good place?" Jackie asked.

"The Top of the Mark," Kitty said. "Do they still dance there?"

None of the other three had ever been there. Kitty had, more than once. Her first time at the Top of the Mark had been when she was still in bobby socks, back during the war. It had been jampacked with young officers, but she had come in with a sailor named Bill Rankin, was it Bill Rankin? Yes. They took a cab all the way from Knapp's Bar over on San Pablo, across the Bay Bridge to a blacked-out city, she could hardly remember the blackout, when San Francisco had been invisible from the East Bay.

All she remembered about the Top of the Mark was that it had seemed refined and decorous compared to Knapp's Bar, no card-game in the corner, no fights, nobody screaming, and of course that magnificent view, all but blotted out by the blackout, but still beautiful, with the buildings looming out of the fog . . . Knapp's had been her hangout as a kid, a riot of a bar, full of sailors from Alameda Naval Air Station, a few soldiers, and a gang of war workers who lived across the street at the Cordenices Village housing project, mostly women out for a good time.

She had been sixteen or seventeen then, just a sweet little girl from East Oakland, ha ha, lucky she hadn't married any of those guys. Half her dates in those days asked her to marry them. They were just out of Oklahoma or Arkansas and hadn't seen anything like the wild life along San Pablo. They wanted to get married because they didn't know how to approach a girl any other way. They had been such innocents, she thought, drinking like maniacs, losing their money over the twenty-four-hour poker table. She remembered one sailor had gone AWOL to stay in the game, thousands of dollars ahead and unwilling to give up the biggest lucky streak anybody around there had ever seen, a lucky streak that had begun before Kitty showed up and was still going on when Kitty left town, dragged back to East Oakland to finish school. She wondered what ever became of the poker-hot sailor. She had been on San Pablo since, many times. Knapp's Bar was of course long gone. It had been a great bar. Or anyway, that was how she remembered it. Great bar.

After dinner they were very civilized, brandy in ponies, coffee in demitasse cups, while they plotted the rest of the evening. There were lots of new bars south of Market, and they thought about trying one or two of them, just to see what the kids were up to these days.

"Let's go down there," Jackie said. "Isn't there a hot salsa club down there, Cesar's or something?"

"We could go there," Richard said. "If I can find it."

"Let's walk," Jackie said. "I feel like a long walk."

"It's a long walk back to the car," Kitty said.

"If I can find the car," Richard said.

"I know exactly where we parked," Dakin said. His veneer as a company president had worn thin, and he was becoming the used-car salesman Kitty remembered. Strange cars he sold, cars for stars, Rolls-Royces with gold-plate instead of chrome and plum-colored flock instead of paint, or a fur-covered Mercedes limo, crazy stuff, sitting out there in the hot sun.

Now it was time for the men to fight over the check, and out came the gold American Express cards.

"It's my party," Richard said quietly.

"But you're doing the driving. The least you can do is let me pay the check."

"Okay," Richard said, and handed the bill to Dakin.

Jackie laughed her loopy laugh and Kitty said to her, "Come on," and took her into the toilet. There was a black maid in there, and Kitty handed her a couple of dollars and said, "Give us a little privacy, huh?" and the maid left.

"Are you okay?" she asked Jackie.

"Just let me do my business and I'll be fine," Jackie said, and went into her booth. "Oops, I almost fell down," she said. "I'd hate to fall into a toilet."

"It's no fun," Kitty said from her own booth. After she was finished she came out, washed, checked her hair, put on fresh lipstick, blotted it, and waited for Jackie. "You okay in there?"

"I'm fine," Jackie said. "I'm just tired." The toilet flushed, and Jackie came out, looking pale.

"You do look tired," Kitty said. "Maybe we should just go home."

Jackie was peering into the mirror, frowning and smoothing down her hair. "No," she said. "I don't get out that much anymore. I want to have a good time."

Out in front of the restaurant they had another decision to make. Down the hill toward the car and the Mission, or up the hill to North Beach? They finally decided to get the car and drive down to the Mission, look around, and if they didn't like it, drive back to Marin and have a nightcap in Sausalito. So they started down the hill, but after only half a block or so, Jackie stopped.

"I want a drink," she said. So they turned around and walked up the hill to Broadway, at this time of night jammed with people looking for a good time. "This is more like it!" Jackie said.

"We could go to Enrico's," Richard said, but Jackie disappeared into a place that had a barker out in front, a little strip joint.

"Oh, Jesus," Richard said.

"Show's just starting," the barker said. He was a young man with a long mustache, wearing a straw hat and a red-and-white striped blazer.

"I'll get her," Kitty said.

"I'm coming along," Dakin said, and all three of them went in. The place was tiny inside, and there were no customers at the little red-covered tables except Jackie. The waitresses all wore black net opera hose and black hotpants, with lowcut white blouses. There was an empty stage with an empty set of drums, just a platform really. The walls were covered with red drapes and there was a tiny bar with three stools. On one of the stools sat a guy who looked like the manager, wearing a tuxedo and a mustache just like the barker's.

"One drink!" Jackie said to them.

"Not in here," Richard said.

"Oh, sit down and don't be such a killjoy," Jackie said to him.

"Show's about to start," the manager said. He was sitting about two feet from Jackie. One of the two waitresses came up to them, holding her tray at her side.

"Hi," Kitty said.

"Hi," said the waitress.

"Just one round," Jackie said. They sat with her, around the little table that was no bigger than a phonograph record.

"Would you like a bottle of champagne?" the waitress asked. "That's our special."

"That would be great!" Jackie said.

"No, no," Richard said.

"Bring us four martinis then," Jackie said.

"No, no," Richard said.

"We don't have them," the waitress said. They finally settled on gin and tonics, and a bartender came out from behind the drapes to make their drinks. Loud music played, otherwise the place was quiet. You could hear a little street noise.

"I've never been in a place like this," Jackie said. "I wonder when the show starts."

The waitress brought their drinks, two apiece, and set them down on the table. "Two-drink minimum," she said. "Thirty-two dollars, please."

"Don't say anything," Richard said to Dakin, pulling out a roll of bills.

"That's a fucking outrage," Dakin said, but he let Richard pay.

"Drink up and let's get out of here before the show does start," Richard said.

"You have experience in places like this, huh?" Jackie asked him. She had already finished one of her drinks, and was toying with the swizzle stick in her second.

"From my college days," Richard said.

"Well, I want to see a striptease," Jackie said.

"No, you don't," Richard said.

"You're gonna have to kill me to get me out of here," Jackie said. But she was smiling and looked happy, full of mischief.

Kitty tasted her drink. She could detect no gin, just the bitter tonic water. That was all right. She was worried about Jackie, who had already finished her second drink and was reaching for Richard's.

"Do you want this?" she asked him, but she took it without waiting for an answer. Richard was staring at the empty stage, as if waiting for the show to begin, and Dakin had taken Kitty's hand under the table. His hand was no longer as dry as it should have been. He squeezed Kitty's hand, and what could she do? She gave him a little squeeze back and took her hand back to plump her hair. She was not being coy, she just didn't like the way this whole evening was going.

The show never started, so they were able to get Jackie out of there before the girl brought them another two drinks apiece. Back out on Broadway, with the mobs swirling around them, Kitty felt better.

"I hate dumps like that," she said.

Dakin gave her a big grin, showing gold. "What do you know about dumps like that?"

"What do you have to know?" Kitty said.

"Right," Richard said. "Let's head for the car."

"Stop raining on the parade," Jackie said.

The ride back to Lincoln's Grove was complicated by a couple of things. Jackie kept yelling about stopping for a drink. First she wanted to go south of Market, and when that became obviously out of the question, she wanted to stop on Lombard Street. When they were on the Golden Gate Bridge, she said, "Turn off for Sausalito, I hate to go home so early," and Richard said, "There's a cop behind us, cool it," and she said, "There's a cop right here in the car."

The other complication was Dakin, who seemed to want to have a little necking party in the backseat. Kitty let him kiss her a couple of times, but when he started reaching for things, she had to say, "Don't do that, please."

They both sat up straight, and he said in a hurt voice, "What's the matter, Kitty?"

"Nothing's the matter," she said. Except that twenty years had passed, and his transfer was all punched out. "Try to pretend you're a gentleman," she said, and smiled to take the edge off, but he couldn't see her smile in the darkness.

"I am a gentleman," he said in a hurt voice.

"Jesus Christ," she said tiredly. "I'm sixty-one years old. When does the grabbing stop?"

"I didn't mean to upset you," he said in a hurt voice. He was as far away from her as he could get in the cramped backseat of the Cadillac.

"I'm not upset," she had to say. Up in front they had the radio going, Stan Kenton.

"Hey," Kitty yelled, "Stan the Man!"

"Yo!" yelled Richard. "I saw him a couple of times. Once at Dantey's in the Valley. You ever been to Dantey's?"

"No," she yelled. "But I used to go to Shelley's Manhole."

"There aren't enough jazz clubs," Richard yelled.

"No money in jazz," Kitty yelled.

"Hey!" Jackie yelled. "You want to change seats with me?"

Up and down two hills and they were in the parking lot next to the Happy Hour. All of them had been quiet for a while, listening to the radio. Jackie said quietly, "Let's go in and have one last drink, and then go over to the Corner for breakfast. Unless you don't want to," she said to Kitty.

"Sounds fine to me," Kitty said.

The Happy Hour was jammed. It was midnight on a Friday, and everybody seemed to be having a great time. Both pool tables were busy and had people waiting to play. The row of game machines was all busy, and the bonging and clicking had to compete with loud sixties rock and roll. Kitty excused herself from a much-subdued Dakin LeFevre and went into the women's toilet, where she had to squeeze past a couple of girls who were obviously tooting cocaine. They looked at her with big eyes until she locked herself in the booth, and then they started giggling and sniffing. When Kitty came back into the bar, she had to look around to find her party. They were crammed over into the corner at the front, by the window. The instant she spotted them she could tell that Dakin was making a play for Jackie, his head bent in close to hers, his eyebrows up. Jackie was moving her head to the music, her eyes shut. Richard did not seem to notice. He was yelling something at the bartender.

"I'll have a virgin Irish," Kitty told the bartender. As far as she was concerned, this night on the town was over.

Now Jackie and Dakin were dancing, and the bartender was yelling at them that dancing was illegal.

"Dancing is always against the law!" Jackie yelled back. Two other people started dancing, and then some people started clapping their hands.

"Come on," Richard said to Kitty. "Let's show 'em," and they started to dance. This was not really dancing, it was more like midair fucking as far as Kitty was concerned, but she enjoyed it, even when some idiot yelled, "Look at the old lady go!" Fuck him, and fuck all his friends. Kitty was having a good time. But real dancing required skill and practice, Fred and Ginger time. She could do a little Ginger, and she did. Richard was a good dancer. For a guy so heavy-looking he was pretty light on his feet. Kitty was glad she had worn her Wicked Witch shoes. They were coming in handy on the high kicks.

Then the unlawful but otherwise terrific dancing was over, and the music went on to the Stones' "You Can't Always Get What You Want." Kitty sat with her back against the wall watching Jackie and Dakin with their heads together. She sipped at her Irish coffee, making plans to just say goodnight and go out and get into her little car and vanish into the night. She was so glad she had brought her own car. She watched Jackie get another drink and drain it in one long gurgle. It was a short little dull orange drink, Lemon Hart rum and orange juice. One hundred fifty-one proof. She wondered if Dakin was going to get to sleep with Jackie. Probably. Jackie was really drunk by now. Kitty still liked her, but wanted no more to do with her this night. Richard was over watching one of the pool games. He probably didn't care. It was sad to see Jackie like this, but there wasn't anything anybody could do. Kitty drained the last of her Irish, and stood up.

Jackie saw her, and a look of drunken compassion came over her face. Jackie was certainly a lovely woman. She came up to Kitty and put her arms around her. "You're my only friend," she said.

"It's okay," Kitty said, and patted Jackie.

"Couple a Lesbos, huh?" Dakin said. So much for the old veneer. He was leering at them both. "Why don't the three of us go somewhere?"

Still clinging to Kitty, Jackie reached for her new drink and drained away half of it. At that moment her face changed. Even her hand on Kitty's waist felt different, as if Jackie had become a different person. Her smile seemed bigger, and her eyes glittered with energy. "Oh ho ho," she said to Dakin in a low voice. "So you want to party, do you? An old-fashioned orgy, is that what you want?"

"That's what I want," Dakin said. "I'm hot to trot."

"I'm out," Kitty said.

Jackie turned to her, still holding onto her, and said, "Oh Kitty, you have to come along. We'll go to my house and have a really good time."

"I have to work tomorrow," Kitty said.

"Not till midnight," Jackie said with that glittering smile. Ah! Kitty recognized that smile—it was the smile of the Perfect Stewardess. Jackie beamed it at her. "We have plenty of time to play . . ."

Dakin's mouth was open a yard or so, his face red, his eyes small and hard. Kitty didn't like him anymore.

At that moment Richard showed up. "We're going to have a little private party," Jackie said to him.

"What kind of party?" Richard asked. He looked wary.

Jackie pulled Richard to her and whispered in his ear.

He said, "That would be fine, but what do we need with all these other people?"

"That's what will make it fun," Jackie said. "Don't you like to have fun? What are you afraid of?"

"I'm not afraid."

"Well, I don't care," Jackie said. "I'm going home, and anybody who wants can follow me over there."

"I'm in," declared Dakin.

"Hey, she's my date," Richard said.

"You can't leave me alone with these two men," Jackie said.

"I won't," Kitty said.

"Good. Then we're gonna have a party," Jackie said. Kitty wanted to slap that smile off her face, but this was not the time.

Outside, Jackie was sort of leaning on Dakin, and he had his arm around her shoulder. Richard was on her other side, and Kitty brought up the rear.

"Let's all take our cars," Jackie said. "It'll be a fucking motor-cade."

"No motorcades for you," Richard said. "Get in my car. They can follow us."

"Don't tell me what to do," Jackie said.

"God damn limey lemon," Dakin said, looking down at Jackie's green Jaguar. "These fucking cars aren't worth a goddamn piss."

"Shut up," Richard said. "I think this party's over. Good night all." He took Jackie by the arm and tried to put her in his car, but she pulled away from him, hitting at him. He grabbed her wrists, grinning, and it might have been a standoff if Dakin hadn't gotten into it. Dakin tried to pull them apart, but Richard let go of Jackie and slammed Dakin up against the Cadillac with a *whump*.

"Oof!" said Dakin.

"Don't fuck with me, you son of a bitch!" Richard said to Dakin.

"Stand back," Kitty said to Jackie, but Jackie was mad. She started hitting Richard.

Richard tried to bat her away, but by accident he got her a good one on the forehead and Jackie went down to the gravel, yelling in surprise. The thumping of the music from the bar kept right on, and nobody came out to see what was happening. Kitty and Richard and Dakin all tried to help Jackie to her feet, but she was thrashing and growling like a madwoman. Finally she got to her feet, her eyes blazing.

"Kitty, ride with me," she said.

Kitty made up her mind quickly. "Okay," she said, and took Jackie's wrist, and the two women got into the Jaguar. Jackie rolled down her window.

"You can follow us, if you want," she said. After they got rolling, Jackie tuned her radio to the classical music station. She was driving pretty well, and Kitty began to relax. Jackie didn't live far away, she could walk back after getting Jackie settled down. Turning around, she could see the two other cars had caught up and were following them. She didn't know what she would do about the men, but it did not seem like a big problem. Just tell them to go away. Jackie was humming quietly to the music. Kitty tried to remember what it was about Dakin she had liked, twenty years ago. It must have been his money.

Jackie parked in the double garage behind her house, and they got out of the car.

"Let's go in the back door and lock'em out," Kitty said, but Jackie laughed and flashed her big smile. "The party's about to begin." The back door was open, and they went into the house. Jackie kept her house nice and clean, Kitty noticed, when Jackie snapped on the kitchen light. The front door was bonging away.

"Jackie, let's talk a minute," Kitty said, but Jackie was already answering the front door. Kitty found a light switch and lit the front hall. The two men came in and Jackie put her arms around their shoulders and led them into the living room. "I have vodka," she said.

"Can I make myself a cup of coffee?" Kitty said.

"I think I have some grass," Jackie said. "But you know what we need? We need some cocaine, to make this party really get perking."

"Too bad we don't have any," Kitty said. She sat on the couch.

"I never had any coke," Dakin said. "I'd like to try it."

Jackie said, "Let me look for that grass," and left Kitty alone with the two men. Dakin sat beside her and put his arm around her. "I hope you're not mad," he said.

"Hell no," Kitty said. She winked at Richard, who was standing in the middle of the room with his arms folded tightly across his chest.

"I'm really tired," Kitty said to Dakin. "Why don't you take me home?"

Dakin smiled glassily. He was drunker than she had thought, or maybe he was just pretending.

Jackie came out of the back of the house, holding up a plastic baggie half-full of marijuana, with some little butts and a package of rolling papers in it. "Only a little," Jackie said. "What about that cocaine?"

Richard pantomimed empty pockets. "No glot," he said.

"Shit," said Jackie. "When I first met you I thought to myself, here's a hip guy who probably knows all the angles. You work for rockers, don't you? Don't the rockers have all the *drugs* they want? Can't you just call somebody and get us some cocaine? Don't you know any coke dealers? Do I have to go back to that fucking Happy Hour and do a deal myself? I can get coke, don't think I can't, but wouldn't it be the gentlemanly thing for you to get us the coke? I mean, what the fuck use are you if you don't bring something to the party? I mean, except your slightly overweight body?" Jackie beamed, holding her arms like a Balinese dancer. "It's a nice body, even if it is slightly overweight." She did a couple of Balinese steps, moving her head from side to side.

"It's late," Richard said.

"Oh shit, it's never late, but if you don't want to do this, then I'll just have to run back to the bar. Okay?"

Dakin got to his feet. "I'll go with you. I'd like to try some cocaine."

"You're an evil man," Jackie said, and gave Dakin a big kiss.

"Oh, hell," Richard said. "I don't want you going back down there."

"Will you get us some *drugs*?" Jackie asked.

"I can try. Look, just sit here and have some coffee or booze or something and I'll be right back."

"Where are you going?" Jackie wanted to know.

"Out for some *drugs*," Richard said.

"You're going to an allnight rocker party, aren't you? I want to come along."

"If you guys are going out, I'd just as soon go home," Kitty said. She got up, and thought about walking down to the Happy Hour in her heels. "Maybe you could drop me off at my car," she said.

Dakin got to his feet. "Let's all go," he said.

"This has been some party," Jackie said. "I haven't even offered anybody a drink," and she was gone into the kitchen.

"I don't need anything," Richard called after her.

"Turn on the radio," Jackie yelled from the kitchen, but Richard just stood by the front door, his face expressionless. Kitty saw the stereo in the corner. She went over and carefully kneeled on the rug in front of it, trying to see how to turn it on. Dakin kneeled beside her.

"You're mad at me, aren't you," he said in a low voice.

"Not at all," she said. She pushed a button and the stereo boomed out loud symphony music. She turned it down and started to get to her feet. Dakin took her hand and helped her up, and then tried to grab her around the waist. They were nose-to-nose, and his breath was sour.

"Don't be mad at me," he said.

Jackie came back from the kitchen, carrying a tray with a bottle of vodka and four glasses, all different sizes. "This son of a bitch isn't going to get us any drugs," she said. "We might as well enjoy the vodka."

The two women sat on the couch and the men sat crosslegged on the floor, on the other side of the coffee table. Jackie poured them all shots of the icecold vodka. Kitty drank hers in one gulp. By now it was welcome.

"You weren't, were you?" Jackie said to Richard. "You were just going to leave, weren't you?"

"Yes," Richard said. "I don't like you when you're in this mood."

"Oh? What mood is that?"

"You know. Drunk."

"I'm not drunk. You should see me when I'm drunk," Jackie said, all with that big smile and the eyes glittering. She poured herself another shot, and started to pour one for Kitty, but Kitty put her hand on top of her glass.

"Kitty's mad at me," Dakin said. His face had come loose, and he really looked his age. "Richard's mad at *you*. So, why don't *we* go in the bedroom?"

Jackie laughed. "It's not that easy," she said. "You fucking old goat. You can't insult my friend Kitty like that. If we get into bed, we all get in together. Wasn't that the whole idea? That's what I want, anyway." She turned to Kitty, her eyes shining. "I can't wait to make love to you."

"To me?" Kitty said with surprise.

"Jackie's mad at me," Richard said. "This whole thing."

"I am not," Jackie said. "I'm going in the bedroom now. Anybody who wants can follow." She got up and left the room, and then came back, poured herself more vodka, and then left again.

"I think she's drunk," Kitty said.

Dakin slowly got to his feet. "I don't know about you two," he said.

"No," Richard said tiredly. "Don't go in there."

Dakin looked at Richard. "Yeah? Why not? Because she's your date?"

Richard got up. "She's so fucking drunk she doesn't know what she's doing," he said. "And I think you're so drunk *you* don't know what you're doing."

"You're the drunk one," Dakin said.

For Kitty it was the same thing all over again. She got to her feet just as Jackie came back into the room, naked except for her heels. The other three stared at her. Jackie held her arms up and beamed at them.

"I love you," she said.

She seemed so innocent, Kitty thought. It might have been perfect for them to take off their clothes, too, and all four of them pile up on the rug. It might have been just the right thing to do. But of course they did not, and Kitty put Jackie to bed while the men waited in the living room. Jackie let Kitty lead her into the bedroom, let her pull back the covers. She slipped into bed and let Kitty tuck her in. Then she said, "Oh, Kitty, did I do the wrong thing?"

"No, baby," Kitty said. "You go to sleep now."

"Aren't you coming to bed?" Jackie asked.

"No, baby," Kitty said.

DEATH

Jackie remembered almost none of it. She remembered coming out naked, but she couldn't remember who had been there, or where they had been that night, or any of the other things she must have done. But she could remember coming out naked and saying, "I love you," to people she could not remember. She held her pillow like a lover and descended into a dreamland where she could not feel any pain, but it did not last, and she came awake again, her mouth dry, her soul filled with dread and humiliation. But she was determined not to face another two-day hangover, not without fighting back, and so she made herself get out of bed.

She was still naked. This embarrassed her, even though she was certain she was alone in the house. She put on fresh underpants and a tee shirt advertising THE GROVE MARKET, and sighing, walked out into the hall. The living room was clean, no bottles or glasses, no full ashtrays, no heavy dead party smell. Maybe it had all been a dream. But no, she knew better. She went into the kitchen, her head pounding, and opened the refrigerator. There were several bottles of ale, but she ignored them and opened the freezer compartment. There on top of the icecube trays were two bottles of vodka, one almost empty, the other with its seal unbroken.

She took out the almost empty bottle. The vodka in it was thick and moved slowly as she tilted the bottle back and forth. There was enough for about two shots. She thought she remembered both bottles being full the night before, but maybe that had been two nights before. There were four glasses upside-down on the counter next to the sink. They looked clean, but she opened the cupboard and got herself a fresh glass, a thick barrel tumbler that was heavy and reassuring in her hand. She emptied the bottle into it, filling it about half-full. Better drink it fast, while it was still cold. But she might burp it into the sink. If she did not have something on her stomach. Not food. She got out a quart of milk, opened it, and drank from it, one, two, three, four, five swallows. The milk tasted foreign on her tongue and hit her stomach coldly. She waited a few moments, leaning against the counter.

"I love you." Oh, God.

She drank her vodka like water, and it began warming her almost at once. Her face was painfully flushed, but she knew it was shame, not sickness. The clock on the stove said it was 11:15, and through the window over the cafe curtains she could see blue sky. She leaned against the counter for fifteen minutes and then poured herself another vodka and drank it down. Did she have anything to do today? She looked at the big calendar over the counter. Nothing in today's square, or for that matter, the rest of the month. Good. With a chill of guilt she went back to bed, but not to sleep.

She knew she was a goner. Drinking to kill a hangover was so obvious a sign that even she could not miss it. This would be the final phase. It occurred to her that she was drinking herself to death. The thought did not bother her nearly as much as it should have. Well, I'm going to die, she thought. There was no reason not to. She had lived her life and it had been a disappointment, but wasn't everybody's life a disappointment? The warmth was creeping through her whole body now, making her pleasantly thoughtful. She should have been frightened, but she wasn't. It was a relief to know it was all over. What had she contributed to the world? One salesman and one long-distance operator. At least they were okay. Or if not okay, out there fighting the world, not needing her help. She would have no more children, and her only regret was that she had not lived long enough to see her grandchildren, if there were to be any. Her looks were shot, her calf muscles cramping if she ran on the mountain, her chances of finding a new companion dimming. Had Richard been there last night? No, or he would have stayed the night. Or had he? It didn't matter anymore, and she didn't feel guilty anymore. That was one nice thing about drinking. It really worked, it killed pain, suffering. And it would kill Jackie. That was nice. You know, funny, when you stop to think about it, it was time for her to die. She had lived through her child-rearing years, her career, all that, her marriage, her life, all over, all gone. There was no real reason for her to go on living except fear, and at this moment she felt no fear. The only trouble on the horizon was that she would have to get up, dress, and go out for more vodka. Soon. Not today, thank God. But as long as she was giving up, she might as well enjoy herself. She sat up and began to fiddle with her bedside radio. She wondered if Derek had left any cigarettes in his room. Poor Derek, he would be saddened by her death. He was a good boy. He was trying. He just hadn't been born with much. Diedre would cry for her, and then wipe away her tears and go back to work. That was all right, in fact, that was fine. Jackie would be mourned but not missed. That was the way things should be. Steven would probably cry in his hands and then feel an immense relief. Trust Steven to get the most out of grief.

Jackie got up and went back into the kitchen for some more vodka, and opened a bottle of Green Death for herself as well. Then she started looking through the kitchen drawers and cabinets, then both bathroom cabinets, then out in the laundry room. She was looking for some way to hasten her death, kill herself, actually, that would not be too painful. She had to admit she hated pain. Of course the house was full of knives, but she had no intention of stabbing herself to death, or slitting her wrists. She could imagine herself, filling the bathtub with the hottest water, and then slipping down into it with her razorblade tight between her fingers, cutting the veins with a quick deep cut and then putting her arm under water with the rest of her body, closing her eyes against the blood, and slowly, warmly, slipping away. Just like falling asleep.

Except that they would find her in a tub full of blood. Whoever found her. Who would it be? Probably Derek. She did not want to do that to him. Or to anybody. That was really the trouble with dying. Sooner or later, somebody would have to find the body.

But enough about dying. She was alive. It was time for another drink, and back to bed. Bed was warm and comfortable, and the radio played softly. Jackie felt fine. The telephone rang. It was her friend Kitty, wanting to know if she was all right, and Jackie could feel the alcohol softening the guilt.

"I'm fine," she said carefully, so as not to sound drunk. "How are you?" she asked, to change the subject.

Kitty was going to the store. Did she need anything?

"No," Jackie said. "I'm on my way out," she said. She did not want Kitty or anybody else coming by. She hung up the telephone and sank back into her pillows warmly. How sweet of Kitty to offer to shop for her. They didn't even live in the same town.

It was another day before Jackie actually left the house. She knew it was coming. She had plenty of food, but she needed fresh orange juice, milk, ale and vodka. She could have driven her car, but instead she made a point of walking the few blocks to Main Street. It was the middle of the day, and there was nobody out on the streets of her little subdivision. The air was hazy, and the trees were changing color. It was quite beautiful out. Jackie was wearing her jeans and a man's shirt, with a pink sweater thrown over her shoulders against the chill, but out in the sunlight it was quite warm, so she folded the sweater over her purse and hooked the strap over her shoulder. There was a big orange cat watching her from the picture window of a house.

She walked down the hill on Main toward the freeway and the bay, passing the Happy Hour. In through the window she saw one of her bar pals, a businessman who wore little bow ties and loud sports jackets. He held up his drink to her, and she mock-saluted him, but did not go into the bar. Drinking in public was too expensive. She wanted no more blacked-out nights, and she could get a whole bottle of booze for the price of a couple of drinks. In the daytime, the free drinks did not flow so freely. But never mind, she wasn't going into that place anymore anyway.

Another bar friend stopped her in front of the Grove Market, a woman named Jane Sindrell, who had her own little computer business she ran from her home. "Isn't it a wonderful day?"

"I love this kind of weather!" Jackie went into the market waving and smiling back at Jane, whom she did not want to talk to, for fear she might say something incriminating. The market was not busy this time of day, and she roamed up and down the aisles looking for things she needed. When she got to the checkout stand she had her quart of fresh orange juice, her two quarts of milk, two sixpacks of ale and two quarts of vodka. It made a heavy load, and Jimmy the clerk asked her if she wanted any help taking it out to her car.

"Do I look helpless?" she joked.

"Not to me," Jimmy joked.

"Oh, give me a couple of packs of Pall Malls," she said.

"Just the necessities of life," Jimmy said. She had known Jimmy for twenty years. He had been working at the Grove Market since getting out of high school, a mild pleasant man who leased a lot of land north of town and grazed people's horses on it. She did not know another damned thing about him. She hefted her load and let a nice older man open the doors for her. Slowly she trudged back up the hill and turned off on Birch Avenue toward home. The mountain looked beautiful, blue in the haze, and she thought about going up there running. She had not been running for a while, she could not remember how long. But no, running was toward life, and she was moving toward death. It was a small matter. She would never run again. She did not regret it.

And so it went. Every two or three days, Jackie would walk downtown and buy supplies. Most of the time she would go to the Grove

Market, but sometimes, to cover her tracks, she would go to the liquor store across the street, which also sold milk and orange juice (although not the fresh, this orange juice came in a carton and tasted metallic). Tamalpais Liquors would take her MasterCard, and so when she was low on cash she would go there. But even so, even though she knew it was the only place she used the card, it was always a surprise to get the monthly bill:

TAMALPAIS LIQUORS
TAMALPAIS LIQUORS
TAMALPAIS LIQUORS
TAMALPAIS LIQUORS
TAMALPAIS LIQUORS
PAYMENT—THANK YOU
TAMALPAIS LIQUORS

It made her laugh to think of the person sending the bill, thinking she must be some kind of terrible drunk, which of course was true. What she couldn't understand is why they didn't just cut her off. Wasn't it obvious? But of course it would not be obvious to a computer. To a computer, a bill was a bill. Rat-tat-tat, pay or die! Well, the joke was on them.

It was amazing how many people Jackie would meet on these excursions to town, people she knew, people who would ask her what she was up to, why they didn't see much of her anymore, how was she doing? She always told them she was fine, she was looking for a good job, her children were fine, and how are you, Mister Wilson? She did not run into Richard Kreach, and he did not telephone her. She was convinced now she had done or said something to him while drunk that sent him away. That was all right. She had no use for him anyway. The telephone seldom rang anymore. Kitty called once or twice to say it got lonely in the middle of the night, and did she want Kitty to come over or anything, but she told her no, regretting it, but not wanting to see her or anybody.

She had her life all worked out. At last she had learned how to live a day at a time. Every day was the same day. She would get up around eight, drink a couple of cups of coffee, take care of the house, make sure she got her shower, and then begin drinking, usually at around eleven or eleven-thirty. First, of course, she had her glasses of milk and orange juice, to ensure the proper nutrition, and then into the vodka, three or four shots before she would taper off to ale for most of the day, going back to the heavy stuff in the late afternoon and on into the night. She usually stayed in bed all day, reading a novel. The novel was John D. MacDonald's *The Empty Copper Sea*. When she got to the end of the novel she would start all over again. It did not matter. Escape was escape. Derek had left four or five of the Mac-Donald novels around the house, but she read only the one. It passed the time, and every fifteen or twenty minutes, she would get up, go into the kitchen, and get a fresh shot of vodka, or a fresh bottle of ale. Then back to bed, back to Florida, back to somebody else's troubles.

And then there was no more money. That was too bad. She had wrung her sisters dry. She had wrung everybody dry. Nobody called her anymore, or if they did, she did not remember the calls. It didn't really make any difference. She just stopped going to the Grove Market and did all her business at Tam Liquors. They had everything she needed, milk, fruit juice, vodka, ale and cigarettes, and that was fine. She enjoyed the dreamy walks to town, even in the rain. There was something wonderfully natural about it. She could pretend she was on the west coast of Florida. The only thing that bothered her was running into people who wanted to talk. She always lied to them. It was none of their business what she was doing.

And then one rainy day she went into the store, got what she wanted, and gave the clerk her MasterCard, and he kept it. "I'm sorry," he said. He was just some little punk. "Take the stuff, but I gotta keep the card," he said. She walked home in a daze. No card? That was terrible. How could they do that to her? She did not blame the kid. He was probably embarrassed about it, he probably hated to do it.

She didn't really mind. It had to happen some day. She had enough booze to last about three days. If she ran out of food she could rummage around the kitchen and find something. But when the time came, she just lay there in her bed. Getting up was such a chore. The idea of cooking some rice and keeping it on hand passed through her mind, but the thought of eating the rice plain did not appeal to her, so she lay in bed without anything to eat and without anything to drink, just lay there.

It was a kind of freedom. She felt no hunger. Quite the opposite. She did not miss the liquor. She did not even read her book. The only thoughts that passed through her mind were fragments of memories, poling that flatbottomed boat across the shallows of Key West, the terrible sunlight turning the whole world white and empty. She knew she was dying. Everybody was dying all the time. Now was her time. It was all right. Everything was warm and white, empty.

She opened her eyes. Nothing had changed. She blinked. It was daytime. She sat up, feeling a little dizzy. Now she knew. She did not want to die. If she kept lying there, she would die. If she kept drinking, she would die. She threw back the covers, feeling something almost like fear. She would have to get something to eat. There was nothing in the house. She put her feet on the floor, wondering if she could walk out into the kitchen. She knew it would be a mess, bottles everywhere, on the counters, on the table, even on the floor, green bottles and clear bottles. She stood up, wobbly, and made it to the toilet. She sat on the toilet with her eyes shut, waiting for the dizziness to stop, for the roaring in her ears to stop. She didn't have much to pee, and it felt like acid. When it was over she wiped herself, bent forward to pull up her underpants as she stood, and swayed so badly she had to grab the towel rack to keep from falling on the floor. She laughed. It sounded like the croaking of a very sick crow. Caw caw cough cough . . .

She would go into the kitchen, forest of bottles or not, and search for something to eat. She knew she had to get something on her stomach. Eat or die, she thought.

She was in the kitchen, very dizzy now, trying to get the cupboard open, when her son walked in the back door.

"Hello, Derek," she said.

Kitty never felt better. She had gotten a case of the flu somewhere, and it knocked her out for a week, flat on her back in her San Rafael apartment. That was the bad news. The good news was that people kept calling her up to see how she was, people from the Buttermilk Corner, customers who missed her, Elizaldo the cook, with his sly humor, suggesting that she was not sick at all but malingering. That was a joke. The whistling shits, fever of 102. And the cat from next door, climbing in her kitchen window and spending his days curled up on the foot of her bed, or sometimes giving himself a wash or coming up to her to have his ears scratched. He was a big tabby, black, white and grey, a handsome animal with scars all over his big fat face. She didn't know what his name was, so she called him Butch and the hell with it. He must have weighed twenty pounds, and for a while, in her delirium, she thought maybe God had sent this big cat to pick her up for the last journey.

But no, the fever passed, and finally she was able to control her bowels. Once again food tasted good, and she was thinking about going back to work. But the weather turned bad, days of rain and wind, and so she decided without consulting anybody that she might as well stay home another couple of days and recuperate. The cat was a big help. She had to keep the kitchen window shut because of the rain, but when Butch wanted in he would jump up onto the ledge and rub his body against the glass, never so much as a meow until she would pull up the window and he could jump down onto her table with a grunt, as if to say, "What took you so long?"

"Sorry, Butch," she might say, and if he was really wet she would get a towel and sit him on her lap, wrapped in the towel, and dry his head and ears. He loved it, and would look at her with his big yellow eyes full of affection. "I love you, too, Fatso," she might say.

But more than cat-love was coming her way. She had gotten rid of Dakin LeFevre. He had only come into the Buttermilk Corner once after the big double date, coming in about three in the morning, dressed in grey slacks, a blue blazer, yellow checked vest and dress shirt unbuttoned at the throat. He looked rich and comfortable, and she didn't like him anymore. He had been a little too obvious in his moves. When poor Jackie had come out naked, Dakin's tongue really hit the floor.

Now here he was, sitting over a cup of coffee, apologizing to Kitty and explaining how tough it was, to be rich, married, and living in Belvedere. He had no freedom, he explained. His life was stuffy and tiresome. He had no real friends. Everybody in the company was afraid of him. His wife did not love him so much as she needed him to maintain her social status. And he felt *terribly* uncomfortable among his peers at the Corinthian Yacht Club. He needed Kitty. Kitty reminded him of younger, happier days.

"You can't live in the past," Kitty told him, meaning she wouldn't go out with him. He got the message, and sat there like a little boy over his empty coffee cup, and then shambled out of the place and roared off into history, or wherever the hell he was going.

No, it was another guy, who came into Kitty's life and promised to make things interesting. He didn't have Dakin's money or even his good looks. He was in fact a short, roundheaded, hard-bellied plumbing contractor named T. Wavell Jones, and of course the T. stood for Thomas. Tom Jones, hey? Wavy Jones was up and around at night, seeing that his fleet of plumbing trucks was on the job, seeing to it that all the drains and toilets in south Marin worked. His plumbers all claimed to hate and fear him, but they said it with a smile. Kitty found him crude but goodhearted, and he was desperately in love with her.

Wavy was her most consistent caller when she had the flu, and he was always offering to take care of her, recommend a doctor, do her shopping, sit bedside and hold her hand, all but don a nurse's uniform and move in. He did come and visit her while she was recuperating. The wind howled and raindrops rattled the windows while they sat and watched television, Kitty in her favorite chair wrapped in her bathrobe and drinking hot lemonade, him tilted forward in her wooden rocker, scowling at the screen, his lemonade untouched on the floor between his high-topped scuffy black workshoes. She went back into the kitchen to rinse out her glass when she saw Butch against the windowpane. "Oh! You poor cat!" she said, and pulled up the window to let him in. She carried the wet cat into the living room. He must have weighed an extra pound from the water.

Wavy's eyes lit up. "Well, where'd you get *that*?"

"Let me get a towel," she said. She sat, with the cat in the towel on her lap. Wavy kept grinning at the cat. "He's a good one," he kept saying, and later when the cat was dry, Wavy played with him, pulling his tail and slapping him vigorously on the sides. The cat loved it, and ended up asleep in Wavy's lap. It was as pleasant an evening as Kitty had spent in she didn't know how long, and when it was over, Wavy acted like a perfect gentleman, not trying to kiss her, but taking out his affection on the cat.

Coming back to work had been a pleasure. Kitty hated being sick, even with the down time. Everybody was cheerful and glad to have her back, and a lot of the regular late-night customers had stories about the girl who had replaced her, evidently quite a beauty. "But we're glad to have you back anyway," somebody joked.

The only thing that bothered Kitty was that she had not heard from Jackie Jay, not since the last time Kitty telephoned her. She had been so drunk she could hardly talk, and this worried Kitty. Jackie seemed to be on the road to hell, and there was nothing Kitty could do about it. Obviously, she was so drunk all the time that she didn't come out at night anymore. It was a shame. Jackie was a good person.

The place was empty except for three kids down by the jukebox. Nothing was playing, and Kitty could hear Elizaldo faintly, singing in the kitchen. She wiped down the counter and then went around checking the booths, seeing that there was salt, pepper, sugar, and sugar substitute, making sure nobody had left anything behind, no wallets or purses. She had found some pretty strange things left in booths, from hats to flashlights, but nothing tonight.

Kitty went behind the counter and poured herself a cup of coffee. She wondered what T. Wavy Jones was up to. He had his office in a little Quonset hut down by the bay, where he would sit yelling over the CB at his plumbers, drinking poison coffee he made himself on an old Silex. He hadn't called her yet tonight, and so he must be busy, or catching one of his catnaps. Which made her think of Butch the cat, wondering if she had left the window open in the kitchen. She was pretty sure she had. She liked to come home and find him curled up on her bed or in her chair. She never fed him, and he never seemed to want her food. The relationship was purely personal. Kitty smiled. She should get a package of fresh napkins from the storeroom. The busboy would be in there asleep on the sacks and boxes. She hated to wake him up. She loved the way Butch the cat would wake up on her bed, stand, arch his back, give her a look, and then curl back up into sleep. As she pushed open the storeroom door she thought about Butch leaping up into her lap so gently she could hardly feel him land, and at that moment, without any warning, her heart stopped beating.

Kitty would have enjoyed her funeral. For one thing, nobody knew where the body was, if it had been shipped to relatives, if it was lying in state at some funeral home, or if the county had it in a body bag awaiting the drop. The body was not what mattered. On the Sunday after her death, people gathered at the Buttermilk Corner, and by one in the afternoon the place was packed.

It was raining again, a heavy misty rain, and the Corner's own parking lot filled up early, making people park down below in the bus parking lot and walk up the steps through wet overgrown acacia trees. You could hear the merriment halfway up the steps. Inside, there was a buffet laid on the counter, and several people brought bottles, which they passed around freely. The jukebox played loud rock music and the air was filled with the smell of wet clothes and marijuana smoke. Groups would go into the restrooms and come out chattering, with bright eyes and loose grins. It didn't seem like a funeral at all. Kitty would have liked that, everyone said.

There were a remarkable number of policemen in the room, state highway patrol, county sheriffs and city police from half a dozen cities. They were all late-night customers and they all said they would miss Kitty's smile, the way she knew what they wanted, the way she charged them full price, relenting every once in a while with a free cup of coffee or hamburger. There were also a lot of hospital workers, nurses and attendants, even a few of the doctors who worked at Ross or Marin General, and a lot of the rock musicians who used to kid her and ask her out on dates. Elizaldo was there, with his tiny wife and four children. And there were a lot of nondescript people who came and stood around and looked lost, the insomniacs who had been Kitty's customers in the long empty hours.

Jackie Jeminovski was there, sitting on the end stool by the window, thinner than ever, sipping tea, smiling and talking to anybody who came up to her. Her son Derek was with her, and his girlfriend Kathy, who was tall and slim and elegant, with lovely blue eyes, not the sapphire eyes of Jackie, but paler, more like opals. At around four, Richard Kreach came in, wearing a huge sheepskin jacket and a cowboy hat. He stood with the rockers for a while, and then made his way over to Jackie. He shook hands with Derek and Derek's girl, and then later he was seen going into the men's room with a couple of cops. T. Wavell Jones did not come. They all said he must have been too broken up. Dakin LeFevre was not there either.

The party went on for several hours, and Kitty would have liked the way it broke up without incident, giving the employees a chance to get ready for the dinner rush.